Bourbon Billy

Three In-laws and a Son of a Bitch
Take Intersecting Paths Through the
Financial Manias which Preceded the
2008 Financial Collapse.

Bourbon Billy

By Ted Fiolek

Copyright 2014 © Enough Already Publishing

Published by Enough Already Publishing
Edison, New Jersey

ISBN-13: 978-0991367009 (Enough Already Publishing)

Printed in the United States of America

4

Table of Contents

Prologue

Wilfredo Rocinante was born on May 25, 1965, the night of the second Sonny Liston/Cassius Clay fight. Clay swung and hit nothing but air, but Liston collapsed nonetheless. As Sonny Liston hit the canvas following the phantom punch, Willie dropped from his mother's womb.

Nothing much of note happened to Willie for the next thirty four years.

1 - A Surly Son of a Bitch

"Bullo Cordardo? He was a surly son of a bitch."

"So, you knew him. Was he a friend of Willie's?"

"Well, I don't know if I'd say 'friend'" said Pete, Willie's onetime roommate and fellow bartender. "He was more of an acquaintance of Willie's than a friend, but probably as close to a friend as Bullo had, outside of the firehouses".

"Firehouses?"

"He was a retired fireman from Staten Island and, also, an accountant. That's what he and Willie had in common, that and twenty something year old girls. Actually, the three of us had that in common."

"I heard that he was from Staten Island."

"Most of the assholes that come to Madison Ave are from Staten Island. They cross that Outerbridge and all of a sudden they're tough guys; single tough guys. Then, when they go back home, they're just married assholes again."

"He sounds just like Willie."

Pete leaned against the bar, revealing a roll of belly and midriff. His extra-large Dan Marino jersey wasn't extra-large enough. "Nah, Tony . . . I know you have your issues with Willie – what he did to you . . . and, the way he treated your cousin and all – but Willie's not malicious. He's a little selfish, I'll admit that."

"A little selfish?"

"Bullo, though. . ." Pete shook his head, "Bullo was just a real bad guy. I don't even know why he came to the club all the time – well, I do know why, to hit on the girls – but, I never seen anyone who seemed to hate people like he did. I never even seen him speak with nobody – hardly even Willie – unless it was a girl he was trying to take home. 'Get me a Heineken' was about the only thing he ever said to me. If some guy would sit down at an empty bar stool by him, he'd just growl or glare at them."

"He never got his ass kicked?"

"Anyone tough enough to give him trouble, he'd just avoid. In fact, the only actual fight I ever heard him getting into was the night he ambushed Willie."

"He and Willie had a fight?"

"You didn't know that? Bullo left Willie for dead out in the parking lot . . . that's why he split for Florida."

"I didn't know that, no one in the family did. We just thought he and Leah were having marital problems. So, why the hell did Willie wind up going into business with the guy?"

"Willie was already working in Bullo's tax preparation office then. They had some dispute over a broad, Fannie LaBrutto – she's an old regular around here. Willie used to see her semi-regular, but Bullo was with her that night."

Willie was working a late-evening shift at Madison Ave while Bullo hastily scrubbed every inch of his body in LaBrutto's shower. LaBrutto tried reaching Willie on his phone, but at Madison Ave you could hardly hear someone screaming at you from six inches away much less hear a cell phone ringtone. LaBrutto only reached his voice mail. "Willie! Willie - you asshole. I'm going to kill you if this piece of shit doesn't kill me first, you fucking asshole."

After toweling off and dressing, Bullo stomped out of LaBrutto's apartment without saying a word to her and drove straight towards Madison Ave. He pulled into the empty parking lot of a daycare center a half mile down the road where Willie wouldn't be able to spot his car. It was late March, but Bullo was drenched in sweat in spite of just having showered. Bullo marched to the Madison Ave parking lot and paced out of sight behind a couple of SUVs for a half hour until Willie left the club for the evening. Bullo spotted Willie walking towards his truck, half-buzzed and looking preoccupied. Bullo crouched behind the car to the left of Willie's Explorer. As Willie fumbled for his key, Bullo walked just slowly enough for Willie's eye to catch Bullo before he landed a straight right to Willie's forehead. The timing was important to Bullo and he got it just right. In spite of being stronger, soberer and more experienced in fighting than Willie, Bullo couldn't resist the opportunity of throwing a sucker punch. On the other hand, Bullo wanted to see Willie's face before he was hit but after he knew a beating was coming. Willie's glance revealed a look more of puzzlement than fear or shock which further fueled Bullo's anger.

"Stop . . . please" cried Willie, as Bullo beat him savagely.

"Ha, you Mexican piece of shit, you spic." Only exhaustion and a growing ache from bruised knuckles on his right hand made Bullo stop. No longer able to put up even a modicum of defense, Willie laid on his belly, with the right side of his head resting on the cracked blacktop next to the front left tire of his truck. Bullo turned, took five steps towards the daycare parking lot and them made an abrupt about-face when it occurred to him to urinate on Willie's ravaged body. For the first time since Willie left the club, Bullo felt concerned about potential witnesses. His eyes made a 180 degree arc. Being reasonably sure that no one was watching, Bullo stared back down at Willie. Willie's eyes were shut but his head faced towards Bullo. He marched straight back at Willie and kicked him just above his left eye - a kick that would leave a permanent scar - before returning to his car and racing back to Staten Island.

2- A shotgun Wedding

Mayday, 1999

"The miscellaneous table, as usual," Tony Violette said to his wife Gwen. "It wouldn't be a genuine Magillicutty wedding if we weren't at a table full of strangers." Besides his wife Gwen, the only one else Tony knew at the table was Pastor Droll the divorced, former failed-stockbroker minister who had performed the ceremony. Joining them at the table were a couple of friends of the bride -who hadn't made the bridesmaid cut-, their dates and work friends of the bride's mother.

"It's not malicious, Tony. You're an only-child in a family full almost entirely of younger and close girl-cousins."

"I know. I'm just not in the wedding-spirit. If it weren't for me, she would have never met this dolt."

"Leah and Willie met at your wedding, didn't they Tony?" asked Pastor Droll.

"I'm sorry you didn't get to do that one. I had to pretend to be Catholic for a few months to marry Gwen.

"Tony!" said Gwen.

"But, yeah, I hired Willie to be the server at the open bar."

"Leah was one of my bridesmaids."

Tony nodded, glumly. "Now, one hundred fifty five days and five White Russians later, Leah is one hundred and fifty five days pregnant, and three hours married."

"We're both due on the same day."

"Well, it was fate then," said Pastor Droll.

"Fate? I only met Willie the week before while he was bartending at Madison Ave Club during my bachelor party, the first guy we hired bailed at the last minute."

"Well, that's certainly fate."

"It's not fate. The only reason we're here is because Willie is just too irresponsible to use contraception."

To Willie, his evening with Leah was no different than any of a hundred or so other one night stands. Willie had caught Leah's eye early during the reception and saw that she had no date. Willie made Leah's White Russians increasingly strong and by the wedding's end Leah wasn't even feigning resistance to Willie's advances. Twenty unromantic minutes after Willie had entered Leah's hotel room, he had already finished his business while Leah passed into a deep, drunken sleep. Without looking back, Willie left the room and drove to the Carteret apartment he shared with Pete.

Six weeks later an enraged, fiery Leah showed up at the office in which Willie was doing some accounts payable temp-work. It was the only time in her life Leah had really lost her temper and presumed to boss anyone around.

"Who the hell do you think you are?"

"Lisa?" asked a confused Willie.

"Leah - my name is Leah, you big jerk."

"I know . . . I remember. What are you doing here?"

"What am I doing here? When were you going to call me?"

"I lost your number . . . I was going to call."

"You couldn't call my cousin Tony? He's been back from his honeymoon five weeks and says no one's left a message asking for me or my number."

"I didn't think of that" muttered Willie, which was both true and misleading. He hadn't thought of it, but why would he? They had their night and Willie forgot about her then next day. On the other hand, she looked great, especially all riled up like she was. Willie thought he wouldn't mind seeing her again sometime. "Let me have your number, we'll definitely go out again."

"What? Are you kidding?" shouted Leah. By this time, more than a dozen staff from the office had gathered to watch the exchange. "Go out again? I'm pregnant - we have to get married .. . like, this week . . . before it's too late."

Leah was a devout catholic, the only Catholic in the Scotch-Irish Protestant Magillicutty family. Leah's mother Frances was a flower-child of the late 1960s and a believer in the natural-childbirth movement. Leah's father, Liam, twenty four years older than Frances and married with children to another woman, hoped to keep the pregnancy secret, and as low-cost as possible. So, Liam went along with the idea of a home delivery in Frances' recently rented Kearny apartment and with only Liam assisting in the delivery. The squeamish Liam passed out at the sight of Leah emerging from her mother's womb, cracking his head on a bedroom dresser. Not being in a hospital, and with Frances giving birth, there was no one to give Liam medical attention. Frances had no phone service in her apartment. Her screams for help - and Demerol – went unheard. Liam became the first man known to have died giving birth.

Frances, at that moment a Buddhist but raised in a Baptist household, decided to raise Leah a Catholic like her Irish father who had been quite devout, except in matters of fornication. Leah needed little coaxing to embrace her father's faith. Even as a child she was fervently Catholic, seeking both god and a connection to the father she never knew through devotion to the Roman Church. The shame of her out-of-wedlock pregnancy drove Leah to a temporary conversion to the Baptist Church of her recently deceased grandmother. Frances was working her way alphabetically through the world's primary religions and cults but was at a temporary agnostic impasse between Shintoism and Zoroastrianism, so the grandmother's Baptist faith was the obvious alternative.

Leah met Pastor Droll at the funeral when her grandmother died the year before. Pastor Droll handed Leah his business card - Pastor Droll always handed attractive unmarried, and sometimes not-so-unmarried, young women his business card - which read, 'For weddings, funerals, baptisms, mutual funds, IRAs & life insurance - call Pastor Droll". His previous card which read 'Let a Pastor "Droll-over" your retirement account for "heavenly" returns' had been rejected by his broker/dealer's compliance department. Leah immediately returned to her Catholic faith after the wedding as a legitimately married women and this pleased the unreligious Willie greatly. Besides it humoring his Roman Catholic mother, Willie resented Pastor Droll for pressuring him into purchasing a heavily-loaded contractual investment plan during a pre-marriage counseling session.

Willie stared at Leah, speechless, like a chimpanzee being asked to solve a Rubik's Cube in fewer than twenty moves. Willie was certainly feeling dissatisfied with his life, but it had never occurred to him that the source of his dissatisfaction was his empty, directionless bachelor lifestyle.

"Okay" said Willie, to the cheers of the office staff audience. Prior to that moment, Willie hadn't given marriage five seconds of thought in his entire life, but now he was trading in the bars and the bimbos for a wife and kid. Or, at least he was going to give it a try.

3 – The worst people in the world

The worst people in the world live in Staten Island. Not worst like Pol Pot or Jeffrey Dahmer worst. It's simply an island filled with cads, louts, wannabes, waxed Camaros and badly built condominiums and attached houses. Staten Island is everything that is bad about New York, but without any of its good qualities. Staten Island is the place where, if you are from New Jersey and have a mangy dog whom you cannot train, you drive over the Bayonne Bridge, open the door and say "so long, Fido."

The legend that Staten Island is actually not an Island but, rather, an ocean garbage patch that had reached surface and been paved over to build houses for New York City civil servants is only a slight exaggeration. The island is mostly inhabited by families run out of Brooklyn and Queens that weren't successful enough to move to Long Island or Manhattan but still retained an unearned sense of superiority that forbade them from making the trip all the way to New Jersey. If you look on a map of Staten Island, it appears geographically to belong to New Jersey and, in fact, there was a half serious movement in the early 1980s for the island to secede from New York State and join New Jersey to escape New York City resident income taxes. However, every other household in Staten Island depends on a New York City government job for their sustenance, a pipeline that would have quickly closed had Staten Island jumped ship. Cooler heads prevailed.

Bullo had contempt for Jerseyans. The Staten Islander, though, did have Jersey roots on his mother's side, but that only gave him a sense of entitlement whenever he crossed the Bayonne or Goethals Bridges or the Outerbridge Crossing. Twenty years of weightlifting and sulking in New York City fire stations had toughened him. He viewed Jerseyites like half-farmers who were easily cowed. Also, for Bullo, the implicit terms of his wedding ring only applied in New York State. In New Jersey, he was single.

"What are you doing with that water?" asked Bullo, as Holly - a Madison Ave regular - filled the Jacuzzi in their Rahway Inn suite.

"You don't like hot tubs?"

"No." Bullo was already in a sour mood from having to pay for a suite, because all of the economy rooms were booked.

"Why?" asked Holly, as she continued to fill the tub. "They're great."

"You wouldn't like baths either, if your mother taught you to swim by holding your head underwater."

"God . . ."

"This is why I prefer prostitutes," thought Bullo, "I don't have to talk to them." Then Bullo said, "Turn that off."

"Fine . . . well, at least your mother never put her cigarette out on your arm because there wasn't any milk left for her coffee after you fixed yourself a bowl of Frosted Flakes."

"Poor you" said Bullo, scratching the stubble on his neck. Bullo purposely shaved before going to bed every night - rather than the morning - to avoid ever appearing clean shaved. "One time she held my hand over the flame on the gas stove until I was able to wriggle out of her grip."

"Ouch! That's terrible. How old were you?"

"Four maybe . . ."

"Four? What did you do?"

"It wasn't terrible, I didn't do anything. She was just teaching me not to touch the stove when things were cooking."

Holly shook her head. "Maybe that's why you became a fireman."

Bullo's, mother, Seweryna 'Sparky' Cordardo, grew up in the Lucchese section of Newark in the 1950s. Schooled in the fine arts of tomato ladders, the Taccetta brothers, picking wild mushrooms from the sidewalk cracks of Stuyvesant Avenue and making homemade wine from Dandelions, Sparky was a sort-of quasi early feminist. Not that Sparky thought women should have the same rights as men. Rather, Sparky simply was a smoldering caldron of willfulness. Born before the era of Prozac, tranquilizers and mania diagnoses, Sparky was a young bull elephant in the body of a tiny Italian immigrant girl.

After being expelled from a half dozen Catholic and public schools, Sparky's parents, unable to handle her, signed her over to the State of New Jersey at age eighteen to be a ward of the state. After a lucky thirteenth electroconvulsive therapy treatment, Sparky was set free on the streets of Essex County. With her synapses fried, Sparky was in her somnambulistic period. This enabled her to find temporary employment and snag a husband. However, the mind-moat created by the electric shock treatment still left the occasional spark of hostile histrionics explode onto whichever unsuspecting next victim was in her path. Today, Sparky would likely be diagnosed as some type of extreme bipolar antisocial borderline personality. In the more civilized late fifties to early 1960s period, she was simply considered bat-shit crazy.

Working in the Rheingold Beer factory in Orange New Jersey, Sparky met her future husband Ryan, probably the only man in the world who could have tolerated her for twenty five years. Sparky landed a part-time job attaching labels to Reingold bottles on a conveyer belt after the labeling machine had broken down and the label-machine repairman's union went on strike. Ryan was carrying three cases of bottled beer and tripped, spilling six gallons of ale and leaving shattered glass all over the floor. A five-foot two - in shoe-lifts -, balding, middle-aged foreman ran up chest to chest to the six-foot three chiseled Irish/German/Italian Ryan and dressed him down in front of Sparky like he was a cocker-spaniel who just took a dump on the new carpet. Ryan just meekly apologized. Sparky had found, if not her soul mate, at least her lifetime lackey. Sparky invited Ryan to her folk's Newark apartment for dinner.

"I never hear Italian called a Ryan," said Sparky's father, in a heavy Italian accent.

"Oh, well I'm Irish, German and Italian, a third each."

"How can you be a third of something?" asked Sparky, pleased to hear Ryan was only partly Italian.

Ryan was a third Irish, German and Italian - which is not an easy combination to be. Even allowing for rounding off, for practical purposes, you'd have to go back to your great-great-great grand-parents and claim to have six of one ethnicity and five of two others to even come close to a third each of three distinct ethnicities. And, that's assuming you were able to track back that far. Even then, it's a highly implausible combination. Throughout his life, though, Ryan had told people he was a third Irish, German and Italian and not a single person had ever questioned him before on it.

"I've only got three grandparents" said Ryan, not even slightly nonplussed to be explaining this for the first time.

"Howa you only got three a grandparents?" asked Sparky's mother.

"Well, my mom and dad grew up next door neighbors. You know, childhood sweethearts. My grandpa Cordardo, who was married to my Irish grandmother, had a fling with the German woman next door – mom's mom – Grandma Mencken. We didn't know until dad made a deathbed confession about mom being his half-sister. My mom still denies it."

"In Italy you a-marry your cousin, not your sister," said Sparky's mom. "You must a shocked."

"No, it was a relief" explained Ryan, "Grandma Mencken's husband was a Jew."

Ryan's anti-Semitism made up for his part Irish and German ancestry; Sparky's parents approved the marriage. So, the Newark daughter of Calabrese cousins and the Brooklyn boy of sibling-parents wed. The Cordardo couple chose Staten Island - located roughly between Brooklyn and Newark - as the compromise place to live, the first and only compromise Sparky would ever make with Ryan. Bayonne is more directly between Newark and Brooklyn but all agreed it was the home of too many Pollacks.

To her disappointment, her first – and only - child was a masculine child. The twenty-five year old Sparky was already looking to groom an eventual successor, but her womb grew as hostile as she, so she would have to settle for Bullo. Bullo would serve a purpose, though. Sparky knew she would almost certainly outlive her husband, whose health suffered greatly under the strain of her emotional abuse. Bullo would be groomed as the future flunkey, after Sparky was widowed and too old to trap another toady. Sparky tamped down on every spark of independence and personality the child Bullo would show, with wooden spoon a-wielding. Outside of obeying Sparky, though, Bullo was scarcely disciplined so as to not squash his natural ruffian leanings. Bullo became a low-end punk in his Forest Avenue neighborhood. More someone to be avoided than feared, he had a constant countenance of discontent, in spite of no apparent grievances.

All Sparky wanted for Bullo was a government job with early retirement. Little academic aptitude is required for most civil service jobs but these positions were so highly prized by New York City residents in the 1970s that the city was able to require a college degree - along with family connections - to secure one. Studies were already beginning to show that applicants with high IQs were poor candidates for police and firefighter positions because they quickly became bored with the profession and often quit after a couple of years. With Bullo, there was no risk of him growing bored with the lack of intellectual stimulation from passing time at the fire hall. Bullo would go on to attend and graduate from Saint John's University with a solid gentleman's C average and a Bachelor of Science degree in accounting before becoming a fire fighter.

The lazy life of card playing and lifting weights suited him and his accounting degree allowed him to earn side money preparing income taxes. Beset with chromes, diverticulitis, GURD and severe irritable bowel syndrome, Bullo's father Ryan died during Bullo's first year as a fireman. Before the funeral, Sparky handed Bullo his father's wedding ring. Without words being spoken, Bullo placed it on his ring finger where it would remain the rest of his life.

4 - Dr. Koop

"Willie, who would have imagined you as a full-fledged member of the bourgeois?" asked Tony, while refilling his glass of Bardolino at the Magillicutty family Thanksgiving Day gathering.

"What do you mean?"

"You and I both grinded our way to accounting degrees, but as far as I could tell you never had much interest in an accounting career."

"In debits and credits? No - that's boring stuff. Accounting is just a means of breaking into the business world."

"But now you've got the traditional bean-counter job and a pregnant wife. Me? I always planned on having a traditional accountant's career, but working in a CPA's office – for me - is unfulfilling."

"You're gonna leave accounting?"

Tony and Willie had been squeezed in the narrow kitchen of Tony's parent's house, just an ear-shot from the dining room table full with nosey Magillicutty women. Tony nodded towards the deck where he and Willie could talk in private. "Gwen and I have come to an agreement. Rather than use our savings - mostly gifts from the wedding - towards a down payment on a house, I'm going to make a foray into the restaurant business. In exchange, Gwen's not going back to work when the baby is born."

"No kidding?"

"It's ironic, a year ago we were both single - you chasing skirts at that bar, while I was, basically, Mr. Rogers with a slide-rule. Now we both have pregnant wives getting ready to pop, but you're the guy with the nine to five job and benefits, and I'm the one rolling the dice."

"Hmmm" said Willie, too embarrassed to admit he had already been laid off from his accounting job and not wanting to one-up Tony by letting him know he was way ahead of him in the dice rolling department.

Willie and Leah had made no particular deal as to how their rolls would change or money be spent once they were married and their daughter had been born. It would never have occurred to Willie to consult Leah or 'come to a deal' to begin with. Of course Leah would continue to work after their child was born with Willie's and Leah's mothers providing the free day care.

Willie's nature wouldn't allow him to continue in the monotonous number-crunching jobs he'd been working fulltime since his engagement to Leah. A couple of weeks after Willie and Leah had returned from their honeymoon, Willie began sowing the seeds for his termination with the staffing agency that was getting him accounting jobs. Willie didn't deliberately set out to get himself fired, rather he passive-aggressively made his way onto the State of New Jersey Unemployment Insurance rolls by calling out sick, coming in late and performing unsatisfactorily. Once married, Willie gained control of Leah's modest weekly check. That, along with his part-time off-the-books bartending income, covered their basic expenses. Now, with plenty of free time, a weekly stipend from the State of New Jersey and the nearly twenty thousand dollars in cash from wedding gifts, Willie planned on day-trading the Rocinante's savings into a small fortune.

"I knew you'd be back to bartending."

"Just part-time, Pete, for some pocket money to supplement my unemployment."

"I've been thinking of getting a job too, so I can collect unemployment."

"Who's gonna hire you, Pete?"

"I know, they should have bartending gigs where they take taxes out, like a regular job."

"You wanna pay taxes now?"

"Only to collect. Anyway, if you're unemployed, why aren't you bartending full-time?"

"I won't be bartending at all after a couple months and I'm done with accounting."

"You'll never quit bartending for good. And, you'll be back

to accounting too, once your unemployment runs out."

"No, Pete I'm done. I'm becoming a trader."

It was nearly December 1999, just weeks before the millennium – numerically, if not mathematically. Barstools across the country were full of middle-aged, - and not quite middle-aged men - living in their parent's basements or married to working women, who were day-trading for a living. Mostly, they were just buying the same stocks back and forth from each other, bidding up the price and creating the illusion of wealth accumulation: a classic bubble. It was really just a form of 'respectable' gambling. You couldn't well tell your family that you had retired at age thirty-seven from factory work, restaurant-management, plumbing, sales, truck-driving or whatever other line of drudgery that paid the bills in the past, in order to earn a living betting football. However, stock-trading had an air of respectability to it and day-trading was down-right sexy. You weren't too lazy to drag your sorry rear-end out of bed every morning at six and put in ten hours of toil to eke out a living for your family. Rather, you were a sharp, shrewd capitalist turning the eight thousand dollar lump sum you took from your 401-K when you got canned and were spinning it into a lifetime annuity for you and your family. Unlike 'gambling', stocks weren't a zero-sum game. Stocks always go up, don't they?

The coalescing of the internet, low-cost online stock trading, massive Y2K capital spending and dot-com IPOs created a perfect bubble-mania storm that would have left seventeenth century Dutch tulip-bulb buyers bedazzled. The unemployed, stock-trading novices sitting in their underwear before their computer screens were simply bidding up the price of valueless dot-com stocks between each other. The founders of these companies and the investment bankers who put the IPO deals together had long since walked away with their take. What was left was no more valuable than a chain letter - the greater fool theory - except nobody realized they were fools.

A racket this dubious could never avoid ensnaring Willie. For a couple of years, Willie had heard story after story of bar-stool Buffets bragging about their day-trading fortunes but he lacked the funds to try it himself. Now, with twenty thousand dollars in cash from his wedding, pocket money from a few off-the-books bartending shifts he reacquired from Madison Ave and his weekly unemployment check from New Jersey, Willie was ready to put the indignity of wage-slavery behind him and begin his day-trading career.

"What are you talking about Willie, Stocks? What do you know about stocks?"

"I bought a book: *Trade Stocks, Chase Skirts and Retire at 30* by Bulbo Tulipanos; he's the fourth wealthiest day-trader in all of San Giuseppi, Sicily.

"Willie, you're already thirty-four, and you've never read past the second chapter of a book in your whole life."

"I'll be retired before forty. And, he's got a cassette course - just five easy payments of five hundred fifty-five dollars."

"You still owe me two thousand dollars for rent after you split to get married!"

Willie certainly did no research. The bare minimum knowledge he acquired in school regarding balance-sheets, income-statements and cash-flow reports had long since been forgotten. The famous dot-com stocks of the day were on the lips of everyone, even non-traders: eToys; Pets.com; GeoCities; Disney's Go.com; and Lou Dobbs' Space.com. Willie simply had to choose one. Willie chose Drkoop.com, a website providing healthcare information. Today, such a site would be called a blog, likely run by an unemployed art-history major/wannabe writer who minored in exercise science. In 1999, such nonsense was considered the next McDonald's or Microsoft. The DrKoop.com IPO raised nearly $100 million based solely on the fact that a million and a half readers browsed through their articles each month. These stocks had no earnings and barely any revenues. Rather than be valued by price/earnings ratios, cash-flow, or even some dubious future profit projection, these stocks were being valued by 'mouse-clicks'. Every twenty-two year old searching the Dr. Koop site to see if the blister on their lip was a cold-sore or herpes, translated into thousands of dollars of market value for the ridiculous 'company'.

The irony of Willie investing in an enterprise of someone famous for advocating condom use, which Willie eschewed, never occurred to Willie. Dr. Koop was President' Reagan's staunchly pro-life choice for Surgeon General who proceeded to horrify President Reagan's socially conservative base by becoming the world's foremost advocate of the use of condoms after the onset of the AIDS epidemic. Willie was scarcely aware of who even the president at any given moment was, much less who was the surgeon general when he was twenty years old. Still, Willie would have failed to see the irony of his DrKoop.com investment even if he had known that Dr. Koop had championed the prophylactic in the 1980s.

"I'll pay you back – with interest – next month."

"That quick, Willie? How are you making that much that quick."

"OPM, Pete. OPM."

"What the hell's OPM?"

"Other People's Money."

"You mean like my two grand?"

"No – I mean leverage - margin. You invest a thousand dollars, but you own two thousand dollars of stocks - you double your profit."

"It kinda sounds like credit cards for stocks."

"It is, except, instead of paying interest, you're getting rich instead of the credit card company."

Willie wasn't a day-trader in the strictest sense. For one thing, Willie seldom got out of bed before 11:00 a.m. His evening shifts a Madison Ave usually began at five and the stock markets conveniently close at four. So, Willie was more of an afternoon-trader. Moreover, Willie didn't trade regularly. Rather, he simply sat in front of his computer screen for hours at end clicking the refresh button to watch the direction of his stock. Thanks to margin, Willie was two hundred percent invested - all in Drkoop.com - and had tripled his money in a couple of weeks before he finally decided to sell. Willie hadn't given up on DrKoop.com. In fact, he planned on reinvesting all his money back into Dr. Koop as soon as he and Leah returned from Disney World after Christmas through New Year's Day week. In addition to needing funds for the vacation, Willie simply did not want to be invested while he was away and unable to watch the stock price on his computer screen all day. What hadn't occurred to Willie was that he had incurred a forty thousand dollar short-term capital-gain which would cost Willie and Leah ten thousand dollars on their federal tax return alone.

Even though Willie could prepare basic tax returns, he had no sense for tax planning. However, even if he realized he was facing a ten thousand dollar tax bill, it wouldn't have phased Willie one bit. He was making more than two thousand a day day-trading - ten thousand dollars was nothing.

When Willie returned from his vacation, he reinvested the fifty-two thousand dollars he had left after paying for the vacation and putting a down-payment on a new Jeep lease. Again, Willie used leverage, so he had a hundred thousand dollar bet on Dr.Koop.com. As earning reports showed Dr.Koop.com loosing tens of millions of dollars, and had only scant revenues from advertising, the stock plummeted. Willie received a margin call on his loan and his entire position was quickly and completely wiped out.

On Leap Day, an exhausted Tony and despondent Willie sat in the maternity waiting room at JFK hospital in Edison waiting for their daughters to be born. Leah and Gwen had gone into labor within minutes of each other. For Tony, it was his first half-day off since acquiring the Lakeview Pancake House in January. Trusting none of his acquired staff, he abruptly closed the restaurant midday. Willie pulled Tony aside for some advice on the quagmire he was in regarding his own tax return for 1999.

"Tony, Datek sent me a form 1099-B for sixty thousand dollars for some DrKoop.com stock I sold."

"Wow!" said Tony, taken back a bit. "Good for you . . . and you got out just in time. How much did you make?"

"Nothing . . . I lost it all - twenty grand."

"What do you mean? What's the 1099 with sixty grand for?"

"I put twenty grand into the stock - you know - after the wedding and it went up to sixty thousand. I sold it to pay for the vacation and whatnot . . . that's really my only profit - the eight grand for the jeep and Disney World."

"Willie, it doesn't matter how much of the profit you spent. You still bought a stock for twenty grand and sold it for sixty. That's a forty thousand dollar gain. You're probably looking at ten grand in taxes."

"I didn't make any money. I bought back into the stock and it went to zero . . . fifty two grand . . . "

"That stock's not zero yet, but it will be - you should sell it now."

"It's already sold - I bought it on margin before it crashed."

"Oh, geez."

"Datek closed out my position without even asking me . . . wiped it out completely. They say I still owe them seven hundred or something for the commissions and interest, or something."

"So, you don't even have the money to pay the taxes?"

"What taxes? I told you, I lost the whole twenty grand - minus the eight thousand I spent."

"When did Datek close out your position?"

"January."

"That's why you're back at Madison Ave full-time . . . "

"Can't I write off the twelve thousand dollar loss?"

"Willie, this is a nightmare scenario. Your loss occurred in 2000, not 1999. You don't have a twelve thousand dollar loss. You have a forty thousand dollar gain in 1999 and a . . . what . . . fifty thousand dollar loss in 2000."

Willie just stared at Tony waiting for him to provide a solution to his mess. "What can I do?"

"You're completely screwed, Willie. You're going to owe ten grand, maybe a little less - I don't know what you guys make - and beginning in 2000 you're going to have a three thousand dollar a year tax write-off every year until 2017!"

"But, it's a wash sale . . . "

"It doesn't work that way, Willie. Wash-sale rules prevent you from taking a loss on a stock for tax purposes that you buy back within thirty days."

"This was less than thirty days."

"It only applies to losses - to keep traders from working the system. When you have gains, you're expected to manage that yourself. What you did is accelerate your gains and then spread out your losses over two decades. It's a worst case scenario."

"We don't have ten grand - I lost it all . . . how can I pay the taxes?"

"Gwen's got a cousin who's a lawyer, maybe he can file an offer in compromise for you to the IRS . . . Sammy Riscatto . . . I can ask Gwen for his number."

"Make sure she doesn't say anything to Leah . . . she doesn't know I blew all the wedding money."

An hour later, the twin cousins – Wilma and Nicole - were born.

5 - Tony Pepperoni's Pork Roll & Pizza

Unable to chew through the duct tape that was wrapped three times around his head, nor Houdini his way out of the quarter inch nylon rope that bound his wrists behind his back, his ankles together and his ankles and wrists to the pitch black stockroom's metal support beam, Tony determined to wait out the evening - maybe even get some sleep - and hope that his opening waitress would have the sense to try the back door when she came in for her opening shift to find the front door still locked.

Upon waking at 2:00 in the morning to find that Tony had never come home that evening, Gwen frantically called Tony's parents who picked her and Nicole up and drove to the restaurant. Tony's car was gone, but the back door to the restaurant was ajar. It was 3:30 in the morning, just ninety minutes before he needed to be up again to open the restaurant, when they found him. They quickly unbound Tony, expecting him to be traumatized, but he wasn't.

"My God, Tony you must be frightened to death. We have to drive you to the police," said Gwen. Tony was only interested in ripping the duct tape off his head without pulling any hair from his scalp.

"Do you know who they were? Someone you fired maybe? I know you like firing people," said Tony's father, Eddie. "Can you describe them to the police?"

"A couple of black guys in ski masks. I'm not going to the police, it's a waste of time. I just want to get home and take a shower so I can open up on time tomorrow?"

"You're opening the restaurant tomorrow?" asked Gwen.

"Yeah, why not?"

"I'm not driving you home until you go to the police department," said Eddie.

"I can drive myself home."

"Your car's gone."

"I forgot about the car."

The car being stolen bothered Tony almost more than being held up at gunpoint and having his till with a day full of receipts stolen. With the car being stolen, Tony had no choice but to involve the police, for insurance purposes if nothing else. The past eight months had left Tony not only nearly penniless - the robbers had left the nickels and pennies in the cash register till – but made him feel more like a prisoner than being tied and taped had. However, lying bound and taped on his stockroom floor for five hours had brought Tony to an epiphany regarding his previous eight months of toil. "It's not only foolish, but also almost mathematically impossible to run an ordinary, cash business profitably using honest accounting."

Armed with an accounting degree, ten years of business experience and a miscellaneous restaurant resume of part-time college jobs, Tony had been convinced he could take a foundering, or marginally profitable restaurant, and turn it into a financial success just by applying sound fiscal and managerial procedures. Tony's accounting work had given him the opportunity to see many small business operations, including restaurants, up close. Tony was seldom impressed with the business acumen of the hamburger-flippers and dough-rollers that ran the typical New Jersey pizzeria, deli or family-style restaurants.

The Lakeview Pancake House had been a fledgling family-style restaurant that catered to the Jersey-shore summer crowd. After Labor Day and until Memorial Day weekend, the restaurant struggled to break even. The restaurant was run by a husband-wife team with the husband doing most of the cooking and the wife helping with food prep and covering open waitress shifts. Tony figured he would keep the successful breakfast menu the same, but change the lunch and dinner menu that focused on low margin, early-bird specials and attracted mostly grey-haired geriatric cases from Ocean Grove. The restaurant owners were tired of the six-day, ninety hour work-weeks with only Wednesday's off, when the restaurant closed. The long hours didn't faze Tony who assumed he would have the restaurant largely run with assistant managers and that he'd take a more supervisory role after a transitionary period. Tony was able to pick-up the restaurant for just a twenty thousand dollar down payment and a monthly note of just over fifteen hundred a month that would last for forty eight months, the length of the lease that Tony assumed.

Tony closed on the restaurant in January. He was either going to work one full last tax season or none at all. Financially, it would have been better to work the tax season and then take over the restaurant in May. However, jumping from a hundred hour tax season work week into a restaurant in May that was largely a seasonal, summer business would have been insane. Besides, that would have given Tony no time to make the changes to the restaurant he planned before the summer rush began on Memorial Day weekend. So, February 1st, instead of twelve weeks of fattening up on tax fees, Tony took over a restaurant that barely broke even October through December and in January through March was lucky not to lose too much. Worse, Tony had a fifteen hundred dollar monthly nut the previous owner didn't have and he had to hire two extra employees to cover the previous owner's wife's shifts. The two extra employees, though, were only a part of Tony's added payroll expense.

"I understand that the previous management had the practice of paying all of you in cash" said Tony, in a meeting with the Lakeview Pancake House staff prior to taking over. "That all ends today. In order to offset the cost of FICA and New Jersey Unemployment and Disability taxes, I'm giving each of you a ten percent wage increase."

"We have to pay taxes now?"

"The ten percent increase I'm giving you will more than pay your Social Security and New Jersey Unemployment and Disability taxes. Your income taxes should be minimal. In fact, many of you will now qualify for an Earned Income Tax Credit that you cheated yourself out of by working strictly cash. Plus, now if you get sick or hurt, you'll be covered with state disability insurance and you'll be contributing towards your future Social Security income. Best of all, now you won't have to worry about anyone knocking on your door."

Tony explained this with the naive confidence that his making them legitimate, legal employees and his picking up most of the tab would be viewed favorably, even gratefully, by the restaurant's staff. It wasn't. First, 'the ten percent increase I'm giving you' was taken as arrogant and patronizing by the staff. They were netting the same, or slightly less in most cases, thanks to Tony putting them on the books. That the payroll taxes were being paid out of Tony's pocket meant nothing to them. Putting them on the books was *his* issue, not theirs. Why shouldn't he pay for it? Further, working off the books provided a certain cultural satisfaction to many in the restaurant-worker subculture. It was a form of defiance, a way of sticking it to the man. The typical dishwasher, busboy or waitress would rather earn ninety dollars in cash then receive a net paycheck of one hundred dollars. Checks were deposited into banks and went to pay bills. Being paid in cash, daily, meant never feeling poor - you always had money in your pocket. Most of the restaurant workers couldn't manage checking accounts anyway. Many of them now had to waste their time and money visiting check-cashing businesses and those with checking accounts often found them over-drawn resulting in their paychecks going to cover fees and overdrawn checks.

The ten percent pay increase, the new employer payroll taxes - which the previous owner never paid -, the workmen's compensation insurance - which the previous owner wasn't required to purchase because he had no official employees as Tony did - and the two new employees to cover the owner's wife shifts weren't the only added labor costs Tony had to meet, although they were the only ones Tony was aware of for a while. Employee theft skyrocketed upon Tony's arrival. February was a slow month for tips for the waitresses and busboys and the dishwashers and cooks all had their hours cut. Increased seasonal thievery was an understood cost of doing business in the winter on the Jersey shore. Under Tony, the winter season stealing soared. The staff simply didn't like him. They couldn't identify with him. Tony wasn't used to working with working-class people and he wasn't relating to them. A little owner-empathy went a long way toward minimizing employee theft. With Tony in charge, even the carpeting and ceiling tiles weren't safe.

The only immediate change Tony made to the Lakeview Pancake House, besides legitimizing its accounting, was opening on Wednesday. So, Tony was out of the accounting business yet he was now working more hours during tax season than a practicing tax accountant. Except, instead of raking in fees, Tony was bleeding cash. After making his down payment on the restaurant, Tony only had a small cache of cash left, and that was earmarked for the new sign, menus, pizza ovens and advertising for when Tony converted the Lakeview Pancake House into Tony Pepperoni's Pork Roll & Pizza.

Tony grinded his way through the winter and early spring under the Lakeview Pancake House banner, firing over half the staff and only replacing half the employees he had fired. By late April, Tony was sucking wind physically and financially. Tony's thirty-five year old body had been trained by ten tax seasons to work like a dog all winter, but also expected rest come April 16th on a huge bed of cash from preparing hundreds of tax returns. Now, Tony was flat broke, juggling bills to keep his checking account in the black but his real work was only about to begin - the Jersey Shore summer season.

Between the payroll, insurance, rent, taxes, food costs, thievery, the monthly business note and utilities, Tony managed to just scrape by, erect the new Tony Pepperoni's Pork Roll & Pizza sign, change the menu, install the pizza ovens and run a few advertisements in the local paper. Better still, Tony's classifieds for summer restaurant help in the Rutgers and Monmouth College school newspapers brought Tony a slew of applicants to replace nearly the entire staff he had inherited from the Lakeview Pancake House. Tony took a cold delight in laying off the old staff, all of whom continued to refer to the restaurant as the Lakeview Pancake House and to Tony as Tony Violette, instead of Tony Pepperoni. Now Tony was surrounded by bright young college students he liked and who could culturally identify with him. Tony had reached bottom financially, but things were looking up. He had a new staff, the restaurant had been converted and his season to cash in was around the corner. Tony had only fallen short on two of his plans. Any hopes of Tony hiring an assistant manager were put off for at least a year. Tony was flat broke and couldn't afford the added expense. Also, Tony wanted to offer delivery as well as eat in and pick up service for his pizza business but learned the liability and workmen's compensation insurance would increase tens of thousands of dollars if he did.

Tony Pepperoni's summer season was a moderate success. Tony worked like a dog, cracking eggs in the morning, flipping burgers for lunch and rolling pizza dough in the evening. The Jersey Shore is full of competition in the pizza business and Tony's pie was no worse and no better than average. Still, it filled the booths and tables better than the Lakeview Pancake House's early-bird meat loafs and hot-opened turkey sandwiches. What Tony would do after Labor Day when his staff went back to school and the Joeys and Paulies who patronized Tony Pepperoni's went back home to Bayonne, Staten Island and Elizabeth, Tony hadn't figured out yet. Some of the students from Monmouth College could continue to work evenings and weekends, but Tony knew he'd have to hire some local scrubs to work mornings and afternoon shifts now.

The day of the robbery was the Wednesday before Labor Day. It was the kind of nasty thunderstorm day that Tony knew not having a delivery service was costing him hundreds of dollars. The slow afternoon, though, gave Tony his long-awaited opportunity to look hard at his financial statements for the past four months - embarrassingly primitive and non-GAAP for a former staff accountant - but for a couple of hours, he felt like a financial professional again, but his figures were troubling. Certainly Tony had accumulated some cash in his checking account - it would be difficult not to make money selling anything in Bradley Beach, New Jersey in June, July and August - but Tony's accounts payable where high and, except for a couple weeks of credit card charges he hadn't been paid for yet, his receivables were zero. Tony's summer receipts, while short of his expectations, weren't so bad. Tony brought in nearly a quarter of a million dollars in both July and August. June was an additional hundred and fifty thousand and September, like May had a chance to hit the hundred thousand dollar mark. The restaurant's sales would exceed one million for the year easily - even without a January - but there was something missing . . . profit.

Tony priced everything on his menu to the exact average price of every competing restaurant within ten miles. Tony was religious about this. Also, Tony's food was average. Nothing on the menu was bad, nor was anything spectacular. This was all by design. Tony's business plan was to simply run a tighter, more efficient restaurant than the competition. Tony didn't have to be better, he just couldn't be worse. He believed he could open an identical restaurant to one next door and earn a profit while the business next store lost money, simply due to Tony's accounting and business smarts. Except . . . Tony wasn't making money.

"It doesn't make any sense" Tony thought. "I'm not charging a dime less than anyone else in the area, they've been in business for years, yet I'm barely going to be able to put enough money aside to survive until next Memorial Day. Gwen's going to have to get a job. Who's going to watch Nicole?

"The dining room is basically full all day. . . we could maybe hope to increase sales another fifteen or twenty percent, but our labor costs are almost fifty percent . . . fifty percent . . . food costs are thirty five percent, which is fine . . . but what's the point of increasing sales if marginal costs are eighty five percent? How are all these pizzerias and delis staying in business all these years on these margins? I'm facing eight months ahead of net breakeven business at best, only to start the whole cycle over again in May?"

Worse, all Tony had to look forward to was a half day off on Thanksgiving and his only day off for the year on Christmas. What would he do if he got sick or hurt? It wasn't even something he contemplated. His dishwashers and cooks and waitresses, though, were all covered now under State of New Jersey short-term disability and Social Security long-term disability should they fall ill, but not him. That's the way Tony was. He wasn't altruistic or a champion of the working man. If anything, he was dismissive of them. He had just assumed his work ethic and smarts would be rewarded ahead of shiftless souls who only seek to work the system. It wasn't.

While taped and tied in his stockroom, it all became clear to Tony. "What have I done? What was I thinking? It would be bad enough if the restaurant was a failure, but business is robust, or at least, fairly decent. I'm employing dozens of people, feeding thousands more and paying hundreds of thousands of dollars in taxes . . . only to break even?!"

The resentment people feel towards people in 'cash businesses' that don't report all their income is often un-warranted and based upon an undynamic understanding of the financial circumstances these people operate in. People in industries in which their reported income and sales are easily concealed do not compete in a vacuum. Having two sets of books in a cash business isn't an unfair advantage - it's a required skill with real costs. The ability to not remit all collected sales tax to the state, to save on payroll taxes and pay a lower wage by paying in cash and the ability to claim the income you want rather than the income you actually earned on your tax return is just a competitive tool that all cash-industry businesses must engage in simply to compete on an even playing field.

"How do I explain to Gwen that I blew our savings and wasted a year of my life because I was the only sucker committed to playing by the capricious rules of politicians and bureaucrats?"

Being in a cash business is actually a burden to its members rather than an advantage. The benefit of being able to hide income and transactions falls to the customer who pays a lower price and thereby benefits society in general rather than the cash business owner who superficially seems to be the one who benefits. The cash-businessman is actually put in a vulnerable position, always potentially subject to tax evasion charges; tax evading that benefits his customers, not him. He is often unable to qualify for the loan terms he should be entitled to because he cannot validate his true income and he cheats himself out of higher future Social Security benefits by underreporting his income during his working days.

"I've worked over twenty-six hundred hours, collected and submitted to the State of New Jersey nearly sixty thousand dollars in sales tax, paid out over a half million in salary, payroll taxes and workmen's compensation premiums and I've got nothing to show for it!"

In fact, the twenty six hundred stolen from the cash register combined with the thirty thousand of employee theft Tony had estimated was more than he was likely to take from the restaurant for the entire year. A restaurant like Tony Pepperoni's Pork Roll & Pizza breaking even with $1.2 million in sales can be transformed into an after-tax equivalent of a hundred thousand dollar annual income by simply using creative accounting.

"The State of New Jersey alone is raking in an average of six thousand dollars a month in sales tax and I'm not even compensated for collecting the tax!" Less than a quarter of Tony's sales were credit cards, the rest was cash. "I can report almost any amount of sales I want. If I only claim fifty percent of the sales I can pocket three of the six thousand dollars of sales tax New Jersey is collecting for doing nothing", a policy Tony quickly reduced to thirty percent. "Thirty-six thousand in cash a year is the equivalent of forty-five thousand dollars of reported income. I'm already halfway to a six-figure equivalent income with just one maneuver." Only reporting half his sales meant Tony couldn't deposit most of the cash he collected so he also started paying his help in cash. "Paying the staff in cash alone will save nearly fifty thousand dollars a year in payroll taxes and workmen's compensation insurance premiums."

In just a few hours of confinement, Tony had transformed his restaurant from a cash bleeding behemoth into an equivalent six figure income enterprise. And, he had his armed robbers to thank for it.

6 - You wanna step outside?

Throughout his firefighting career, Bullo Cordardo had bounced around between more than a dozen CPA firms in Staten Island who hired extra accountants to help during tax season. Bullo became a cancer at every firm he worked and seldom was invited back for a second season. CPA firms generally focus on business taxes. Fees from individual returns during tax season are considered gravy that there often isn't enough time to attend to. Seasonal accountants like Bullo are hired to prepare returns and hand them off to CPAs to sign, take credit for and bill at CPA rates.

During his final tax season before retiring as a fireman, Bullo worked for Debitetto & Credle, CPAs on Victory Boulevard in Staten Island. It was his first and only season with Debitetto & Credle. Accountant Arnold Dainty had handled the surplus simple tax returns himself for Debitetto & Credle for years and received a twenty-five percent commission for the fees charged. Besides working as a tax season accountant, Dainty was a math teacher at Port Richmond High School. His full time teaching position limited the hours he could work and with business robust, Debitetto & Credle brought in Bullo to share the extra returns.

Thanks to his flexible hours with the fire department, Bullo was beating Dainty to the office, grabbing the majority of available files and cherry picking the clients he left behind for Dainty, typically the time consuming returns with numerous stock trades or boxes of receipts that were a nuisance to prepare. Dainty felt a twinge of anxiety as he passed Bullo's cubical, scrupulously avoiding eye contact. "Grrrr" muttered Bullo, annoyed by Dainty's mere presence. The bin on Dainty's desk was empty.

"Where are my files?" asked Dainty, to no one in particular, but only Bullo was in earshot. Bullo said nothing. Dainty headed to the office of a senior partner, Craig Credle. Dainty counted on his tax season income to pay off Christmas credit card bills and fund the family summer vacation. In spite of his tenure with the firm, Dainty's complaints about Bullo's greed were dismissed.

It was late February and Credle was swamped with work. Seasonal accountants like Dainty weren't greatly respected, particularly since they didn't bring business into the firm, they simply fed off the crumbs of others. If anything, Credle respected Bullo's aggressiveness. "Just do your best to get along with him."

In frustration, and in front of the office secretary and afternoon receptionist, Dainty pleaded with Bullo. "You are not being fair. Please, only take your fair share of the files."

"You wanna step outside?" asked Bullo.

Dainty just shook his head and slunk out of the office. Immediately, Bullo took to badmouthing Dainty when he wasn't in the office and finding petty reasons to confront him when he was. Worse, Bullo started surreptitiously removing documents from the files that he did leave behind for Dainty and tossed out phone messages left on Dainty's desk to undermine him. As the returns Dainty completed started coming back from IRS and New York State with corrections, the embarrassed CPAs, who had signed - but never looked at - the returns Dainty completed, gave less and less work to him.

Dainty appealed again to Credle, this time complaining of Bullo's abuse. Worse, Dainty made the mistake of letting Bullo know he was going to Credle. Once it was apparent that there would be no repercussions from Dainty's latest meeting with Credle, Bullo stepped the harassment up further, referring to him as 'Daintily' in front of others and mercilessly staring him down. Dainty was stung that he received no support or defense from any of his coworkers. Most of them simply were relieved that it wasn't them suffering from Bullo's wrath. Raising his voice and pointing to the ceiling, Dainty shouted "Remember Martin Niemöller!" and walked out.

Likely, none of them knew the reference to begin with, but Dainty proved prophetic. With Dainty gone, Bullo's abuse spread. First, it was only the office staff who suddenly were alarmed by Bullo's viciousness and controlling behavior. However, with Bullo now the only tax season accountant on staff, the partners were even less inclined to discipline him. Later, the junior accountants were targets for Bullo's malevolence. Bullo resented that they were younger and better paid them him. Only the senior partners were exempt from his grief. Bullo knew it would likely only be a one year assignment with no offer to return again. Further, with his pending retirement from the fire department, he had thoughts of opening his own office anyway. His workload was heavy now with Dainty gone and threats and intimidation always seemed like less work to Bullo than persuasion to get people to do what he wanted.

In addition to the returns he had prepared for the various CPA firms that had employed him, Bullo prepared taxes for many of the firefighters he worked with. Unlike the accountants he worked with, Bullo didn't strong-arm any of his fellow firefighters - quite the opposite. Bullo was easily intimidated by many of them and learned early on that the best way for him to please them was to get them juicy tax refunds. Although he was under no restriction from pursuing side work by the accounting firms he did seasonal work for, Bullo adopted the practice of most accountants who work for large firms and do have contracts forbidding them to do work outside the firm, namely, Bullo refused to sign any of the returns he did for the other firefighters and was always paid in cash. The returns were all done by hand - in Bullo's handwriting - and marked "self-prepared" in the paid preparer section of the tax return. In his laziness, Bullo even had a stamper made with the words 'self-prepared', never considering how ridiculously obvious it would be to anyone paying attention that no tax filer who prepared their own taxes would bother to get a stamp to save them the trouble of printing out the twelve letters in 'self-prepared' once a year. Clearly, these returns had an anonymous preparer. Fortunately for Bullo, no one was paying attention most of the time.

Bullo learned early on that line-by- line scrutinization of tax returns for middle income earners by the IRS was extremely rare. This emboldened Bullo, especially on his unsigned, fireman returns. Bullo's side practice thrived by providing fellow firefighters with eye-popping refunds. "I knew H & R block was screwing me" was the usual reaction to Bullo's work. Thousands of dollars of unmade charitable contributions, ridiculous uniform and equipment deductions and even business meals for their own lunches were written off - after all, they couldn't leave the fire house, so their meals were business meals, right? - reducing the firemen's tax liabilities typically fifteen hundred to two thousand dollars less than had it been prepared legitimately.

No one ever questioned Bullo on how he was able to get them such high refunds. Most of the firemen were fairly dull when it came to financial matters and fairly quick to believe they had been getting screwed in the past. The smarter ones figured the returns were not square and knew enough to play dumb and not think of potential consequences.

The tax returns became even more bogus when Bullo started to prepare returns for some police officers who had been referred to Bullo by their fireman friends. The cops to a man were even more dishonest and aggressive on their returns than the firemen and they were even more intimidating to Bullo than his fellow firemen, even though they were seldom in as good of shape. The cops, mostly Irishmen - as opposed to the firemen who were almost all Italian - spent their days shaking down pimps and drug dealers and busting gangbangers. They were barroom brawlers with a badge and free-agents when it came to following the law. They were New York City's cowboys.

"Can't you do any better than this?" they'd grunt at Bullo, handing them over a 'self-prepared' tax return done by another accountant, but not yet mailed in. One thousand dollars in range fees, seven-fifty for ammo, fifteen-hundred in uniform dry cleaning, thirty-five hundred dollars in church donations - these were returns that even made Bullo cringe – but they felt entitled to more. Bullo never disappointed them. If their previous non-signing accountant inflated the deductions by four thousand, Bullo inflated them by six thousand. The well paid firemen and police officers were usually in the twenty eight percent tax bracket - plus the State of New York and New York City taxes - so, two thousand dollars of extra write offs would be worth seven or eight hundred more to their already inflated refunds.

"You gonna start looking for a fulltime accounting job soon?" asked Sparky, as she ladled tomato sauce onto his plate of sausage and pasta, intentionally ignoring Bullo's hints of opening his own office.

"I've already got my own clients. I just need to expand some."

"Side-work doesn't make for a business, it's for cash pocket money."

"I've been putting in two full days every week at the firehouse for twenty years; I'd like to know what it's like to have a summer off." Bullo had no experience in business accounting and that was year-long work. "I want to focus on individual returns. I just have to expand beyond the firemen. They all expect miracles and they all expect a discount because I'm also a fireman."

Bullo wanted to expand beyond his aggressive fireman and police officer client base. These were risky returns with clients who were extremely demanding - not a promising business model - but Bullo's demeanor and his general dislike of people made it difficult for him to attract and retain legitimate clients, and even he knew that.

"Just tell them you'll get them bigger refunds if you can charge them more."

"I'm already taking too much risk for fifteen grand or so in cash, now. Besides, if I want to expand and open an office, I'll have to start signing most of the returns. I can't advertise or have business cards printed up, when I'm not even signing the returns or reporting the income from them."

"What about all these Puerto Ricans on Forrest Avenue with the big signs in their windows? You can do that, can't you?"

"Those are refund mills. If I was a Mexican or Filipino, mom, or colored, maybe . . . I don't want to go to jail for an extra twenty grand each year."

Out-in-the-open phony tax return mills are surprisingly common and often stay in business for longer than one might expect. They usually target-market particular ethnic minority groups, often immigrants who are often only half aware that they are involved in a scam and in a single tax season can turn a simple storefront with a crudely painted 'fast refunds' or 'reembolsos rápidos' sign into a two or three thousand tax return business, profiting hundreds of thousands of dollars, mostly in cash. These firms fearlessly exploit every gimmick, conjure up ridiculous deductions and even engage in the trading of personal exemptions from poor, single mothers with apartment loads of children.

In poor black and Hispanic areas, the Earned Income Tax Credit is the main instrument for fraud. The low-income residents in these areas pay little to no income tax to begin with, so doctoring up fake deductions doesn't work there. The income tax code, however, provides for refunds - refundable credits - for low-income workers with dependent children. A single parent with a couple of children earning fifteen to twenty thousand dollars qualifies for refundable credits up to five thousand dollars but the credit also maxes out with two children, or at least it did in the 1990s, so single mothers with more than two children had valuable names and social security numbers which could be transferred to another's return, without any dependents, generating thousands of dollars of fraudulent refunds. Also, married two-income families with children could falsely be filed as two separate head-of household singles, each taking a kid or two, magically transforming one barely break-even return into two, multi-thousand dollar Earned-Income Tax Credit refund returns.

In higher income target-markets, bogus deductions replaced the Earned Income Tax Credit scams. Doctor and nursing shortages in the 1980s and 1990s brought waves of Filipino immigrants into the New York/New Jersey area. Hardworking Filipino nurses who could no more file their own tax return than rebuild an automobile engine often were making over one hundred thousand dollars working multiple jobs. They were quickly in crushing tax brackets and the chronic under-withholding of taxes from wages from part-time positions left many of them owing thousands of dollars every year. Dozens of phony refund mills catering to the Filipino market sprung up in Brooklyn, Queens, Staten Island, Jersey City and elsewhere to exploit and profit off them. Nurses normally do incur more legitimate work related deductions than most other professions and that is all the opening a phony refund mill requires. Uniform expenses, work related seminars, union dues, travel expenses between jobs are common and legitimate work expenses, costing most nurses a couple of thousand dollars each year. A refund mill, without flinching, will inflate these figures to ten thousand dollars or more and add a few thousand of church deductions, to boot. Suddenly, the two thousand dollar tax bill that H & R Block has handed over to the hardworking immigrant has been transformed into a twenty five hundred dollar refund and they now had a fellow Filipino preparing their returns. Referrals within tight immigrant groups in a shared profession spread at lightning speed. Soon, these refund mills are standing room only and get more brazen every year.

These tax returns can clearly be seen as bogus after a ten second glance over by any marginally competent IRS agent or experienced tax preparer. Still, it was surprisingly rare for one of them to be pulled for a line by line audit. Eventually, yes, they were called in and audited, leaving the filers with tens of thousands of dollars of back taxes, penalties and interest. But, it wasn't their return that would snag them, it would be their preparer. The IRS can quickly pull all of the returns prepared by a single preparer or firm. Once it has been made aware of a bogus refund outlet, it will pull for audit several years of returns for thousands of filers based on a single, fraudulent preparer. No wonder the IRS audits so few individual returns prepared by legitimate firms or 'self-prepared'. Refund mills provide IRS agents enough cases and overtime to make the painstaking, needle-in-a-haystack auditing of ordinary returns a poor and needless investment of time. What happens to the preparers? The smart ones return to their home countries before the operation blows up, but few of them do. These refund mills can operate for a surprising number of years before being shut down and criminals by nature tend to be poor long-term thinkers. Most of them end up doing jail time while their client's finances are devastated.

Bullo wasn't the sharpest pencil in the draw, but he wasn't stupid either. He was more than capable of opening a refund mill, but he would soon have a pension and health benefits for life. He wouldn't be that foolish. Better to stay small and under the radar, he reasoned. Only, how could he get just a little bigger?

7- The Rumson House for the Homeless

While Tony was fibbing down his revenue numbers at Tony Pepperoni's Pork Roll & Pizzeria in order to save on taxes and earn a living, Willie was fibbing up revenue numbers for his new employer. Sammy Riscatto failed to get IRS to accept an offer in compromise on Willie's Dr. Koop tax liability and had to settle for an extended payment plan. Sammy did, however, set Willie up with a new employer: Net Noise.

"Willie, a corporate client of mine – Net Noise – would like to go public or find a buyer. They're looking for an accountant to clean up their financial statements."

"What do you mean 'clean up their financial statements'? I only do accounts payable and receivable work."

"Let's just say, they've got cash-flow problems. They didn't even have money to pay for the contract work I did for them. I accepted stock options instead, which will be worthless unless someone buys them."

"How am I supposed to help them with their cash-flow problems?"

"For one thing, Willie, they need someone who will work cheap – but they'll backload your salary with stock options. So, if they go public, we all win."

"Okay, but I still don't see how I can help with their cash flow problems, other than by working cheaper than someone else."

"Just talk to them Willie – unless you've got something else better to do."

"No."

"There located down in Rumson, near the shore."

"Rumson? That's where Springsteen lives. How are they in Rumson if they've got cash-flow problems?"

"They got a good deal on the rent." Sammy handed Willie Net Noise's President Henry Clarence's business card.

"There's no phone number on the card."

"They're strictly internet-based, Willie. They purposely maintain no phone – that's the future. Just go there and ask to speak to Henry. He's expecting you. Just follow the directions and walk in. They share office space with another operation. Just put the exact address into your GPS and you'll be fine."

Net Noise was an internet music site that offered new bands - at a price - internet exposure. Pre-YouTube, it wasn't an entirely bad idea, a sort of legalize payola. Rather than bribe a DJ to play a new act's record, the new act paid Net Noise to promote their songs and videos on the Net Noise website. Since few sensible record agents were willing to pay Net Noise to promote their bands, Net Noise tried to position itself as a way to cut out the middlemen: the agents, the record companies and the radio stations. Bands could contract with Net Noise directly. Net Noise made no artistic judgments. Whoever paid got promoted. The problem for Net Noise was that startup wannabe singer-songwriters and bands had no money. The profit potential of the venture was bleak. Net Noise's owners reworked their entire business model towards cashing in on an IPO or, better yet, a buyout from a larger internet company.

Willie stopped home to put on his best Hugo Boss double-breasted suit and drove to the Net Noise corporate headquarters on Main Street in Rumson. The business card's address sent Willie to the Rumson House for the Homeless, instead of Net Noise. Worse, the business card contained no phone number, so Willie couldn't call for directions.

Willie pulled into the Starbucks next door. After using the bathroom and ordering a coffee, Willie asked the barista, clad in a Che Guevar T-shirt, if she knew where the headquarters for Net Noise was.

"Of course" she said, pointing next door towards the homeless center. "They're our neighbors."

"The homeless center?"

"Yes – isn't it wonderful?" Willie was too dumfounded to respond. "Oh, and two cents of the six dollars you paid for that coffee goes to help fund a political action committee demanding a livable wage for Indonesian coffee-bean harvesters."

"What time do you get off work?"

"I'm a lesbian, if that's what you are getting at."

"Okay, well I've got an interview next door, anyway."

"Good luck."

Willie grabbed his coffee and walked over to the Rumson House for the Homeless. Inside the spacious, pristine barracks were just two bearded, unkempt men behind two computers. The younger one to the right was playing solitaire. The older, frog-faced man up front was eating a day-old scone and a roasted vegetable panini. He looked up from his screen.

"No more clothing or furniture donations. The sanitation guys won't take them and Starbucks won't let us throw them in their dumpster anymore."

"I was looking for a Henry Clarence from Net Noise."

"Oh – that's me." Henry stood up and offered Willie his hand. "You must be Willie Rocinante. Sammy left a message at the Starbucks that you'd be coming. Sit down."

"I thought you were with Net Noise."

"I am, I'm the president. That's Babu, our computer engineer."

"I don't understand, where's your office?"

"This is my office, Willie. May I call you Willie? In that thousand dollar suit, you look more like a Mr. Rocinante to me."

"You're homeless?"

Henry laughed. "I own a home in Middletown, although I'd like to move here - to Rumson - once Net Noise goes public."

"Why is the office in a homeless shelter?"

"Cash, Willie – there ain't any. I hope Sammy explained that to you."

"He said you had cash flow problems. I'm an accountant – I don't know anything about marketing."

"It's too late in the game for us to try to turn this into a cash generating operation. I need someone who can put lipstick on this pig for a couple of quarters so our financials look promising and we can go public, or maybe get bought out by a large tech company. I wouldn't be able to pay you, Willie, but there's free day-old food from the Starbucks and unlimited hour-old coffee. Once we've got a buyer, you'll make hundreds of thousands of dollars with your stock options."

"How long will that be?"

"Nine months to a year Willie, tops."

"You have no money at all?"

"Less than a thousand dollars in the corporate checking account, plus a couple hundred a month income we get from the website via PayPal."

"How can you even survive nine months with less than a thousand dollars?"

"We don't have any expenses."

"How can you not have any expenses?"

"Well, we have no overhead, we've got free Wi-Fi with the Starbucks next door and we pay everyone with stock options only. This place: a wealthy widow in town, probably senile and with no family, left her entire estate to the Rumson House for the Homeless. Only, *there was no* Rumson House for the Homeless. So, a foundation was created and this building was built with the money from the estate. But they couldn't find any homeless people in Rumson. Now they've got this big place built with no one to use it and, worse, between construction costs and director salaries, there was no more money. So, they applied for federal funding, which they receive to maintain the place, but it's contingent on them actually having homeless people here. For a while they were busing in poor people from Asbury Park, but they grew tired of the stale food. Besides, the economy's so robust, even around Asbury there's more openings than applicants, so the businesses are hiring the homeless now for room and board. They work for free all day and just let them sleep overnight when the businesses are closed.

"Anyway, I made a deal with them. We get free use of the facilities. In exchange, we have to look like we're homeless. So, ditch that fancy suit and wear your workout close to work. And, don't shave until you get home."

So, after taking a beating at day-trading, Willie had a second crack at cashing in on the internet boom. Willie's job was to puff up the startup's phantom income stream as high as he could so the company would look healthy to potential investors. Willie had Net Noise offer bands exposure on their website which they could pay - or, in most cases, couldn't pay - on terms. Who cares if anyone paid anyway? The important thing was that a promise to pay -

even if it was a sixteen year old with a fake email account - would be booked by Willie as revenue. The phantom revenues allowed Net Noise to create a couple of quarters of promising income growth on their financial statements.

Nine months after Willie joined Net Noise they were purchased by a large search engine company looking to throw cash at any web company for sale. Willie walked away with a quarter million from his stock options, netting him nearly a hundred fifty thousand even after paying off his Dr. Koop tax bill. Sammy profited nearly one hundred thousand dollars for less than forty hours of billable legal fees which was mostly his legal assistant printing out boilerplate contracts from legal software.

Tony, meanwhile, spent the next eight months living mostly off skimmed New Jersey State sales taxes and, in May, put Tony Pepperoni's Pork Roll & Pizza up for sale. Tony did what he felt he had to do to survive, but didn't want to spend his entire life juggling two sets of books simply for the pleasure of surviving. By the end of the summer, Tony had found a buyer and unloaded the restaurant for two-hundred fifty thousand dollars. After paying off his business note and income taxes for his capital gain, Tony had enough money to purchase the income tax practice of retiring accountant, Thomas 'Blinky' Potzandpan.

8 – Mom's Rental Property

Frankie Valentine was a retired fireman who had been referred to Bullo by his nephew Tommy who worked with Bullo. Valentine had been griping about his taxes at a family gathering so Tommy recommended he see his guy, Bullo, "a fellow fireman." In addition to his firefighter's pension, Valentine's wife had a pension from her work as a school teacher. Their kids were grown, so they had no extra exemptions plus their home had long been paid off, so they had no mortgage interest deduction. Relatively low property taxes was perhaps the only good thing about living in Staten Island. So, even with income in excess of one hundred twenty-five thousand dollars, the Valentines couldn't even itemize their returns. They were taking a standard deduction like some sixteen year old working at McDonalds and were getting crushed in taxes.

Valentine brought Bullo his prior year's tax return along with the new one that showed he owed over five thousand dollars. They sat at a flimsy folding poker desk in the coffee room of the firehouse. Bullo was retired now but still used the firehouse like a satellite office of his shabby, two room Hylan Boulevard suite. Bullo compared the two returns. "I've been taking it in the ass ever since I retired" cried Valentine, "but now this? Five fucking grand? I can do fifteen hundred, I'll live with two, even. But, this is bullshit."

"I see what happened." said Bullo "You had this partnership loss in 1990, almost ten grand. What happened to it?"

"That house? You're telling me my mother's house made that much difference?"

"Your mother's house? What do you mean?"

"Five or six years ago when my mother started with the 'old timers', my brother and I sees this lawyer. He took us for five grand too, come to think of it. Anyways, he sets us up in this partnership to transfer the ownership of mom's house into this trust or family partnership or something, with me and my brother as beneficiaries, or whatever. A year later, moms went into the nursing home and we started renting her place out to this Pakistani family who run this deli on Richmond Ave., and then we rented the upstairs to these other Indians, or whatever." Valentine grimaced, but then conceded, "they do everything in cash, these A-rabs, you gotta love them."

"So this partnership is your half of the rental property?"

"We never claimed the rent, so we took a loss on the taxes and whatnot. The jerk off lawyer charged us another six hundred bucks a year to file a partnership return every year. All I got from it was a K-1 form, a piece of paper for three hundred bucks - my half."

"That three hundred bucks saved you almost three thousand in taxes every year. How did that house loose so much money?"

"Stupid . . ." said Valentine, shaking his head. "My dad thought he was Donald Trump - eighty three years old at the time - and he sold their house in Canarsie they lived in for forty years - the house my brother and me grews up in - he sells the house and has the bright idea to 'move out to the country' – Staten Island - and buys a two family house by the ballpark with a mortgage, he figures the rent will pay for the mortgage he was taking on. But he died only a couple of months after they moved in and moms never wanted strangers living up stairs, so she never rented it. . . It made that much difference?"

"So, where's the K-1 for this year?"

"There is none. Moms died a year and a half ago. The house isn't worth much after taking off for the mortgage. We put it all in my brother's name - he doesn't have a pot, anyway. He lives downstairs now - still rents the upstairs. I don't know how he can stand the smell."

"I don't know what I can do for you" said Bullo, feeling a great deal of anxiety and not accustom to disappointing people.

"What do you mean? Tommy said you were the man."

"You and your wife are both retired - I can't add any work expenses. Maybe we can put down a few thousand of charity so you can itemize some, but that will only make a few hundred dollars difference."

"The house made that much difference?"

"A partnership is a page one write-off - an above the line deduction. It's subtracted before we calculate your total income."

"Well, why don't we put it back in again . . . just for one more year?"

Even Bullo was taken aback by the audacity. "Put it back on again? You need a K-1 with a loss on it. That's as good as a W-2 with a negative number for income."

"I can't go back to the jack-off attorney, he transferred the property into my brother's name already and he knows it. You can't make a K-1 for me? The partnership was never closed. Jack-off wanted another six hundred bucks for that."

"I can't just make a K-1 up for you. A partnership return has to be created and filed."

"What would one of these CPA firms on Richmond Avenue charge me for a partnership return?"

"The same: probably five or six hundred bucks."

"Not bad . . . five hundred bucks to save three thousand" said Valentine, thinking out loud.

"How are they going to generate a partnership return? Based upon what?"

"The same way jack-off did. I just gives him a sheet of paper and a list of expenses. Couldn't have took him more than an hour to do, either. I can do the same with one of these CPA assholes, just change a few numbers around, and bring you back your goddamn K-1 sheet of paper."

"I guess if you had a K-1 from a CPA firm . . ."

"Just this one time, Bullo."

Bullo was stunned by the brilliance of it. No busy CPA firm is going to examine, or even question, the numbers Valentine gave them, especially in the first week of April during tax season and especially for a measly five hundred dollar fee. Heck, the CPA probably wouldn't even do it, he'd just had it off to some part-timer who'd generate the forms with the CPA firm's name and EIN number on it and a clean, pristine K-1 would be generated. The CPA would scarcely even look at the return he was signing.

It was well known that partnerships and S-corporations were even less frequently audited than individual returns. This was ten times cleaner than any refund mill's operation angle. A K-1 was generated by a third party. It was exactly like a W-2 and the loss came straight off the front page of a tax return - no loud write-offs to attract prying eyes. The taxpayer didn't even have to itemize their deductions to save thousands on their returns. S-corporations and partnership returns with less than two hundred fifty thousand dollars of assets and revenues are not required to include balance sheets in their annual tax returns. This makes these small enterprises reporting requirements more like a simple profit and loss statement as required of sole-proprietors on the annual schedule C attachment to their income tax return. Without a balance sheet, there is no accounting for the business's capital, it is just an annual snapshot - income minus expenses. No explanation of how the business continues to operate, in spite of losing money every year, is needed.

The key in Bullo's mind was keeping it small and low profile. Bullo figured he'd be able to sell shares of stock into phantom real estate companies to greedy types like Valentine who were never satisfied with their refunds and who viewed the entire income tax system as a racket to either play or be a victim to. The investment would be sold strictly as a 'tax shelter' whose only return would be higher tax refunds. Bullo would be able to pocket the entire purchase proceeds in exchange for generating an annual K-1 with a negative number.

Bullo felt he had conceived the world's first honest Ponzi scheme. His investors, after all, would be profiting four to five times as much as he was and he'd be taking most of the risk.

9 – The Bastard

Willie took one hundred of the one hundred fifty thousand dollars he netted from Net Noise for a down payment on the most expensive three bedroom ranch in Fords, New Jersey. The other fifty thousand went nearly as quick: a Mediterranean Cruise- from which Leah returned from pregnant -, a second Jeep, a week in Cancún and about a dozen new suits, even though Willie lacked a new accounting job to wear them to.

Willie's position with Net Noise ended with its acquisition. The acquiring search engine company had no need to continue to puff up sales on a business it had already purchased, so Willie was of no use to them. Had Net Noise gone public, rather than be purchased, Willie likely would have found himself in a great deal of hot water from his ridiculous revenue numbers. However, having been bought out by an internet giant awash in cash and just as eager as the former Net Noise executives to have its shady books disappear, Willie's fraudulent Net Noise accounts receivable numbers never came back to bite him. The $25 million the search engine wasted on Net Noise was of less concern than the embarrassment that its lack of due diligence would have brought to the company had they sued Net Noise. The Net Noise investment was simply written off and the website shut down.

Fortunately for Willie, his one hundred thousand dollar down payment made his mortgage payment modest because he was back bartending at Madison Ave. Being back at Madison Ave allowed Willie to resume his philandering ways. During his previous return to Madison Ave Willie had also began cheating on Leah, however at that point Leah was still pregnant and Willie limited his dalliances to women he had already been with. That was the deal he had made with himself. It wasn't really cheating since he had already been with these women before. By limiting himself to women he had already been with, it couldn't be said he was pursuing other women. To Willie, this was effective fidelity. These were all strictly sexual relationships with no *Fatal Attraction* risk.

In his second post-wedding stint at Madison Ave, Willie loosened up the rules for himself a bit. Willie allowed himself relations with fellow bartenders and waitresses at Madison Ave. They were colleagues, after all– friends, really. He wasn't having a relationship with them – they were just helping each other take care of a physical need. It would have been almost stupid had they not hooked up from time to time, given the opportunity. Willie had given Leah a daughter and now a home. He was providing for her, so why shouldn't he provide for his own needs too? The women who worked at Madison Ave all knew Willie was married – a few of them were married themselves – and certainly none of them had any serious designs on Willie. Again, Willie had sworn off pursuing the patrons at Madison Ave – at least the ones he hadn't been with before – and for this sacrifice Willie felt he was maintaining a high level of faithfulness.

In spite of the limited income Willie earned while bartending, he was spending as if his quarter-million dollar windfall from Net Noise was his annual salary, rather than simply a once-in-a-lifetime blessing. Having recently qualified for a mortgage and purchased a home, Willie's mailbox was now stuffed daily with credit card offers. When the fifty thousand left from Net Noise ran out, Willie's lifestyle remained the same, only now it was funded by Visa, MasterCard and American Express.

The easy cash from Net Noise corrupted the little honest work ethic Willie had. With the bursting of the NASDAQ and dot-com bubbles, there were no other fledgling internet firms looking to employ Willie and an ordinary staff accounting position held no appeal to him. Bartending was one thing. Surrounded by drunk twenty-five year old girls, bartending was only quasi-work to Willie. However, getting up at six every morning to balance debits and credits for sixty grand a year was something entirely different. That was work. Worse, Willie had gotten himself into a new pickle that was going to put even more pressure on his finances.

"Willie, what brings you before me again?" asked Sammy Riscatto, sporting a warm grin. Sammy had a fondness for Willie due to their shared disinterest in societal mores. "That Net Noise racket we cashed in on - that should have solved all your problems. I heard from Gwen that you bought a house."

"A waitress from the club, Sammy . . . I was only with her one time."

"Oh geez, you already got a kid, right?"

"Yeah, and I don't want Tony or Gwen to hear about this."

"This is a tough one to keep secret. The girl's determined to keep the kid?"

"Yes. I have to stay away from these Catholic girls."

"Maybe she heard about your Net Noise payday and she's just shaking you down."

"I don't see how she knows about that."

"Does she know you're married?"

"I told her I was married."

"Before or after you knocked her up?"

"It didn't come up before. The thing is, Leah's pregnant again now too - they're both due the same week."

"Irish-twins, right? That's what you call it when you have two kids the same year. What is it when you have two kids by two women the same week, Willie?"

"Puerto Rican twins."

"This is a mess, Willie."

"She's already threatening to go to my wife."

"You've got to settle with this girl - child support. I don't know how you keep it secret from your wife and if the girl knows you want to keep it secret that's a lot of leverage too. What's this girl's name?"

"Marissa something, some Italian name."

"Willie, we're going to have to make this girl a child support offer. You don't want a legal case here . . . if the court looks at your 2000 income taxes, with those Net Noise stock options, you're looking at two thousand a month child support."

"Two thousand a month?! I'm barely making that in tips now."

"I'm guessing this girl's not too bright, huh? How much of that two thousand dollars a month is reported?"

"None of it. I've been collecting unemployment since the Net

Noise buyout and that just ended. That's been paying my COBRA insurance and credit cards."

"Credit cards? What are you running up credit cards for? You went through that Net Noise money already?" Willie just nodded, glumly. "What about insurance? Does this Melisa have health insurance?"

"Marissa. No, she's just waitressing now but she wants to move to Seattle and become a weather girl, or something, someday."

"She'd have to go to college and become a meteorologist for that, Willie. My bet is she'll be waiting tables in Jersey for the next forty years, that probably pays better than reading weather reports anyway. Okay, she'll probably qualify for Medicaid, but that kid's gonna have to go on your policy. How old is this Marissa?"

"Nineteen or twenty - lives with her mother and sister in an apartment over some Pollock deli in Sayreville. Their place always smells like cabbage."

"You know Willie, maybe you should think about getting yourself snipped, before you become the Abraham of Middlesex County, with twelve different families, one in each town."

"Vasectomy? Leah's a strict Catholic, fanatic. She doesn't believe in birth control of any kind."

"A strict Catholic, huh? What would she think of you impregnating one of the handmaidens?" Willie had no response. "You want to keep news of this bastard kid from her, right? Well, a vasectomy is a smaller secret than that; everyone will just assume your plumbing went bad after the second kid. As for child support for this Marissa, offer her two-fifty per month. That's the IRS personal exemption amount - three thousand - divided by twelve, the least amount you can legally pay."

As usual, Sammy Riscatto was the only one who offered Willie any sensible advice that Willie would actually listen to. Sammy saw Willie as a younger, doltish version of himself and looked after him like a younger brother. Sammy almost admired Willie's impudence, or at least, he was envious of it in some way. Although Sammy shared Willie's disregard for social mores and values, Sammy was too aware of the consequences of ignoring them like Willie. Willie viewed society's standards and values as a minor nuisance and the consequences of ignoring society's standards and values like the occasional stone caught in one's shoe. Willie looked to Sammy as the man who could remove that stone.

10 - The Asbury Memorial Arms

The two hundred fifty dollars a month kept the gestating Marissa quiet and content for the time being, but it only made Willie's cash flow problems worse. More down and dour than usual, Willie filled the ears of an unsympathetic Bullo with his woes and misfortunes while Bullo ate a veal parmesan sandwich at Madison Ave bar during lunch. "Get me another Heineken" said Bullo, without looking up at the rambling Willie.

"Sure."

"Willie, you working this afternoon?"

"I'm off from two to six."

"You wanna go for a ride? Can you get out now?"

"A ride? Where?"

"The shore: Asbury Park. And, we can stop at Heartbreakers for a couple beers while we're there."

"Asbury?" asked Willie with a shrug. "That's a ninety minute round trip, without traffic."

"I want to show you something" said Bullo, staring at his half eaten sandwich, "I've got a business proposition for you."

"What kind of business? What are you talking about?" Bullo knew Willie had an accounting degree. A new tax season was around the corner and Bullo was in need of help beyond a part-time receptionist. Bullo needed someone with some accounting background but also someone who'd be morally indifferent towards Bullo's accounting shenanigans. Willie was just the guy.

"Come on, I've got something to show you. See if you can leave early, it's slow here today."

Ten minutes later, Willie was sitting in the passenger seat of Bullo's Mitsubishi Montero. An odd choice of a vehicle, thought Willie. He could have bought a Jeep or Pathfinder for the same price. "Where are we heading, Bullo?"

"You'll see, Willie . . . or, really, you won't see." Bullo turned and smiled at Willie - and Bullo never smiled - "you'll see."

Willie chuckled and shook his head as Bullo tail-gated and lane-changed his way down the Garden State Parkway. Traffic was light this time of day and Bullo's foot was heavy at any time of day. Bullo cut people off intentionally close without using his blinkers, he met honked horns with threatening stares and he flew through the toll plazas without paying, When Bullo finally reached Asbury Park, he drove to Memorial Boulevard until he reached its very end and pulled over. "How many shares would you like to buy into my apartment property?" Bullo pointed to the empty lot beyond the end of the boulevard, "The Asbury Memorial Arms."

"You're building an apartment building over there? The lot's too small."

"Building?" asked Bullo, feigning confusion, "It's already built. You don't like it?"

"What are you talking about, Bullo?"

Bullo went on to describe his new K-1 operation to Willie. "I'm creating S-corporations, which invest in low-income housing units, and selling shares in them for ten annual payments of seven hundred fifty dollars. For their seventy-five hundred dollars, I'll generate ten years of losses in a range of nine to ten thousand dollars a year. Depending on their tax bracket, this is worth as much as three thousand dollars a year. I use the money to pay for some filing fees and expenses and pocket the rest as management and accounting fees. After ten years, I buy their shares back for a dollar."

Bullo would have gone on but Willie showed only minor interest in the details, which was even more than Bullo would have hoped for. Willie was a perfect candidate to assist him. Willie could replace a part–time receptionist and free up time for Bullo by completing simple form 1040s. Bullo could then focus on selling shares in his tax shelters and generating the bogus corporate returns and K-1s.

As for the S-corporation returns and K-1s generated, they were completely fictitious. Bullo's companies were all registered in New York, but he chose for the apartment's addresses all distressed New Jersey towns and on real streets. Bullo felt the

New Jersey locations would make it less likely New York State would show any interest in his operation. For the street address, Bullo would drive to the very end of a street and simply add one number to the last house number and that would be its address. Bullo's Hylan Boulevard office served as the address of record for all the businesses but Bullo still liked to drive to the fictitious properties. It somehow gave them a sense of legitimacy. Also, his gas and restaurant receipts from his trips to his apartments - which he claimed as expenses on his own tax return - established a history of visiting the properties should he ever be subject to a very cursory audit. He always made a stop at Heartbreakers go-go bar in nearby Neptune on his trips to his Asbury apartments and was likely their only customer who ever asked for a receipt. Bullo's trips to his fictitious apartments also gave him windows to pursue his hookers and hook ups.

Six weeks later, Willie began working for Bullo in his accounting office, Monday through Saturday, 10:00 a.m. to four in the afternoon during tax season. Willie answered the phones, returned calls, took care of the mail and handled Bullo's files. For all this, Willie was paid nothing. Between getting coffee and being hollered at by Bullo, Willie was also given tax files by Bullo - the simpler ones he figured Willie couldn't screw up - and Willie prepared them himself for a fifty dollars cash commission. Willie's secretarial duties were simply viewed as a cost of doing business, Willie's cost of doing business. Mostly, Willies simply served as Bullo's punching bag.

The previous year, Bullo had hired a lazy Korean accounting student to handle his mail and phone calls, but Bullo hated like hell paying him nine dollars an hour to mostly listen to the radio and do his homework. Bullo had wanted his phone covered during all business hours, but simply didn't have enough work to keep a secretary busy. Bullo unmercifully abused the student, Kim, calling him a "goddamn Chinaman" and threatening to take him outside when Kim complained about being paid as a contractor instead of an employee. Kim did unwittingly get some payback by calling out sick on the final day of tax season, April 15th. Kim wasn't really sick, but he wasn't looking to retaliate for Bullo's cruelty either. He simply was frightened at what the pressure of April 15th would bring out of Bullo, so he stayed home on his last day of work. "Goddamn Chinaman" Bullo repeated dozens of times that day.

Willie earned enough working tax season for Bullo to pay off a couple of credit cards. Instead, he and Leah took a Mediterranean cruise. Willie learned enough working tax season for Bullo to know better than to ever work for him again. Instead, Willie – short on funds as always – would be back in Bullo's line of abuse the following tax season.

11 - Valentine's Day Brownies

Potzandpan Tax & Financial was an odd fit in many ways for the straight laced Tony Violette. Blinky's office was buried in the back corner of a wraithy Edison New Jersey shopping center/office complex consisting mostly of empty pizzerias, massage parlors, check cashing businesses and Indian and Pakistani owned offices whose business purposes weren't completely clear. Behind Blinky's windows ran the New Jersey Transit lines between the Metro Park and Metuchen train stations. The sound of each passing train was an endless distraction one never got used to. The locomotion would rattle Blinky's windows, which were usually open in spite of the train noise due to the building's unreliable air conditioning. In the winter, Blinky's windows were also opened to due to the building's too reliable heating system and the insistence of the building's predominantly Indian and Pakistani tenants that the building thermostat be kept at eighty degrees. With only screens between the office and passing trains, Blinky's office was an extraordinary magnet for dust. The squeaky floors were covered with old, stained Berber carpeting containing more pulls than carpet and the vinyl waiting room furniture was covered with duct tape to cover the rips. Storms with even modest winds caused door frames and latches to become misaligned making half of the building's doors almost impossible to open and the other half almost impossible to close. Blinky's old file cabinets barely opened, too. The suspended ceiling tiles were all water stained and the wallpapered hall walls all curled at the sanitest seams and were covered with tacky pictures. The parking lot outside of Blinky's office was littered with paper plates and empty cat food cans. Dozens of feral cats filled the broken black top, sustained by a dozen or so of round-faced, depressed, middle-aged women who fed the cats. After dusk, the cat population was replaced by a half-dozen raccoons that fattened up on the left-over cat food and hid under Tony's car.

"You know, I think that Chinese acupuncture place down the hall may be a front for prostitutes" said Tony, to his unconcerned but somewhat amused receptionist, Rickie Rose.

"Why do you say that?"

"The door's always closed. The only time I see customers go in there is after 9:00 p.m. and it's always grubby-looking middle-aged men."

"Middle aged-men need acupuncture too" said Rickie, in a south of I-195 accent.

"You're not concerned? We share a bathroom with them. Although, I don't think any STD could survive that stench."

"I think they have their own bathroom, I've never seen any of the Chinese women in the hall bathroom."

"I heard both phones ringing off the hook the past four hours yet I don't see any new appointments in the book."

"Thursday is Valentine's Day . . . I was scheduling my dates." Rickie smiled and Tony shook his head. "Don't worry, your girl Sarah Shah comes in for me in ten minutes, she'll fill up your appointment book."

"The Shah of Iran? She's crazy, that one . . . moody. She told me to go 'f-myself' last week. I would have fired her but I'm worried she might be one of those suicide-bomber types," said Tony.

"Believe me . . . she's not religious at all. I've talked to her a couple times between shifts. She's a little off, though."

"She wore one of those headscarves to her interview."

"That's only because her mother probably drove her. Her parents are Muslim fundamentalist or something. She's gone the other extreme."

"What do you mean?"

"She went on some rant last week about Jack Daniel's and of having already made her way through half the Crips in New Brunswick already."

"Crips?"

"Crips or Bloods . . . I don't remember. Now she's got a

boyfriend who's half Jewish and half Lebanese Christian who she says her parents would kill if they found out she was dating him."

"I told you she was nuts."

"She said she doesn't even like him that much but that it would upset her parents so much if they knew, she stays with him, anyway."

"God. Or should I say, Allah?"

"Her only regret is that she isn't lesbian."

"Don't go . . . don't leave me alone with her. Tell her you're working on files - you can just do your homework. I don't care."

"I've got class and you should know Melanie's coming with me Spring Break week, so it will be just you, Ben and Sarah that week."

"You know my whole family goes away that week too? I can't even have my wife cover your shifts. We won't have anyone to watch Nicole."

Tony purchased Blinky's tax practice for eighty thousand dollars - one year of expected billings - that fall, with the stipulation that Blinky would work part-time during the first tax season at a nominal salary to ease the client transition over to Tony. After Blinky died of norovirus gastroenteritis during a Mediterranean cruise meant to celebrate his retirement, Tony took over a rudderless practice consisting mostly of individual tax returns, a shiftless seasonal staff and a shabby office in a dilapidated building. Without Blinky to smooth over the transition, what Tony had purchased wasn't much more that a mailing list and a broken down office. The majority of Blinky's clients did return to the office and have Tony prepare their returns though. They had to find someone new anyway after Blinky died and Tony had their old files. However, after years of dealing with the charismatic Blinky Potzandpan, many of the clients were a bit standoffish to the smugly Tony.

"You're going to owe taxes again, like last year" said Tony, to Veronica Velcheck. "You need to have taxes taken out of your Social Security."

"That is because Ronald Reagan taxed Social Security. Social Security was tax-free until Ronald Reagan."

"That is a fallacy. Social Security was not taxed until Jimmy

Carter began taxing Social Security - fifty percent of it - and then Bill Clinton taxed up to eighty-five percent of it."

"That is not what Bill Clinton says."

"Nobody with any sense listens to anything that Bill Clinton says."

"Well" said Velcheck, about to veer off on an odd tangent, "George Bush knew the planes were going to crash into the World Trade Center and all the Jews stayed home."

"Uh . . . what did you say?"

"The Jews flew the planes into the buildings and George Bush knew about it ahead of time."

"You are a horrible person."

"I am the best person in the world!" declared Velcheck, and then adding this odd non-sequitur she thought validated her patriotism in some manner. "My uncle fought in World War Two."

"Yeah" said Tony, dismissively waving his hand, "probably for the Germans."

"You are anti-German . . . you hate Germans."

"I am not going to prepare your taxes."

"Yes. Yes you will."

"No. I am not."

"Yes you will."

"Get out of my office."

"I will not" shouted Velcheck, with admirable boldness for a seventy-two year old woman.

"Leave."

"No."

"Get out."

"I will not"

"Get out" Tony repeated as he stood up, picked up Velcheck's crutches - which were leaning on his desk - and carried them to the front waiting room.

"Where are you going with my crutches?"

"Get out."

"I don't understand why you're so angry" cried Velcheck, as she struggled to stand without her crutches, "all the old people on the bus *say* that.*"

"Leave" is all Tony would say, as Velcheck struggled down Tony's hall.

"Can your girl call me a cab?"

"I don't care" shouted Tony. Tens of thousands of American soldiers were risking their lives in Afghanistan following the 9-11 attacks. It was the least Tony could do to throw an old anti-Semite out of his office. However, the screams from Tony and Veronica Velcheck's shouting match were heard throughout the building.

"He's so uptight" said Sarah to Ben, who had just walked into the commotion to replace her at the front desk. "It's only February 11th and he's already close to a mental break down."

"We should get him some weed."

"If anyone should smoke pot it's him - but, he'd never take it. He's too tight assed."

"What if we slipped him some? Snuck it in some brownies or something?"

"If you make them, I'll give them to him on Friday. I'll tell him they were leftover from a Valentine's Day party."

"Done . . . but don't say anything, unless he's in a great mood and wondering why."

"It takes a few hours for pot-brownies to hit. My shift will be over . . . you deal with him."

Tony grinded his way through Blinky's client base, throwing about twenty percent of them out of the office. It was bad enough keeping two sets of books in order to survive at Tony Pepperoni's Pork Roll & Pizza, but Tony was not going to risk his freedom signing off on bogus tax returns for a hundred bucks a pop. When he wasn't battling his clients, Tony was fighting the Pakistani neighbor over the thermostat that controlled the heat in both of their offices, arguing with the owner of the math tutoring business across the hall about their students urinating all over the toilet seats in the shared hall bathroom, spying on the hooker/acupuncturists down the hall and installing web cams to catch the women leaving cat food in the parking lot that was turning the local raccoon population into virtual panda bears. When he wasn't battling his clients or his neighbors, Tony was battling his receptionists.

"The breath on that last guy" said Tony, "and I couldn't get him to shut up. We were back there for almost an hour."

"I know, Buddy, and I've got like ten thousand messages for you" said Sarah, fixed on her half-eaten BLT sandwich while

Tony poured himself a coffee between appointments.

"I'm returning no phone calls," said Tony.

"Yeah, I know that, you damn misanthrope. I just need you to answer their questions so I can call them back. By the way, your answering machine is the worst piece of shit ever shat from a butt. Why don't you get a digital machine? This tape machine is from the dinosaur age."

"Well, according to my mom, the dinosaurs were around only six thousand years ago . . . so, that's pretty modern."

"Well, let me remind you, even in that deluded sense of time, answering machine technology has advanced quite a bit in the past six thousand years. I was taking, like, the twenty fifth message when someone said, 'Tony, it's Saturday morning.' . . . a six day old message."

"People don't rewind it after they've taken the message; people are the problem."

"No, people just aren't used to using technology from the 1970s. This piece of shit is probably older than I am."

"Yeah, older than an Iranian bride."

"Your ass-backwards notions about Iranian-brides better take a hike too, bro."

"I just read *The Persian Bride* by James Buchan and *The Art of Mackin* by Tariq Nasheed, so I'm an expert."

"Yes, obviously, you are the cultural paradigm which we should all aspire to" said Sarah, as she finished the last inch of her BLT.

"Thanks, but really Laura Ingraham would be a better choice for a role model for you, being a woman."

"I'd sooner vomit on her shoes then look to her as a role model and Jesus, son, I think I hear something walking on the ceiling tiles."

"We've got squirrels in the building, I think. I'm pretty sure it's not the raccoon. If raccoons get in here we're finished."

"Anyway, try one of these brownies from the Valentine's Day party last night, before I eat them all."

"Thanks" said Tony, taking a quick bite from one of the four brownies sitting on a paper plate on the receptionist's table. "Not bad."

"Take them all," said Sarah. "I had three yesterday and two more already this morning."

"Thanks - I'm starving" said Tony, who took the plate full of brownies back to his office.

Ben, whose shift followed Sarah's came in early, eager to see if Sarah had gotten Tony to try a brownie. "Where are all the brownies?"

"You gave me five - I had one about twenty minutes ago - and I gave the rest to Tony."

"Four?! You gave him four? Do you know how strong those are?"

"Actually, I'm just starting to feel it now . . . this is pretty good shit." Sarah would know. Besides bacon - pork of any kind, really - Sarah consumed nothing more than cannabis.

"He's never had pot before - who knows how that will hit him?"

"Oh well." Sarah smiled as she got up to leave. "Thanks for the brownie. Good luck with him today."

Ben went straight to Tony's office hoping he would offer him a brownie or two, so Tony wouldn't get too stoned. "Sarah said you've got some brownies back here."

"The Shia apostate? Well, sorry Ben . . . he who hesitates is lost. I just finished them all."

"Hesitate? I just got here."

"This afternoon - for this afternoon only - if I hit the doorbell button it's not for you to come and rescue me from a client that I can't get out of the office. If I hit the button, it means I see one of the cat women on my webcam feeding the cats. I want you to go down stairs. I've got a disposable camera in the top drawer out there. I want you to go outside and take a picture of them and get their license plate number."

"Take a picture of the cat woman?"

"Actually, take a picture of the license plate number too."

"What are you going to do with their license plate number?"

"I'm gonna call the cops."

"Call the cops for feeding cats?"

"Feral animals . . . it's against the law. Plus they leave the food out and I've got raccoons under my car every night. I'm gonna get bit and die of rabies."

"Okay . . . whatever . . ."

"Also, these Chinese women, after dark, I wanna get the license plate numbers of the guys going in there. I think they might be hookers."

"Those are hookers? They're pretty nasty looking."

"I know - that's the only reason I have any doubts. They've got a billion people over there and they couldn't spare three or four good looking Chinawoman to be hookers here? A bunch of dogs - no offense."

"Why would I take offense?" asked Ben. "Not all Koreans eat dog!"

"I know, I know. Are you South Korean or North Korean, Ben?"

"I'm an American, Tony. My parents were from Seoul, if that's what you mean."

"That's south, I know. I just thought if you were North Korean, you might be able to get in good with these Chinese."

Tony was rambling worse than usual. 'He's paranoid enough without weed - this was a big mistake' thought Ben. "Sarah left me a mess out there, I better get to work on those files," said the usually lazy Ben.

"There's almost nothing out there, plus it's Friday - not too busy tonight. You're covering for Rickie Rose tonight, right?"

"Yes, she said she had to leave early this afternoon for a funeral back home in Delaware."

"I want you to drive over to Metzger dorm in Piscataway and see if her car's still in the parking lot. It's already the third Friday night shift she hasn't come in for."

"I don't know what car she drives."

"An old white Mustang - I've got her license plate written down here somewhere."

"You wrote her license plate number down?" asked Ben, increasingly weary of Tony's paranoia.

"I wrote all of your license plate numbers down . . . due diligence."

"Route 1 will take me ninety minutes back and forth to Busch campus, this time of day. I've got a friend at Davidson Hall. I'll ask him to take a quick walk over there to check."

"Okay, good idea" said Tony, to Ben's relief. "I've got a great burst of energy for some reason – a real clear head all of a sudden. I think that Iranian is spiking the coffee. I complained one time that she made the coffee too weak and now she makes it super-strong just to try to piss me off. What she doesn't know is that I like it super strong. I've never felt so clear-headed . . . focused."

It couldn't have been more than forty-five minutes since Tony ate the pot-brownies but they were already affecting him. Ben knew the full effect of the brownies wouldn't be for a few hours and he was bracing for the worst. "You don't have an appointment for a couple of hours, why don't you open up that army cot from the closet and grab a nap. You've only been getting four hours a night sleep, you said."

"I only need four hours. I'm wide awake . . . starving though. For some reason, those four brownies made me hungrier" said Tony, now getting the munchies.

"You look a little clammy, though. You might have caught a bug from someone. You should grab some winks while you've got the chance."

"I'm not clammy - that's perspiration. It's February and it's ninety degrees in the building. I'm having it out with the Pakistani once and for all." Tony grabbed a can of Febreze and marched out into the hall outside of Blinky's office, wildly spraying the Febreze while loudly chiding - to know one in particular - about the 'deplorable hygiene' of his fellow tenants. Then, Tony banged on the door of his Pakistani neighbor. All Ben could hear from inside the office was Tony ranting on about 'Bombay', 'cholera' and 'the plague'.

When he returned to the office, Tony asked Ben to inform him when the "brats from the math school started running up and down the halls" so that he could confront the math-tutoring business owners regarding the students who always urinated on the toilet seats in the men's room. "In the meantime, I'll be in my office keeping an eye out for the cat women."

The already paranoia-prone Tony was in a full-blown cannabis-fueled paranoid fit. Within minutes of returning to his desk, Tony spotted a high-cortisol-faced cat woman leaving plates of wet cat food right next to Tony's car on his webcam. "Ben - I caught a cat-woman!" shouted Tony, as if he had just hit the pick-six lottery.

The normally non-confrontational Ben was glad to have any excuse to get out of the office. "I'm on it, Tony" said Ben, as he grabbed his coat and the disposable camera and headed outside to take a picture of the cat-woman. Tony stuck his head out of his back window and watched the cat-woman angrily confront Ben after he took a photo of her next to the cat food by Tony's car.

"It's against the law to feed feral animals" shouted Tony to the woman, who then bolted to her van. "What's her plate number, Ben?"

"P-L-Y-M-94," shouted Ben.

"Okay . . . good work - get a picture of the van too" shouted Tony, as the cat-woman nearly ran over Ben while backing out of her parking spot and darting away.

By the time Ben returned to the office, Tony was up front, waiting for him with an excited grin, like he had great news that he wanted to keep to himself, but was too exciting not too share. "Was that really necessary?" asked Ben. "The woman almost killed me with her van."

"Thank god she tried to kill you, otherwise the cops would never be on their way over here" said Tony.

"The cops?!" cried Ben, "You called the cops?"

"Of course, that's why I wanted you to take the pictures, so we'd have evidence. But they didn't want to send someone just to catch a cat-woman – these damn municipal unions - but when I told them she tried to hit you on purpose, they had to send somebody."

"Tony, I don't think she was trying to hit me on purpose. She was just trying to leave as quickly as possible - you sounded like a lunatic screaming out the window. Besides, I didn't take a video out there - the photos will probably all turn out blurry, anyway."

"I'm not looking to get her on attempted murder. I just want her to stop feeding the cats so the raccoons will stop hanging around out here. I only told them about her trying to hit you to get them to come over."

"Tony, it's really not a good idea for the cops to come over here right now."

"Why not?"

"Uh, no reason."

The cops arrived an hour later, Tony was down the hall haranguing the owners of the math-tutoring business - Future Eggheads -regarding the condition their students left the building's men's room. "We got a call about someone trying to run somebody over in the parking lot" said Officer Gatto to Ben, only to be drowned out by Tony's shouting from down the hall.

"I've never seen hygiene like this! There's piss all over the toilet seats every day."

Ben just pointed with his thumb towards Tony's shouting. "My boss - he wants to report some women who have been feeding cats in the parking lot."

"Cats?!" asked Gatto, annoyed. "Get him in here." Ben walked down the hall and returned with Tony. "Sir, we got a call about someone intentionally trying to hit someone with their van."

"I don't know if it was intentional or not," said Tony.

"Was anybody hurt?" asked Gatto.

"Well, no . . . but she nearly clipped Ben" said Tony, gesturing towards Ben. "He was taking a picture of her license plate while she was backing out. P-L-Y . . ."

"Why were you taking a picture of her license plate, son?"

"I asked him to," said Tony. "She's the one who's been feeding the feral cats . . . at least, she's one of them."

"How is it your business if she's feeding cats, sir?"

"It's against the law to feed feral animals. My wife got two tickets for it last year in Woodbridge."

"This is Edison, sir. The township website on rabies only *recommends* against feeding wild animals, but it's not a crime. Why would it be a crime? If I saw a cat, I'd feed it too."

"But this is private property and she leaves the food right by my car every day. I've got a family of raccoon under my car when I leave every night."

"Unless you can prove she feeds it every day the only way you can get her to stop is if the landlord gets a restraining order on her."

"Every day? I don't know how often she comes."

"If she feeds the cats every day, legally they would be considered to belong to her. Then, maybe I could write her up for not having a license for the cats."

"I've got her license plate number. Can't you at least let me know where she lives so I can go throw chicken feed or dog food on *her* property?"

"Sir, if you plan on harassing this woman further, you're going to wind up getting yourself arrested."

"Harassing her? I'm gonna get bit by a raccoon and die from rabies one of these nights."

"Sir, have you been drinking?"

"Drinking? Of course not. It's four o'clock in the afternoon."

"Are you on any medications, sir?"

"No."

"Your eyes are red, sir. I heard you screaming and cursing at someone down the hall when I walked in."

"My eyes are red from only sleeping four hours a night. They're peeing all over my toilet seats, the Pakistani's got the thermostat up to one hundred degrees, I've got cat-women trying to get me bitten by raccoons and you're asking me if I'm on drugs?" asked Tony, now completely unhinged. "Try busting the acupuncturists down the hall. It's a front for a hooker operation."

"Sir, you have the right to remain silent . . ."

Normally if 'you eat it you beat it', but the level of tetrahydrocannabinol in Tony's blood was sky-high from Ben's potent brownies. Three days later at Middlesex County Adult Correction Center, Sammy **Riscatto** sat down with Tony.

"Tony, what happened here on Friday night? Normally if the cops find you with a joint or something, they hit you with a fine or let you off with a warning, but you were screaming and hollering at everyone at the station, challenging them to give you a drug test. You pissed them off, that's why you're still here."

"I never took a drug in my life."

"Tony, the tests came in an hour ago - THC positive."

"Then they set me up - I've never even smoked a tobacco cigarette."

"Come on Tony, this isn't the O. J. trial here. Have you been around anyone smoking in the last couple of weeks? Second hand smoke maybe?"

"Labor Day: Willie was smoking pot in his backyard."

"That was five months ago. Tony, everybody in America has smoked pot in their lifetime. It's not that big of a deal."

"I didn't smoke anything."

"Okay, I'll choose to believe you, but you're going to have to plead guilty to something, a disorderly person's charge maybe and pay a fine. It's tax season - jail's no place for an accountant during tax season. If you get arrested again, at least let it be for tax evasion or something else worthwhile."

12 - Multi-level Mumbo Jumbo

With his small tax-season income over, a new two fifty
dollars a month child-support nut to add to his Jeep leases and
credit card minimum payments, plus the prospect of Leah's
income ending for a few months later in her pregnancy, Willie
knew he needed to boost his income. Without the dangled
prospects of quick stock options to cash in on, Willie had no
interest in returning to the corporate world. A regular paycheck in
exchange for an honest week's work always seemed like a
depressing proposition to Willie, and a few months assisting Bullo
in his tax office extinguished any last flicker of interest Willie had
in accounting. Buried in bills, and having tasted quick money from
Net Noise, Willie was even more primed than usual to get
ensnared by a multi-level marketing pitch.

"You must really like tending bar" said Jack Edwards to
Willie, as he sat down at the bar. Jack Edwards was all cheap-suit
and hair-spray and with a smile so contrived it would have made
anyone with five more IQ points than Willie cringe.

"It's OK" said Willie, "it pays the bills."

"If it's only paying the bills . . . why bother?" asked Edwards.
Jack Edwards was a sales manager for Sam's Way, a new multi-
level marketing company. Of course 'paying the bills' is an
entirely sensible reason to tend bar or engage in any other lawful
form of employment, but it was the type of nonsensical idea that
scratched Willie right where he itched.

"That's a good question" said Willie, nodding as if Edwards

had said something profound. "What'll you have?"

"Just a club soda for me. I've got an exciting new business opportunity I'm sharing with some friends in about an hour, so no alcohol for me right now."

"Why'd you stop at a bar, then?" asked Willie, showing some momentary sense, even if not enough skepticism.

"I'm like you," said Edwards. "I'm a people-person, if I can't spend my day talking to people and making money - I couldn't get out of bed in the morning . . . and let me have the receipt for the club soda, this one is on the IRS."

"You can write this off?" asked Willie - the accountant - a bit jealous, even though he was working off-the-books, effectively making everything he paid for paid with pre-tax dollars.

Edwards grinned. "I just got back from ten days on Royal Caribbean, wrote it all off and I made money on the trip."

"Made money? We just got back from the Mediterranean - wiped my bank account out."

"I go away the first ten days of every month, give or take a day. I ain't had a trip yet that didn't pay for itself."

"What kind of business are you in?" asked Willie, already hooked.

"You don't look like the kind of guy who'll be bartending his whole life" said Edwards, as he stood up, put a five dollar bill on the bar, left his club soda undrunk and pulled out a pen to write on his bill. "What's your name, my friend?"

"Willie."

"Willie, like I said, I've got this meeting I'm running late for. Let me have your number. I'll get back to you, probably not tomorrow, but two or three days the latest. We'll sit down somewhere and I'll tell you about my business." After Edwards wrote down Willie's phone number, Edwards picked up the receipt and shook Willie's hand. "I've got a good feeling about you, Willie."

Edwards turned, sprinted out of Madison Ave and headed out to his car on his way to the next stop - be it a diner, a burger joint or another bar - to start the whole process over. Edwards had no business meeting with friends, Edwards was simply collecting business leads up and down routes 1, 9, 18, 27 and 35 across Middlesex County. Trying to sell a new multi-level marketing scheme cold on an initial introduction was far too big of a bite for anyone to swallow. Edwards, who had spent four years honing his sales skills and developing this recruiting shtick with Amway, was hawking Sam's Way.

Sam's Way was a fledgling multi-level marketing company formed by a group of breakaway Amway recruiters - led by a guy named Sam - who formed their own organization hoping to leapfrog a few rungs up the ladder. Sam's Way's primary sales pitch to the public - almost all of whom by 2003 had been either recruited to or attempted to be recruited into Amway - was this: Amway was a great idea, but you got in too late. The key to success for any pyramid scheme - or, multi-level marketing business, as they called it - was to get in at, or near, the ground floor. Although they had a much smaller product line, the former Amway salesmen thought they could peel off a lot of Amway dealers by offering them higher bonuses - commissions - because they wouldn't be starting as far from the top of the pyramid. Their limited product line and the threat of a lawsuit forced Sam's Way towards recruiting new multi-level marketing recruits, rather than converting Amway dealers.

As unsympathetic as he was, Edwards was a bit of a tragic figure. He was tenacious, had an exemplary work ethic and, although he was unburdened by conscience in matters of veracity in business, he was an honest fellow when not engaging in business. Of course, a multi-level marketer is seldom *not* engaging in business, at least not while awake. He could have made an excellent salesman - or country preacher - but four years of Amway perverted a potentially fine salesman into a con-man (or evangelist into cult recruiter). Edwards lived in a shabby Menlo Park Terrace studio apartment and drove a twelve year old Toyota Corolla. "I'm not into cars" Edwards would say when someone saw what he was driving, pretending indifference rather than finances was the reason he owned a twenty-two hundred dollar car.

Edwards did 'vacation' monthly and did legitimately deduct it from his meager earnings, but these were for, first, Amway and then Sam's Way sales conferences. Edwards' Corolla was cluttered with Sam's Way demo products, Sam's Way recruitment brochures, sales tapes and Hagstrom maps. Edwards' apartment was the same, minus the maps. Thirty four years old, Edwards didn't have a wife or kids or girlfriend or any friends at all outside of his Sam's Way associates. It was his life, career, future and faith. To objectively evaluate his progress, or potential for success, would have required doubt - the worst sin in any religion - and the consideration of negative outcomes - the worst sin in sales. Two days later - almost to the minute - Edwards placed a call to Willie.

"Hey Willie, this is Jack Edwards. I'm sorry I'm late getting back to you. I know it's been almost a week but I've just been swamped."

Willie paused. He had forgotten Edwards and was not recognizing who was calling him. Edwards' cheap cell phone, combined with the noise at Madison Ave, didn't help either. "Who's this?"

"Jack, Jack Edwards. We met at Madison Ave a couple of days ago. You were asking about my business opportunity."

Willie vaguely remembered. "Yeah . . ."

"Honestly" said Edwards, dishonestly, "the partner's don't want us bringing in any new members right now - we're too swamped as it is . . ."

"That's all right," said Willie.

"So . . . I guess making a lot of money isn't a priority for you right now, Willie?"

"Well, no . . . I didn't say that."

"Wouldn't you like to have enough money to pay off your house, go on a dream vacation and retire while you're still young enough to enjoy it?"

"Well, yeah, sure. Of course."

"You got kids?" asked Edwards, now on a roll.

"Yeah, I got kids," said Willie.

"How many, Willie?"

"Actually, that's a good question. One, really . . . but a couple on the way."

"You're wife's having twins, Willie - god bless you - but tending bar's not going to put the twins through college."

"Yeah . . . I know . . . you're right."

"Don't you want to be able to provide for all their needs?"

"Yeah, I know it."

"Look, Willie, I'm late for a meeting, but I like you. I believe in you. What time do you start work tomorrow?"

"Five."

"Why don't we meet for coffee around 3:30 tomorrow, at the McDonald's around the corner from your club?"

"Yeah, why not? Thanks, Jack. Tomorrow at 3:30."

And with that, Jack had his date, almost as slickly as Willie picking up a twenty-six year old girl. Who was this Jack? What in Heaven's were they meeting about anyway? And, why at a McDonald's? Doesn't Jack have an office? All obvious and valid questions Willie only briefly contemplated, not unlike the sauced single girls seduced by Willie who fail to ask, 'Who is this Willie? Why is he taking me to my place, doesn't' he own a home? Is he married? What am I doing with this old guy?' and so on. When an emotional need is being stroked, the brain takes a breather.

Edwards beat Willie to McDonald's the next day. Edwards always arrived early to business meeting so he would only have to purchase his own coffee. Willie would be a much easier sale than Edwards realized, so he wasted time early in the meeting with his usual script. "What do you truly want out of life" and "What would it be like, Willie, to earn a consistent six figure income and spend all the time with your family you'd like?" Rather than feeling like a trapped rat, like a normal multi-level marketing recruitment prospect, Willie was simply impatient to get to the details. He could have been sold on almost anything at this point in his life.

"Is this like that Amway I've heard about?" Willie didn't ask that in the usual, 'is this Amway?!' manner as is usually the case about twenty minutes into an Amway pitch when the recruiter is still trying to disguise his purposes and whet the prospect's appetite. Willie was genuinely excited that it *might* be Amway. Willie was one of the few people in America over twenty-five who hadn't been recruited to Amway and the schemish nature of multi-level marketing appealed to, rather than appalled, Willie.

"It's not Amway" assured Edwards, to Willie's temporary disappointment. "Amway was a great idea twenty years ago, but it's too late. Sam's Way is a chance to get in on the next Amway . . . at the ground floor."

Less than an hour later, Willie had charged nearly a thousand dollars to his new Discover Card for his Sam's Way enrollment fee, sales tapes, literature and more shampoo, soap and other cleaning supplies than Willie and Leah could use in five years. The only frustration for Willie was that he had an eight hour shift ahead of him at Madison Ave and that he'd have to wait until the next day to begin calling friends and family to get them to sign up for Sam's Way. At the club that evening, Willie was desperately tempted to start sharing the Sam's Way gospel, but Edwards was insistent that Willie wait until he had listened to the tapes and learned the recruiting scripts and formula. In a week's time, Willie would be warned by Madison Ave's management to stop trying to push Sam's Way while at the club, otherwise he'd be out on his ass.

Willie focused on family, particularly the Magillicutty family - Leah's cousins - all of whom signed up with Sam's Way, mainly to not offend Leah, everyone in the family's favorite cousin. The only cousin left to recruit was Tony. Willie purposely waited to contact Tony last, expecting him to be both his most difficult sale, but also his most important, given all of Tony's clients in his newly purchased accounting practice. Willie envisioned hundreds of Sam's Way dealers recruited by Tony who would be a part of Willie's pyramid because Tony would have been recruited by Willie. Willie had Leah invite Tony and Gwen over to play cards. Tony wasn't used to being invited over by any of the cousins and seldom had anyone over to his place due to the general state of disrepair that Gwen left his house in.

"Willie, let me ask you something. A client of mine in the office today was complaining that his kid couldn't qualify for some scholarship because they were from Brazil - which is Portuguese, not Spanish -, because they're not considered Hispanic. Why is that?"

"They're not from Spain"

"You're not from Spain, either. You were born in Weehawken, right?"

"West New York . . . but they're not Latinos."

"But they're from Latin America, right?"

"I guess."

"So, is Latino is an ethnicity or nationality?"

"It's an ethnicity . . . Brazil is in Latin America but they're not Latinos" said Willie, already exhausted by Tony.

"Well, Portugal and Spain are part of the same peninsula, right?"

Willie didn't have the slightest clue if Portugal and Spain were part of the same peninsula or not. "It's different people."

"Why would somebody, whose ancestors are from Seville, be considered the same ethnicity as someone from Barcelona, but different from someone from Lisbon? It's like people who say humans aren't apes, even though we're closer to chimps than chimps are to gorillas. How would you explain to a chimp that you considered him an ape - like a gorilla - but you weren't one yourself?"

"Because of Adam and Eve," said Leah.

"Right!" said Gwen.

"I got no idea, Tony . . ." said Willie, shaking his head, not remotely interested in what Tony was saying.

"Okay, what about this" asked Tony, as Gwen dropped her head to her palms and Leah shook her head, "What if those people from the Basque region gain their independence from Spain and then you found out your ancestors were from Basque. Would you cease to be Hispanic then?"

At this point, Willie almost regretted inviting Tony over. "Basques never refer to themselves as Spanish to begin with. We don't really get along with them - the Portuguese neither. Even among different Latino groups, there's a lot of strife."

"Willie won't even go into Elizabeth anymore" said Leah, "the Colombians have taken over."

"Morris Avenue: they painted the street the colors of the Colombian flag - for the parade - and they just kept it that way . . . permanent" said Willie, now shaking his head in disgust, instead of exasperation.

"I thought after the English and Irish made up all we had to worry about was the Jews and the A-rabs . . . maybe India/Pakistan" said Tony, with mock concern.

"So, Willie's got a new business venture he wanted to tell you about" said Leah, hoping to move the conversation along.

Willie, who was shuffling the cards, shot Leah a cold look. She had interrupted his script.

"What are you up to Willie, Amway?"

"It's not Am's Way it's Samway" said Leah, bungling the names.

"Leah!" said Willie. She had spilled the beans before he could make his sales presentation.

"Willie, why are you getting involved with that? You're just going to spin your wheels for six months and have everyone you know let the answering machine pick up when they see your name on caller ID."

"Tony, aren't you tired of just working all the time just to pay the bills?"

"Yeah, that's why I got out of the restaurant business."

"You're back to accounting . . . but you're still paying bills."

"Yeah, my own bills, Willie, not just the restaurant's. That's the point of working - to pay for stuff."

"Don't you want to retire someday and spend time with your family?" asked Willie.

"I'm with family right now, Willie," said Tony. "And I've got these things called IRAs, paying into Social Security and paying off a mortgage someday to pay for retirement."

"Aren't you tired of the grind? I know *I* sure am."

"Grind? Willie, you're back to bartending. You haven't spent more than two cumulative years in your adult life using your accounting degree."

"Tony!" said Leah.

"Maybe we should get going," said Gwen. "It's getting late."

"Sure, it's a Ponzi scheme" Willie admitted, before delivering his 'Hail Mary' pass before Tony left. "Amway worked, it's just that it's gotten too big. The only people doing well now are members of new immigrant groups, like the Indians and Filipinos. Sam's Way is a chance to start in at close to the ground floor."

"Technically, it's a pyramid scheme, not a Ponzi scheme, Willie, but it's an original marketing angle, I'll admit, where you admit upfront that it's sort of a scam, only that you're getting in on it early, so you'll be one of the benefactors of the racket."

With that, Willie's even marginally plausible plans of creating a multi-level marketing empire fizzled. Willie continued to recruit a few other members to Sam's Way - a couple of bartenders and waitresses at Madison Ave and some cousins from his side of the family - but none of them went on to add their own recruits after filling their cabinets up with lifetime supplies of Sam's Way soap and shampoo. Even after Willie had ended his recruitment pitches and began avoiding Jack Edwards' phone calls, Willie continued to blame Tony - and Leah, who interrupted his sales pitch to Tony - for his Sam's Way business not taking off. In Willie's mind, Tony's entire client base rightfully should have been part of his pyramid. Tony was just too cocky to listen to anyone else's ideas. There was nothing wrong with Sam's Way or multi-level marketing, it was just that Tony had blocked Willie's path to success.

As the due date for Leah and Marissa's babies approached, Willie continued to keep the bastard child matter a secret and he continued to juggle bills by going deeper and deeper into credit card debt. Complicating matters further for Willie was that both Leah and Marissa were expecting boys and that both had determined to name their child John. On Valentine's day, 2003, Leah and Marissa both went into labor. Willie drove Leah to Robert Wood Johnson Hospital in Rahway and missed running into Marissa and her mother in the emergency room by just minutes.

At 10:40 that evening in room 507, John Wilfredo Rocinante was born. At 10:40 that evening in room 509, John Wilfredo Rocinante was born.

13 - Credit Cards

"Willie, Robert Wood Johnson has been double billing us for Johnny on everything," said Leah. "Did you look at the bills?" Willie's primary technique for dealing with bills he couldn't pay was simply not to look at them, but Leah looking at them caught Willie off guard.

"Leave that alone, I'll take care of those," said Willie.

"They're more than sixty days past due and there's two of everything. Two emergency room charges, two charges from the anesthesiologist, there's even a second obstetrician - some doctor I've never even heard of." There were two bills for everything because Willie was receiving bills for both baby-John and bastard-John Rocinante. Willie didn't have money to pay the deductibles and copays for either.

"I know," said Willie. "There's some confusion . . . that's why I haven't paid anything yet."

"We've also got letters from American Express and Bank of America threatening to send your accounts to collections."

"Why are you reading that? Those are in my name." All of the credit cards were in Willie's name except for a gas card.

"They came certified mail yesterday - I signed for them. There were calls yesterday too, from Too Big to Fail Savings & Loan. They said you never made the April mortgage payment."

"Don't worry about it - and stop picking up the phone unless you recognize who's on caller ID."

Leah's only involvement in the Rocinante family finances was handing over her signed paycheck to Willie and receiving her twenty dollars weekly allowance. The only credit card Leah had was a Standard Oil of West Keansburg gasoline credit card, which required her to drive ten minutes out of her way whenever she was short on fuel, but it was the only gas-card Willie could get approved for. In a couple of days, after the banks holding Willie's credit cards began turning his accounts over to collection agencies, the phone began ringing non-stop. Willie's first response was to disconnect the answering machine, after a tearful Leah listened to a couple of the collection agency messages calling Willie a "deadbeat" and threatening to "have him arrested". Soon the phone began ringing incessantly, so Willie turned off the ringer.

Leah scrolled through the caller ID list to see if any family had called only to see that they were receiving dozens of phone calls every hour from collection agencies. Willie then discarded the caller ID and instructed Leah to have her friends and family only call her at work. "Just tell your family we're having trouble with our phone line - squirrels or something." Willie used his cell phone exclusively, so not having a functional phone at home had no real effect on him. Leah was the only one suffering.

After the Standard Oil of West Keansburg station in Perth Amboy refused to let Leah use her gas card to fill her nearly empty SUV, Leah had to scrounge around the floor mats and between the seat cushions for change in order to put two dollars and sixty-three cents of gas in her truck and drive to work. Upon reaching the doctor's office where she worked, Leah was admonished by the office manager, Anita.

"It's bad enough you've been receiving a half-dozen personal phone calls every day lately, but today we've gotten a dozen calls from some agency regarding a Standard Oil gasoline charge account. When you started making personal calls from the office, I assumed you were having some trouble at home. But, if you're having financial troubles, the doctor is not going to tolerate having his phones tied up with collection calls for an employee."

"I don't pay any of the bills. Willie does that."

"Well, it doesn't sound like Willie pays them either."

Willie, who was officially unemployed, never received any collection calls at work at Madison Ave where he worked off the books. Willie scarcely would even have been aware of the collections except that he got the mail most days while Leah was at work including the now regular requests for his signature on certified letters.

Willie slept through repeated rings coming from his front doorbell. It was before noon and Willie normally slept past one. Then, the doorbell rings were replaced by harsh knocking that jarred Willie awake. Willie thought the mailman must be early with another certified letter. He opened the door.

"Yes?" asked Willie, to the man in a black suit and red tie.

"Nice Lincoln out there . . . is that the 2004 already? I didn't even know they were out yet" said the man, with a southern accent and with intentionally fake sounding politeness.

"Do I know you?" asked Willie, groggier than usual due to a late night rendezvous between work and arriving home the previous evening.

"Mister Rocinante, how do you own a fifty thousand dollar vehicle like that but you can't make your Big City Bank Visa card payments?"

"Get the hell off my porch," said Willie. "That's against the law."

"No, standing on a porch is not against the law. What's against the law is not paying your bills."

"It's not even my house," said Willie. "I'm housesitting for my sister and her husband."

"So you're not Wilfredo Rocinante?"

"No."

"Well, do you have a number I can reach Mr. Rocinante? He hasn't been answering our phone calls."

"He doesn't have a cell phone" said Willie, as the cell phone in his pocket began ringing.

"Well, when do you expect him back, ah, what did you say your name was?"

"I didn't. I'm Bullo Cordardo, from Staten Island . . . and they won't be back for a long time. Now, I've got to get some sleep."

"Why do you have New Jersey plates on your vehicle if you're from Staten Island, Mr. Cordardo?"

"Get off the porch or I'm calling the police."

"Well, maybe I'll just knock on some of your neighbor's doors . . . I mean, Mr. Rocinante's neighbor's doors . . . maybe they'll know how I can reach him."

Willie slammed the door and rushed to the bathroom, as the

sudden onslaught of stress had his stomach churning. From the toilet seat, Willie watched through the slits in the blinds as the collection agent strolled next door to his elderly neighbors. After watching him wait on the neighbor's porch for a couple of minutes, Willie could see the agent pointing towards Willie's house with a feigned look of confusion and asking the woman, who had come to the door, for help. Thirty seconds later, the old woman began limping away from her front door, with the collection agent holding her arm for support, and heading towards the Rocinante's house. Soon the doorbell was ringing again, followed by loud banging.

"Are you sure you saw Mr. Rocinante yesterday, ma'am? Because the gentleman at the door said Mr. and Mrs. Rocinante had been gone for some time and that he was house sitting for them." Willie stayed in his bathroom, waiting for them to leave.

"It was Mrs. Rocinante I saw. I'm sure I seen her - she waved 'hello' like she always does. She's so nice. She was with her two babies. The husband always pretends like he don't see me when I wave."

"But this man says he isn't Mr. Rocinante and that Mr. and Mrs. Rocinante have been gone for a week."

"Oh my goodness, it must be a burglar. Let me go to my house and call the police."

The collection agent helped walk the woman back to her home. He waved to her as she closed her front door and he got into his car and left. Willie, damp with perspiration, stumbled out of the bathroom, walked to the living room and lied down on the couch. Ten minutes later, Willie was woken again, this time by the sound of a police siren and then startled by banging again on his front door. Willie lumbered over to the front door and looked through the peephole. He could see two Woodbridge Township police officers with guns drawn.

"What's going on?" shouted Willie through the closed door.

"Open the door slowly and raise both your arms." Willie opened the door and raised his arms, showing both palms to the officers. "What is your name sir and what are you doing on this property?"

"This is my house," cried Willie. "I'm Wilfredo Rocinante." After a few minutes of persuasion, Willie was allowed to get his wallet and show one of the officers his driver's license while the other officer walked the old woman back to Willie's house to identify Willie. After the officers had left, Willie got on the phone to Sammy Riscatto and met with him at his office the next day.

"Can't I sue this guy, and Big City Bank, for false charges?" asked Willie.

"Willie, what was a collections agent doing over your house in the first place? How far underwater have you gotten yourself with these credit cards?"

"Four or five cards, the hospital bills for the baby and the bastard . . . plus, I'm thirty days late with the Lincoln leases. Can't we threaten to sue Big City Bank for harassment and then get them to waive the balance due in exchange for us not pursuing charges?"

"First, Willie, all you can do is file a complaint with the FTC under the *Fair Debt Collections and Practices Act*, and that's against the collection agency, not Big City Bank. Why do you think these banks send these accounts to these collection agencies, rather than handle it themselves? Most of these collection agencies are based out of Texas, or something. They can get away with almost anything, short of killing you. The best thing when they're harassing you - especially on the phone - is to threaten them with an FTC collections complaint. That usually restrains them a bit until the debt gets handed off to another collection agent."

"I got the phone disconnected at home. Actually, it's on, but we turned the ringer off and got rid of the answering machine, but now they're calling Leah at work."

"If they call you at work, you can tell them you're not allowed to get personal calls at work and they're supposed to stop. It's hard to prove though, if they keep on calling."

"They tell them at her job to stop calling, but Leah's never the one who gets the call."

"We can send them a certified letter asking them to validate the debt. That wastes their time for about a month. They have to send you proof. Then they start calling again or hand it off to a new agent. Next they'll start calling your family and neighbors on the pretext of just trying to locate you. It's all designed to simply embarrass you and pressure you into making payments. Are you doing any accounting work now, Willie, or just working at that club?"

"Just the club."

"Off the books?"

"Yeah."

"Well, your income makes this an easy bankruptcy, Willie. We'll just tell them all to stick it. How much money did you put down on that house?"

"A hundred thousand - from the Net Noise money."

"Shit - no good, that's too much equity. How much do you owe on these cards, plus the hospital bills? And, give me the real number, Willie."

"Forty, maybe."

"Which means it's closer to fifty. I want you to call my guy - Sandy Kirkland - a mortgage broker. Interest rates have fallen since you bought that house. He can probably roll all that debt - the cards, the baby and bastard bills, your mortgage and maybe even buy out those car leases - and have you paying about the same monthly nut you have right now."

"Really? You saved my life, Sammy. What do I owe you for this?" asked Willie, not used to *asking* for a bill.

"Just use Sandy for the re-fi. He gives me half a point in cash for all my referrals. And Willie, disconnect the GPS devices on those Lincolns and start parking them around the corner until you are up to date on your payments. Ford Credit isn't going to call you for payments or come knocking on your door. They'll just come and take the cars back while you're sleeping."

14- Your money is no good

Now retired from firefighting and working solely as an accountant and tax shelter huckster, Bullo found himself with the opposite problem he feared – too much business. The seven hundred fifty dollar annual installment Bullo charged for investing in the rental partnerships provided an annual write off, reducing tax filer's liabilities typically over three thousand dollars. A four hundred percent immediate return on investment. Word spread quickly of the tax shelters (refunds) Bullo was selling. In 2003, S-corporations were still limited to twenty-five members and Bullo quickly reached the twenty-five member ceiling of investors in The Asbury Memorial Arms and Palisade Park Pines.

"Bullo, you know I've got my brother in-law and two more guys from the old firehouse coming to see you. That's on top of my two buddies you saw last week" said Valentine, while rubbing his right thumb over the tips of his index and middle fingers. "One hand washes the other, right Bullo?"

"Greedy bastard" thought Bullo, "I've already saved you four grand on your tax return and you're looking for finder fees?" Then Bullo shrugged and spoke. "Actually, I'm kinda maxed out on the tax shelters – they both sold out. Maybe next year."

It would be little extra work for Bullo to open a third S-corporation and continue to take in investors, but Bullo was already concerned his tax shelter scam was growing out of control. Fifty tax shelter investors brought Bullo nearly forty thousand dollars in cash annually, besides the additional tax return filing fees and Bullo's other semi-legitimate accounting client fees. Bullo already had a municipal pension that paid his bills, and he had benefits for life. More income – crooked income – wasn't worth the additional risk.

"Bullo, my brother in-law's a captain. He's not used to being disappointed." Valentine's brother in-law was a police – not an organized crime– captain but, being in Staten Island, Bullo assumed the latter.

"I'll see what I can do."

"What about the other thing?"

"What did you have in mind, Frankie?"

"I'm still in good with the union, Bullo – those guys are always looking for good investment ideas. You're charging seven hundred fifty dollars for those tax-shelter plans plus another two hundred fifty dollars to do their taxes . . . I think one hundred fifty dollars a year is a lot cheaper than the yellow pages, Bullo. I'll get you forty or fifty more guys here. That's fifty grand a year for seven or eight grand – you're way ahead, Bullo."

Bullo nodded, afraid now to turn Valentine down on anything. He reached into his pocket and pulled out a wad, mostly of fifties and hundreds. "How much do I owe you so far?"

Valentine waved Bullo off, as if to politely say 'your money's no good here.' Then, like he was offering a convenience to Bullo, "I'll have Tommy come by once a month to square things."

After Valentine left, Bullo drove over to Madison Ave to do some thinking and avoid Sparky. Before reaching the club, Bullo had what he felt was an epiphany. "I'm already bringing in more cash than I can blow on broads and beer from the first two tax shelters . . . why not actually buy real properties from now on from new investor payments?"

Making genuine investments with money people gave you to invest shouldn't seem like a flash of inspiration but, to a cynic like Bullo, it was a novel idea bordering on genius. Of course, Bullo had no notion of becoming above-board, but why not go semi-legit and use the cash people invested with him to buy a vacation house down the Jersey Shore that he himself could use or invest in actual rental properties he would own himself outright once he bought out the investors for one dollar apiece?

15 - Donald Chump

"Willie, it's been a year since I saw you last" said Sammy, "I thought you found yourself another attorney."

"Well, my PBA cards have kept me out of a couple of jams, but money has been getting tight again lately and I've got a problem with Marissa and the bastard."

Expecting a long and interesting story from Willie, Sammy clasped his hands together behind his head, leaned back in his chair and placed his crossed feet on his appointment book which sat at the right corner of his desk. "Start with the girl and the bastard-baby."

"She moved in with this guy - into his trailer actually - right after bastard-John was born. So, she never really complained about only getting two hundred fifty dollars a month child support because she didn't have any bills. At one point she even said they were going to get married and that he might even want to adopt the bastard."

"That's the dream scenario, Willie."

"Well, it looks like it ain't gonna happen. She hasn't worked since she had the bastard. He's been paying for everything - minus the two-fifty which she spends on clothes for herself and going out, when her mother can watch the bastard. Well, he's had enough. He wants her out of the trailer by the end of the week."

"He can't kick her out. It's been her home for a couple of years. Plus, she has a baby."

"Sammy, he owns the trailer - it's his. She doesn't pay rent or anything and it's not his kid. She and the bastard, basically, are guests."

"Have this Marissa call me today. In fact, give her my cell phone number so she'll get me even after 1:00 p.m. when my day is done" said Sammy, already with ideas of hitting on her himself. Sammy had never seen Marissa but he knew Willie had a good eye for women and he also knew a girl with a bastard child living with a guy in a trailer would be an easy score. "This is New Jersey, Willie. It doesn't matter if he owns the trailer or not. No judge is going to let him throw a woman with a kid out with a week's notice. I'll have her there three to six months more - depending on the judge – and, if the guy's making it difficult for her, I can have him forced out during the period, too."

"Wow, that's great."

"Now, the other thing . . . money."

"You sent me to Sandy Kirkland. He consolidated all my hospital bills for the baby and the bastard, plus some credit cards, and he rolled it all into one mortgage. He saved me - cash-flow wise - for a while, but he used all my equity. Now I've got another twenty-five in cards. Can't I wipe them out in a bankruptcy or something?"

"Have you read a newspaper in the past two years, Willie? Do you see what's going on in America? There's a residential housing boom. If your house was worth two or two-fifty two years ago, it's worth at least four hundred now."

"Four hundred thousand?!" cried Willie, suddenly feeling rich only forty-five seconds after asking Sammy if he could file for bankruptcy."

"Willie, I bought a two-family rental in South Amboy a year ago and just this month I'm pulling the equity out of that and out of my own house and I am buying two more two-family homes. You think I want to work ten in the morning until one in the afternoon for the rest of my life? Land, Willie, they ain't making any more of it."

"So, you're saying Sandy can refinance my house again?"

"Willie, not only can you refinance again, you ought to pull about a hundred thousand of cash out and use it as a down payment on some rental property. I know that club isn't giving you any pension plan when you retire."

Willie walked solemnly into Sammy Riscatto's office that morning simply hoping he could use bankruptcy to keep a roof over his head and avoid paying too much more to keep a roof over the bastard's head, as well. A half hour later, Willie left Sammy's office feeling like a shrewd real estate investor. Willie's home had more than doubled in value since he purchased it, the bastard would have another six-months rent free at the trailer and, soon, Willie would be making the first of what he anticipated would be many rental property purchases.

A month later, Sandy refinanced Willie's mortgage again. Willie's house appraised for four hundred thousand dollars, twice what he originally paid for it. Sandy gave Willie a three hundred thousand dollar primary mortgage which paid off his prior mortgage and cleaned up Willie's credit card bills. Then Sandy arranged an eighty thousand dollar line of credit for Willie that Willie planned on using for a down payment on a rental property. Encouraged by Bullo, who promised Willie fifteen thousand dollars for repairs in exchange for a twenty percent stake, Willie made an offer on the first house his realtor showed him, a three-family home on Market Street in Perth Amboy. The house was a foreclosure sale and Willie agreed to purchase it 'as is' in exchange for it selling twenty-percent less than what it would have appraised for had it been in pristine condition. The house had been owned by Jimmy Branch who still lived on the first floor, but who had stopped making mortgage payments soon after he joined the Christ Crusaders & Choir mega-church.

The Christ Crusaders & Choir Church, whose building can be seen while driving over the Turnpike Bridge in West Carteret - and more resembles an arena than a church -, preaches Prosperity Theology. Its portly Caucasian preacher promises prosperity in exchange for donations beyond the budgets of it's mostly black working class congregation, an especially disturbing racket from a socio-historical perspective. Thousands of congregants tithing - and some more than tithing - as they fall behind on their rent, mortgage and other obligations while being told that all of their troubles were nothing more than a test of faith from God who at any minute was about to pour financial blessings upon them. The good-hearted Branch emptied out first his checking account and then his 401-K account trying to donate one hundred fifty dollars a week to Christ Crusaders & Choir based upon he and his wife's seventy-two thousand dollars of annual income. After Branch pledged an extra twelve hundred dollars a month for a church building campaign to add a new TV studio to the church, Branch fell behind on his mortgage payments. Each letter from Subprime Financial, warning Branch of pending foreclosure should he not catch up on his payments, was simply seen as a test from God - "the Lord will provide" - or the work of the devil - "be sober-minded; be watchful. Your adversary the devil prowls around like a roaring lion, seeking someone to devour." Finally, when Branch had his tax returns prepared, he found himself deeply in hock to the IRS for taxes, penalties and interest from his 401-K withdrawals. His church donations didn't even help him much on his tax returns because he could barely itemize his deductions since he stopped paying his mortgage and property taxes. Throughout it all, though, Branch remained upbeat. "All this talks on the news about people losing they homes . . . they always emphasize the negative. What about all the peoples still *in* they homes?" Branch asked.

Branch himself *was* still in his home, after all. When the realtor was showing Willie Branch's house, Branch approached Willie and asked if he could stay on as a tenant in the downstairs unit after Willie had purchased the foreclosed home from Subprime Financial, and Willie gladly agreed. When he didn't have his rent money the day after Willie purchased the property Branch explained, "It's been so long since I've paid rent or a mortgage, I forgot to put it in my budget. But don't worry, the Lord will provide for you - just looks at me. I'll catch up with you next month."

The second floor of the rental home was occupied by an animal obsessed shut-in, living on Social Security disability and alimony checks. Though Willie never cleaned a thing in his life, he was spoiled by growing up with an OCD mother - who vacuumed and dusted compulsively - and then marrying Leah who always kept a spotless home. Willie nearly fainted from the stench emanating from the apartment when Connie Conroy open the door after Willie knocked to introduce himself as the new landlord and collect the first month's rent. Conroy's carpets reeked of urine from the cats and dogs relieving themselves. Uncaged parakeets could be seen flying through the screen door that separated Conroy and Willie. The hallway where Conroy stood contained three boxes of cat litter that were weeks over due for changing. Prior to 2009, tenants in homes that had been foreclosed upon could have their leases voided by the new owner. So, cupping his hand over his mouth and nose, Willie informed Conroy that she'd have to sign a new lease, get rid of the animals - except for either a cat or one small dog - and replace the carpets. Otherwise, she'd have to leave. Conroy, who had been Branch's only reliably paying tenant, tore up the rent check right in front of Willie, threw the confetti at him and slammed the door.

A week later, Conroy responded to Sammy's certified letter demanding that she vacate the apartment within thirty days, with a certified letter of her own. "By the time you have received this letter, me and my dogs already have vacated your client's goddamn apartment. I left plenty of water for the twelve cats, but please feed them right away as I ran out of Fancy Feast this morning. And, don't worry about the birds as the cats have likely eaten them by now. Signed, Connie Conroy. XOXOXOX."

Fortunately for Willie, he had the perfect replacement for Conroy, someone who could move right in and wouldn't mind the stench left behind by Conroy's animals, Pete. Pete was Willie's old roommate before he got married and a fellow bartender and skirt chaser at Madison Ave who Willie still owed two thousand dollars for his share of his last three months' rent while living with him. Willie's two thousand dollars of debt to Pete was the only debt - besides mortgages - Willie had after his most recent refinance. Pete's wife had thrown him out of their apartment after finding a prophylactic wrapper in his car and Pete had been sleeping on Willie and Leah's couch the past five nights. Pete figured he would be back home in a few weeks after his wife cooled off, so he didn't want to move somewhere that he'd have to sign a lease. Since Willie already owed him money, Pete simply moved right in, rent-free, into the middle apartment. Well, almost right in. First Pete emptied the apartment of the cats. Not sensitive to the nuance and niceties that most New Jersey pet-ridders display by crossing over the Outerbridge Crossing before releasing unwanted animals, Pete simply emptied the laundry bag meant for dirty towels, which he had stolen from Madison Ave and had been using to keep his own dirty laundry while he was thrown out of his own home, and made three trips - four cats in the bag per trip - to the Perth Amboy Ferry Slip and tossed the felines into the Arthur Kill.

On the top floor of Willie's new real estate empire resided Frank The Liar. Neither Branch nor Willie ever found out what Frank's real last name was. Even Branch, who was constitutionally incapable of seeing bad in anyone, knew Frank was no damn good and named him Frank The Liar. In the eighteen months Frank The Liar lived in the Branch's top floor, he never paid his rent a single time. Yet, he was always promising Branch that he was close to receiving a large sum of money from an estate, or a lawsuit or his divorce settlement and that not only would he pay Branch for all the back rent he was owed but that there'd be a little extra something included in the payment - which Frank implied would be in the five-figure range - to express his gratitude. For a year, Jimmy Branch not only believed Frank, but was convinced that the pending windfall from Frank was the blessing-from-above he was going to receive for his generous donations to the Christ Crusaders & Choir Church. Once Subprime Financial began foreclosure on Branch, rather than viewing his mega-donations as simply naive and foolish, he began to view Frank as a sort of Satan incarnate who had stolen his blessing. Making matters worse, in spite of his failure to ever make a rent payment, Frank The Liar was constantly calling Branch with complaints about the condition of the building. "Mr. Branch, if you're going to expect me to make good on those fourteen months of back rent, you're gonna have to do something about these squeaky floorboards in my bedroom closet," was the typical Frank The Liar two in the morning phone call.

After Frank The Liar failed to respond to Willie's door knocks for ten days straight, Sammy sent off a certified letter, addressed to 'Frank T. Liar', which the post office returned a week later as undeliverable. After three weeks, Willie decided to enter Frank's apartment and summoned a locksmith after Branch's key failed to work because Frank had changed the lock. The locksmith jimmied the front door wide open as Willie and Branch stared in to see an apartment stripped bare. Frank had not only stolen the copper piping and appliances, he had removed trim from the ceilings and around the doorways, the interior doors themselves, all the fixtures in the kitchen and bathroom - including the toilet-, the refrigerator, the bathroom and kitchen sinks, the oven, the carpeting, the spotlights from the recessed lighting cans and the knobs from the kitchen and bathroom cabinets. He'd even cleanly peeled off the wallpaper. "I'm glad I never installed that Wainscoting he'd been asking for," said Branch. Willie was just silent.

Willie's final tenant came at the request of Sammy Riscatto, who knew Willie would need someone to replace Frank The Liar. Part of the terms Sammy had negotiated to allow Marissa and the bastard to remain in Larry Hayes's trailer - until she qualified for section-eight housing - was that he'd find Hayes a low-cost, temporary, apartment. Sammy told Willie he'd have to rent Hayes the upstairs apartment for half of the eight hundred a month he was asking for. When Hayes saw the apartment with no water, lights, toilet or functional kitchen, he just stared menacingly at Willie - whose bastard he knew was staying in his state-of-the-art trailer - and said, "We'll call it even."

A week later the first mortgage bill for the three-family Amboy house arrived in Willie's mail. He had the house fully rented, but was without a single paying tenant. Without a dime in rental income, Willie viewed the mortgage bill from Ohio Lending & Spending like a piece of junk mail, as he did the equity loan bill for his eighty thousand dollar down payment, which arrived a week later.

Willie never collected a penny of rent nor paid a dime in mortgage payments to Ohio Lending & Spending, who financed his rental property. Instead of funding repairs in Willie's rental building, Bullo put a down payment on a Point Pleasant beach bungalow. Willie knew his career as a real estate speculator, house flipper and land baron was over, but it was not without benefit. Within six months, Ohio Lending & Spending Bank had foreclosed on Willie, but he was free of his two thousand dollar debt to Pete and the property had provided him nearly a half year of free shelter for the bastard by allowing Hayes to live rent free. Also, before Ohio Lending & Spending took possession of the house, Willie, Pete and Branch emptied the rest of the house of its copper plumbing, appliances and fixtures and split the cash three ways. Branch forwarded ten percent of his portion to the Christ

Crusaders & Choir Church.

Willie's third request to Sammy to file for bankruptcy proved a charm. Sammy was able to carve out Willie's equity loan in his *Chapter 13* bankruptcy filing and keep Willie in his home and cars. Best of all, Willie was six hundred dollars richer for *his* share of the copper piping loot.

16 - Mixed Beans

With his receptionist Melanie late as usual, Tony was up front in the waiting room making the first pot of coffee of the day. After hearing heavy breathing and clumsy steps from down the building's hallway, Tony darted back to his private office and closed the door, trying to avoid being trapped into a chit-chat. It was Monday morning, April 14th, the next to last day of tax season and Tony's brain was fried. Through his security monitor, Tony could see the old man, Albert, pause before the threshold of the waiting room door. Albert gasped for air as his walker set off Tony's door chime. Even behind the closed door of his back office, Tony could hear the clomping sound of the hundred twenty pound Melanie galloping towards the office. Melanie cut in front of Albert and shouted down the hall to Tony. "Sorry. Rickie was supposed to wake me before she left for class."

"When are you going to get an elevator in this building?" Albert asked Melanie, as he followed his walker into Tony's waiting room and struggled to regain his breath.

"Tony decided to invest in a security system rather than an elevator," said Melanie. "We've got more cameras here than a Las Vegas casino or jewelry store."

"The Jews?" asked Albert. "What?"

"Tony doesn't own the building," said Melanie. "It was built about a hundred years ago before the handicap laws."

"You did what a hundred years ago?" asked Albert, still bent over, leaning on his walker and gasping for air.

"No, the building" said Melanie, nearly shouting. "It was built before you were born. They didn't have elevators then."

"The hell they didn't" said Albert, who paused again to try to catch his breath. "There were horses back here when I was a kid."

"Are you Mark Finkelstein?" asked Melanie, looking at the first name listed in the appointment book that morning.

"I am Albert - Albert Botti, can I go back in?" he asked while pointing with his right arm which also held an old duct-taped vinyl attaché which contained his tax papers.

"Do you have an appointment?"

"I've been here before" said Albert, beginning to catch his breath, but struggling to hear Melanie.

"Do you have an appointment?" asked Melanie again, oddly quieter than she asked the first time.

"Huh?" asked Albert.

Melanie looked down at the schedule book. "I don't see an Albert in the appointment book today"

"I have to make an appointment?" asked Albert, with his face nearly as white as copy paper from the strain of trying to remain standing.

"Can you come back tomorrow?" asked the twenty-two year old, unsympathetic, Melanie.

"I have to make an appointment?" asked Albert again, nearly about to pass out. From his security monitor, Tony recognized Albert and knew he'd be a quick appointment that he could fit in. So, he hit the doorbell button to summon Melanie.

"That's Tony" said Melanie, "maybe he can see you now."

"Oh . . ." said Albert, "maybe two o'clock tomorrow?"

"No," said Melanie in even a softer voice, as if Albert was having trouble processing the vast decibels coming from her voice rather than being hard of hearing, "Tony just rang me. I'm going to ask him if he can see you now."

Pointing down at the appointment book, Albert asked "Is this tomorrow?" and then glared fiercely at Melanie, hoping to read her lips.

Even softer, Melanie said, "Maybe he can see you now."

"Oh, he can see me now?" said Albert, as he began slowing turning his walker towards Tony's office. "Good."

"I don't know" said Melanie, as she walked around the receptionist's desk, cut in front of Albert for the second time and marched down the hall to speak with Tony.

"What a fucking idiot," Albert said to himself. Except that Albert was the only one in the office that morning hard of hearing. Melanie's jaw dropped as she opened the door to Tony's office and pointed back with her thumb.

"He just dropped the f-bomb on me."

"I know," said Tony. "I could hear him. They could hear him in China."

"He's coming back. Can you fit him in?" asked Melanie, as the phone rang.

"That's alright" said Tony, looking at the caller ID. "I don't think I have any choice, but I'm not taking this call. Delbert Robertson . . . he's a nice guy, but he's brutal. I'm not talking to him until after tax season."

"Why don't you just talk to him on speaker phone while you're doing Albert's taxes? He can't hear anyway" said Melanie, as the answering machine picked up the call.

"If he calls back, just take a message" said Tony, "and I need Albert's file." Melanie turned around and headed back to the front office, cutting off Albert for a third time as he struggled to enter Tony's office. Tony, nearly shouting, spoke to Albert. "Albert, we don't have a lot of time. I've got a nine-thirty appointment."

"Why should I be in a hurry at my age?" asked Albert.

"Why? It's simple math, if you've only got a few years left you should be in a hurry to do everything, And, I've only got a few minutes, so we both should be in a hurry."

Albert, who was annoyed at Melanie for not speaking loudly to him, was annoyed to hear Tony yelling as well. As he struggled to position his walker next to Tony's desk, Albert fought to catch his breath. "You need to learn about COPD" said Albert, as the phone rang again. Tony peaked at his caller ID, worried it was Delbert Robertson again, but it was his wife Gwen to whom Tony had pleaded the night before 'not to call the office' during the last two days of tax season. "You need to have more compassion for people with COPD" said a now angry Albert, trying to reach the back of the flimsy black client folding chair with his left hand while holding onto his walker with his right.

"What are you talking about?" asked Tony, intentionally quieter, to get back at Albert for his lack of gratitude for Tony agreeing to see him on April 14th without an appointment.

"COPD" said Albert, as he plopped in the chair.

"I don't know what that is" said Tony, as Melanie walked back into his office and placed Albert's file on Tony's desk. "Your wife's on the phone and she says it's an emergency."

"She always says that. I told her not to call this week unless the house was on fire" said Tony, while raising the volume of his Brahms' Chamber Music CD to drown out the sound of his anticipated hollering at Gwen. Melanie left the room. Albert stared angrily at Tony while Tony picked up the phone. "Gwen, what is it? I asked you not to call today."

"Nicole's nursery school teacher said Nicole has a poor attention span for her age. She might have ADD," said Gwen.

"Goddamn it!" shouted Tony, "She's only four years old, that's ridiculous. Don't call me again. I don't care - unless someone dies - don't call. Wait until I get home if you've got something to tell me." Tony hung up the phone. All Albert heard was 'Goddamn it'.

"Don't curse at me . . . someday you'll have COPD too, maybe" said Albert, as Tony watched Mark Finkelstein on the security monitor enter the waiting room.

"Albert" shouted Tony, "I don't know what you're talking about, but I only have a couple minutes to do your taxes."

"Chronic obstructive pulmonary disease . . . someday, you'll see . . . it's very hard to breathe. You should be more compassionate."

"Disease? Why will *I* see someday? I don't smoke. I can smell the cigarettes on your clothes; I'm getting an allergy attack."

"It's addictive. You would have smoked too in my day."

"No, I wouldn't have," said Tony. "It stinks. Even if smoking was healthy I wouldn't do it, because of the stench."

"Bullshit," said Albert.

"I don't eat broccoli because it tastes awful even though it's healthy. It's the same thing."

"You don't have any compassion," said Albert.

"No" said Tony, "what I don't have is time. You show up on the last Monday morning of tax season without an appointment and you're arguing with me. Well, I've got an appointment now and I'm booked all day. You're going to have to come back tomorrow, if there are any openings."

"Come back tomorrow?"

"I need you to leave."

"I can't get up. I need to rest . . . at least ten minutes."

"You have to go."

"I need help getting out of the chair . . . two people . . . one under each arm" said Albert, huffing harder. Tony got up and walked out to the waiting room.

"How are you doing, Mark?" asked Tony to Finkelstein and then to Melanie, "I need your help with Albert."

"You want me to do his taxes?" asked Melanie, facetiously. "I'm only a marketing major."

"I need you to help me lift him out of his seat. He can't get up."

"I'll give you a hand" said Finkelstein, a retired teacher, while directing a dismissive glare towards Melanie for her indolence. "I minored in phys-ed." Finkelstein followed Tony back into Tony's office. They lifted the silent but heavily breathing Albert out of his seat. Finkelstein pointed Albert's walker towards Tony's door. Albert stepped into it and began to trudge back towards the waiting room. "I hope at least he got you a nice refund, young fella" said Finkelstein, nearly shouting to get his voice over the *Academic Festival Overture in C Minor* blasting from Tony's speakers.

"I didn't get no refund" said Albert, walking away. "He wouldn't do my taxes. He threw me out." Albert continued down the hall until he reached the waiting room and plopped into one of the chairs.

"You kicked an old man out?" asked Finkelstein, retired at age fifty-five with full benefits for life.

"He came in without an appointment. I tried to work with him but he kept on complaining about his CODP or something," said Tony.

"And, will you please turn that music off?" In the commotion, Tony didn't notice how loud the Brahms was playing.

"It's the last week of tax season. Brahms is the only thing keeping my sanity. If you want a refund, deal with the Brahms. Beethoven will get you a refund too, but you'd probably get audited."

"COPD . . . that's because of Bush . . . we've got the worst health care of any industrialized nation in the world," said Finkelstein.

"He's got Medicare, which only costs him one thousand dollars a year, plus he probably has veteran's benefits from the Spanish-American war."

"Medicare doesn't cover drugs . . . and you watch, New

Jersey, they're trying to make the retired teachers contribute to their prescriptions too. They're talking about raising our co-pay from two dollars to ten bucks for name-brand drugs."

"Bush wants to add prescriptions to Medicare, even though we can't afford it."

"You work your whole life and you still have to pay for medicine?"

"Work your whole life? You're fifty-five years old, sitting on your porch all day. We've got the highest property taxes in the country. Why should some twenty-five year old, just out of school with a hundred thousand dollars of student loan debt, pay for everyone else's health care?"

"The twenty-five year old shouldn't have to pay for his health care either," said Finkelstein. "You know, my neighbor told me you threw her elderly aunt out of your office a couple years ago over an argument about Bill Clinton."

"No," said Tony "I threw her out because she was an anti-Semite; you should be on my side about that."

"I don't believe you. I think you just fundamentally hate old people" said Finkelstein, as Melanie rushed back into the office.

"Albert stopped breathing . . . and Delbert's called two more times. He says it's an emergency."

"He and my wife: everything's a damn emergency. I already did his taxes. Stopped breathing? You mean, heavily, he's breathing normal now?"

"No" said Melanie, "like, not breathing at all." Finkelstein got up and rushed to the front office.

"Well, call 9-1-1, I guess. I'd say, empty the rest of the TV dinners out of the freezer and uh . . . you know . . . but Finkelstein would rat us out."

"You're terrible," said Melanie.

"No" said Tony, "I'm just shot, completely shot. It is April 14th . . . I've got nothing left. I've had less than twenty hours of sleep the entire week. I have fifteen appointments scheduled. Everyone keeps bothering me on the phone and now I've got Albert dying in my waiting room. I'm just trying to survive until the 16th. I'm like one of those guys after a whale capsizes their boat, floating around the Pacific for three months with three day's rations of beef jerky, fighting off sharks, licking rain water off my rubber raft hoping I'm going to randomly float onto some tropical island, deserted except for the small tribe of non-English speaking nymphomaniac Amazon women." In the front office, Finkelstein was already trying to call for an ambulance.

"I can't get a dial tone," he shouted.

"Hit 'pound'" Tony and Melanie shouted, simultaneously.

"This is a disaster" thought Tony. "I've got fifteen appointments, we're probably gonna have like fifty people picking up their returns today and I'm probably gonna have paramedics and a dead guy in my waiting room all day."

"I don't want to go out there" said Melanie, "what if he dies?"

"My ten o'clock just walked in, send them back early . . . tell Finkelstein to reschedule."

"I don't want to be out there while someone's dying."

"Work on files at the back desk and don't look. He probably just ate something bad for breakfast and has gas or indigestion."

"Okay, and what about Delbert? He says he *has* to talk to you."

"He doesn't have to talk to me. He's a nice guy, Delbert, but he's brutal on the phone. He moved out to Arizona a couple years ago - spends the winters there - but his wife still lives up here. She's ten years younger and has to work a few more years for her pension. The thing is, he's lonely and he gets me on the phone and I can't get him off. He'll have me on the phone for two hours talking about the Yankees or his landscaping or something. It's April 14th - I'll call him next Monday."

Melanie walked to the waiting room. It wasn't Tony's ten o'clock appointment, it was Betty Bean returning another client's folder that Rickie had mistakenly given to her Saturday afternoon. "This folder is for a Barry and Becky Bean. I'm Betty Bean and my husband is Robert."

"Okay, I'm sorry. So, you never got your own file?" asked Melanie. "Rickie must have mixed it up with the other Bean file, only I don't see either Bean file in the pickup draw. Do you want to take a seat next to Albert? I'll call Barry Bean and see if they have your folder.'

"Is he breathing?" asked Betty Bean.

"The ambulance is on the way," said Finkelstein.

Melanie only got through a half sentence with Becky Bean over the phone. "You gave our papers to someone else? I'll be right over."

"Mrs. Bean says she's coming right over" said Melanie, to a still standing Mrs. Bean, not wishing to get closer to an increasingly pale Albert.

"Does she have my folder?" as Mrs. Bean.

"I think so . . . she really didn't say . . . she just said she was coming right over and hung up" said Melanie, as two EMT workers and Edison police officer Gatto entered the office.

"What's going on here?" asked Gatto, as the EMT workers began CPR on Albert.

"I came in about fifteen minutes ago for an income tax appointment and the accountant - Mr. Violette - is yelling at this old guy in his back office and then comes out and asks me to help drag him out of his office."

"This isn't the first time we've been called out to deal with Mr. Violette's temper," said Officer Gatto. "Where's the young man who used to work here?"

"Ben?" asked Melanie. "Tony blamed him for getting arrested and didn't hire him back."

Mrs. Bean then walked into the office. "I'm Mrs. Bean here to pick up my papers."

"That was quick," said Melanie. "Don't you have a folder for Mrs. Bean too?"

"I live right around the corner . . . and, no, I *am* Mrs. Bean."

"Yes, but this is Mrs. Bean too" said Melanie, "She was given your papers by accident."

"You gave my papers to another person?" shouted Mrs. Bean. "I want to speak to Mr. Violette."

"Who has my papers?" screamed Mrs. Bean. "I want to speak to Mr. Violette." The phone rang again with Delbert Roberson *again* pleading to speak to Tony. Gatto shook his head, further convinced his contempt for Tony was well founded, and backed up to the doorway threshold – setting off the door chimes - to make more room for the EMTs - who were trying to resuscitate Albert - and the Beans. Next, Tony's ten o'clock appointment arrived, as well as two more clients coming in to pick up completed returns.

"I gave him your message, Mr. Robertson. It's just busy the last week of tax season. I'll let him know it's urgent."

The phone rang again. It was Gwen. "Melanie, could you put Tony on the phone, it's an emergency." Melanie stepped over

Albert, who the EMTs now had lying on the floor, squeezed past Finkelstein and rushed back to Tony's office.

"Tony, there are two women named Bean in the office. One says she's got the other Bean's paperwork in her folder, but we don't have her file. The other Bean is angry that the other Bean had her paperwork."

"Did you make a new pot of coffee yet?" asked Tony. "I'd like some *brewed* beans."

"There's no room left in the waiting room. Both Beans are angry and won't leave - they are insisting they speak with you. Meanwhile, I think Albert's dead. There are two paramedics, plus the cop that arrested you last year, in the waiting room, your ten o'clock is here and there's a line of people outside in the hall who want to pick up their returns, but they can't get into the office. And, all they hear are these angry Beans complain about us mixing up their files."

"Mixed beans - it sounds like a salad."

"Oh, and Gwen called; she's on hold, another emergency."

"Damn it, I told her not to call unless somebody died."

"Well . . . it does look like Albert died."

"Funny - a loop hole - you deal with these mean Beans, I finished their taxes Saturday and handed the folders to Rickie to finish."

"Well, your ten o'clock is waiting, the Beans both are insisting they talk to you and Gwen is on hold."

"I can't believe I'm going to say this, but I think I'm gonna choose to speak to Gwen. Get rid of those Beans."

"I'm not going back out there, it's a mob scene" said Melanie, folding her arms, defiantly.

Tony picked up the phone. "Gwen, dammit, I told you not to call unless someone died."

"Someone did. My uncle died, Sammy Sr.," said Gwen.

"Alright, I'm sorry . . . but I can't talk right now. I've got my own dead guy in the waiting room, I've got the cops, EMT people, angry Beans, plus my ten o'clock is waiting."

"You're busy with your Beans? I just told you my uncle died. The wake is at one tomorrow," said Gwen.

"The wake? Tomorrow? Are you crazy? It's April 15th, I'm an accountant: I can't go to a wake on April 15th."

"My cousin Sammy took off work when your grandmother

died. You're not going to go to his father's funeral?"

"First of all, you Italians with these funerals . . . the mailman's third cousin dies and they expect you to take a week off from work. I never expected Sammy to show up at my grandmother's funeral. He mostly just handed out his business cards and hit on my little cousins. Besides, Sammy's a lawyer - he can take off any day he wants; he only works an hour or two a day anyway." All Tony heard in response was dial tone, Gwen had hung up after 'you Italians with these funerals'. "Finally, a break." Tony unplugged his phone and handed it to Melanie. "Put this in the trunk of your car. I'm not taking another call until next week. If anyone calls and asks for me, you can tell them the truth, 'He can't talk to you because he doesn't have a phone in his office anymore.'" Melanie shook her head and took the phone from Tony.

"So, what do you want to do about the Beans?" Tony scratched his head and shrugged.

Melanie walked wearily toward the front waiting room with Tony following her. Gatto, who arrested Tony two years earlier, just stared contemptuously at Tony from the threshold of the entrance door, unperturbed by the constant sound of Tony's motion sensor door chime going off. Behind officer Gatto was Lester, Tony's ten o'clock appointment, and behind him were four increasingly agitated clients who had come to pick up their completed tax returns but couldn't get into the waiting room. Albert was laid out on the floor, just in front of the receptionist desk with the two EMT workers crouched beside him, trying to resuscitate him. Squeezed between the EMT workers, the file cabinets, and blocking Melanie's path to her seat behind the receptionist desk, were the two Bean women with arms folded and scowls on their faces. Melanie stepped over Albert and tried to squeeze past the Beans to her desk, but the Beans wouldn't budge.

"Were my papers in his office?" asked Betty Bean.

"I completely understand that you're upset, but I can't begin to look for your papers until you let me get behind my desk. I've got hundreds of files to go through.

"You gave all my papers to this woman?" asked Becky Bean. "I don't know who she is."

"I'm Mrs. Bean" said Betty Bean, with the police officer still setting off the door chime.

"You're both Beans, that must be the mix up," said Melanie. Then to Tony, who was now standing between Albert's head and the receptionist desk, "Rickie must have mixed the Beans on Saturday." The door chime continued, unabated.

"I remember Bobby Bean and Barry Bean both had appointments Saturday morning."

"I'm married to Barry Bean," said Becky Bean.

"Robert Bean is my husband," said Betty Bean.

"I remember Barry Bean and Bobby Bean because Nancy Alfalfa also had an appointment that afternoon," said Tony. "Alfalfa is a legume, technically, not a bean, but it's similar."

"I don't understand what your point is," said Becky Bean.

"He's joking" said Melanie, picking her head up from a filing cabinet she was rummaging through looking for Betty and Bobby's documents.

"I don't appreciate you pooh-poohing this. This woman had all my documents, bank statements, my W-2s, Social Security numbers . . ." said Becky Bean.

"I'm not pooh-poohing" said Tony, "and, Officer Gatto, would you please step away from the door. I enjoy hearing that chiming, but some people find it irritating after five straight minutes." Gatto stared menacingly at Tony for a second or two, but then stepped back a foot. "Lester, why don't you go back to my office? Step over Albert, it's alright, they're just doing chest compressions on him until it's safe to put him on the stretcher."

"What are you saying?" asked Betty Bean, to Becky Bean, "I brought your papers back. I picked them up Saturday afternoon. I didn't even notice until Sunday they were for a different Bean. You don't have *my* papers?"

"You had all my paperwork all weekend?" asked Becky Bean.

"I'm sure Mrs. Bean isn't going to steal your identity, Mrs. Bean" said Tony, trying - but failing - to assuage Mrs. Bean's concerns. "Although, I have to admit, with the same name . . . it would be pretty easy for her to . . . never mind."

"I don't understand, we were recommended by someone who went to Blinky for years and they saw you the past two years. We come one time . . . and this," said Mrs. Bean.

"I know" said Melanie, "I completely understand and it's unfortunate that this had to be your first experience, but we have hundreds of clients and something like this happens every once in a while. We're human."

"Which Bean are you, again?" asked Tony.

"Betty . . . Robert and Betty Bean," said Betty Bean. "I'm the one who was given the wrong Bean file. I don't know why this Bean is so upset, she has all of her papers."

"Can you folks step back" asked one of the EMT workers, "we're going to put him on the stretcher now."

Becky Bean went on. "All of our information is in this folder, names, and addresses . . . all my personal information."

"I didn't look at your damn documents, Mrs. Bean," said Mrs. Bean. "As soon as I saw Barry Bean instead of Robert Bean I brought the folder back. I thought it was a typo until the girl said they mixed Beans."

"You never looked at any of the papers, Mrs. Bean?" asked Melanie.

"Do you mean me?" asked Mrs. Bean.

"Are you speaking to me?" asked Mrs. Bean.

"Either one of you," said Tony. "Did either one of you go through all the papers? Rickie was a little hung-over last Saturday from too much Jim Beam. Maybe she mixed the Beans and all the Beans are in the one salad, I mean, folder."

Six days later on Easter at Tony and Leah's Uncle Mark and Aunt Lorraine's house, Tony and Willie were sitting in front of the television set watching the Yankees play the Minnesota Twins. "How can you watch this? They're already up three runs and the Twins haven't even hit yet. They're not going to get three runs the whole game against Mussina," said Tony.

"So? That's good," said Willie.

"It's not interesting. Why isn't Mussina still on the Orioles? Every team is just a farm team for the Yankees. They steal everyone's best players. Every team should have the same payroll. Sports is the only place where socialism makes sense." Willie didn't respond. Even marginally philosophical arguments, like Tony was making about team-sports payrolls, didn't register with Willie. It was nothing but gibberish to him. Willie just zoned out and watched the game as Uncle Freddy sat down.

"You missed a great cruise last month, Tony" said Freddy. "How's Loraine's bean casserole?"

"Good," said Willie.

"Compared to the broccoli casserole she usually makes, it's delicious," said Tony.

"Gwen's still mad about her uncle's funeral?" asked Freddy. Gwen took Nicole to the Riscatto Easter dinner and still wasn't speaking to Tony for skipping her uncle's funeral.

"What am I supposed to do? It's April 15th! I'm an accountant. I'd probably get arrested if I wasn't at the office. I managed to make it through the whole tax season this year without getting arrested."

"How *was* your tax season?" asked Freddy, laughing at Tony's torments.

"Well, a couple of deaths," Tony said. "I mean, besides Uncle Sammy."

"A couple of deaths?" asked Freddy.

"Some old guy stopped breathing after I argued with him and threw him out of my office and another guy hanged himself first thing in the morning on April 15th after he left twenty messages at my office on the 14th asking to speak with me. I was wondering why he didn't try me on Tuesday."

"Wow" said Freddy, "do you feel responsible at all?"

"April 16th . . . May 1st . . . even Christmas - I call him back in five minutes. But, it's the last two days of tax season. Only, now the family sees all these cell phone calls to my office the day before he killed himself and they're leaving messages for me now - you know - wanting to know what we spoke about all day . . . what was his state of mind and whatnot. Basically, you just can't have a phone anymore - nothing good comes from it. What am I supposed to tell them? He called twenty times, but I refused to speak to him? Before he kills himself? They'll blame me . . . maybe I could have stopped him, or something. I've already got this Finkelstein character trying to get me charged with involuntary manslaughter for arguing with the old guy and dragging him out of my office, but he's just mad because I had an argument with him about the teacher's union and their benefits."

"You dragged him out of your office?" asked Freddy, while Willie remained glued to the baseball game and finished off the rest of the bean casserole.

Tony just shrugged and then put his palm on his chest. "You know, I don't feel right."

"You look like hell, too" said Freddy, "but I just thought

maybe you hadn't recovered yet from tax season." Then Freddy spoke to Willie. "What do you think? Tony looks kind of pale . . . Willie . . . Willie . . ." Willie wasn't watching the Yankee game, he had passed out. "Lorraine . . . Mark . . . maybe we should call an ambulance."

"For who?" asked Uncle Mark.

"Whom" shouted Tony, holding his clammy head up with both hands.

"Both of them," shouted Freddy.

In twenty minutes an ambulance had arrived taking Tony and Willie with identical symptoms to Chilton Hospital in Pompton Plains. A wallet biopsy revealed a Blue Cross/Blue Shield card and Tony was whisked into the emergency room. Willie had let his insurance lapse after baby-John and bastard John were born. Willie's wallet biopsy only produced seven credit cards, a wrapped prophylactic and a VIP card from the Go Go Rama in Laurence Harbor, showing Willie was only two dances away from earning a free lap-dance. Willie was placed in the waiting room and given a bottle of water. An hour later, a nurse approached a groggy - but conscious – Willie, still seated in the waiting room between a gunshot victim, who had been accidentally shot by a fellow bear-hunter, and a large Guatemalan family of illegal aliens at the emergency room for their annual wellness check-up. "What have you eaten today?" asked the Nurse.

"Just chips and some bean casserole my wife's aunt made," muttered Willie.

"Okay, finish your water then walk over to the pharmacy down the road and pick up some Beano and Pepto Bismol. We'll charge the ambulance run to your friend's insurance."

"Tony?" asked Willie. "How is he?"

"They ran about twenty thousand dollars of tests. They've got him on Beano and Pepto too. He'll be out in about an hour."

"If you've got Beano and Pepto Bismol here, why do I have to walk to the pharmacy?"

"Beano's thirty dollars a pill in the hospital and Pepto Bismol is five hundred dollars a pint. Don't worry about your friend, though, after insurance pays, he's only looking at four or five grand out of his own pocket. And, stay away from your aunt's casseroles."

17 – Card Shark

As usual, Willie was taking a beating at the poker table. "Willie" said a grinning Pete, in front of a stack of bills and quarters, "you're welcome over to my apartment for poker anytime you like. You don't need an invite, you don't even need to call."

"Funny," said Willie.

"Weekends . . . holidays . . . the middle of the night . . ."

"I get it."

"Why don't you let Willie work your shift tomorrow?" asked Neil, another player at the table. "You took him for four hundred bucks tonight - at least."

"I dropped five yesterday at A.C., so, I'm still a hundred behind for the week."

"I told you that you weren't going to beat Trump at blackjack, Pete" said Nick, the fourth player at the table.

"What? Are you trying to count cards, Pete?" asked Neil. Pete grinned.

"What are you talking about, 'count cards'?" asked Willie.

"Blackjack, Willie" said Pete, pointing his nearly empty Corona Lite bottle at Willie's forehead. "Blackjack is the only game in the casino that you can beat the house." Then Pete chugged the rest of his beer.

"You can't beat the house" said Willie, hoping to be convinced otherwise.

"You can at blackjack."

"How's that working out, Pete?" asked Neil.

"I just have to practice more."

"Maybe you should stick to poker" said Neil, as he reached back to the kitchen counter and opened both boxes of Dominos to find no pizza left. "I told you, we should have ordered three pies."

"Look in the fridge, if you've got the guts to try any of Filly's leftovers," said Pete. "Blackjack can be beaten. Science says it can be beaten. Cards aren't like dice, cards have a memory."

"What do you mean, Pete?" asked Willie.

"Blackjack already has the best odds for the player in the whole casino - forty-nine percent -, if you play 'basic strategy'. You do what the chart says - even if it don't make sense –, like, you hit with a sixteen when the dealer's got a seven," said Pete.

"Hit a sixteen? Only if the dealer has a picture card, ten or an ace."

"This is computers, Willie. Science says to hit the sixteen against the seven."

"But you lost five hundred bucks."

"Forget the 'hit the sixteen.' The point is, if you follow what the computers say to do, you can almost break even. If you're playing ten bucks a hand - a hundred hands an hour - you're only losing twenty bucks an hour."

"So, you must have played twenty-five hours yesterday, if you dropped five hundred bucks" said Willie, with a rare attempt at wit.

"Mr. Accountant, you should appreciate this better than anyone. There's a second element to it. You play basic strategy, making the minimum bet, and try not to lose too much, but all along you're keeping track of which cards have been played. It turns out, when there are a lot of tens, aces and picture cards left, the odds swing to you. Maybe twenty percent of the time, the odds are in your favor. So, when you know there are a lot of picture cards and aces left in the deck, you raise your bet to the maximum."

"That's great!" said Willie, already prepared to quit bartending to become a fulltime card-counter.

"And, how much have you made so far?" asked Nick.

"I'm down about two grand."

"Ouch! That's four hookers, Pete."

"That's eight hookers, where I go," said Neil.

"The mistake I made was going down too soon, before I was good at counting."

"Even if you believe the books, you've got to be one hundred percent perfect and spend hours and hours at it," said Neil.

"You know about this too, Neil?" asked Willie.

"It's very difficult to do," said Neil.

"What's so hard once you're good at counting?" asked Pete.

"First of all, you've got to have a big bankroll," said Neil. "Even if you're working the system, if you're taking your profits every day you're gonna hit a dry spell now and then and get wiped out if you've only got a few grand to play with. If your max bet is one hundred dollars, you should have a bankroll of twenty, thirty grand."

"I plan on banking all my winnings until I hit ten grand," said Pete.

"Second, you've got to be real disciplined. If you've got a six-deck shoe and the count is only up two or three, you can't be betting a hundred dollars trying to make a killing."

"You know a lot about it, Neil," said Nick. "How come you're not counting cards too?"

"I don't think it can work."

"You don't believe the numbers?" asked Pete. "The computers say the system works."

"You not a computer," said Neil. "When you're practicing at home - and I assume you're practicing . . . ."

"Every day. First, I run through eight shuffled decks - count right through them - for an hour a day. I'm back to zero at the bottom at least fifty percent of the time and am usually only off by one or two the other times."

"You've got to be one hundred percent, Pete, and not just sitting home in your bathrobe at your kitchen table. You've got to be one hundred percent at the casino, with fifty things going on around you and the dealer dealing a hundred rounds or more an hour. And, you gotta look like you're not counting - like you don't know what you're doing - or they're gonna catch you."

"What do you mean, 'catch you'?" asked Willie.

"You're not allowed to count cards," said Nick.

"You're not allowed?" asked Willie, already feeling cheated although he hadn't counted his first card. "That's not fair."

"Of course it isn't," said Pete. "These scumbags rake in

millions a day. *Our* tax dollars!" It wasn't clear what Pete meant by '*our* tax dollars.' "If they see that you know what you doing, they change the rules on you."

"In Vegas they can ban you from the casino if you're a known card counter," said Neil. "In New Jersey, they just make it impossible for you. They slow the playing down and shuffle after every round so the count never gets too positive. This is what I mean, Willie, I don't think they can be beat."

"But, the computers say they *can*" said Willie, already practically a card-carrying member of card-counters anonymous.

"In theory, Willie" said Neil, "but not in practice."

"You'll see, when I quit the club in two months," said Pete.

"It's a lot of time to invest to get good at counting, but let's say you do it and you've got the bankroll," said Neil. "And, let's assume you've got the discipline not to try and make a killing every night but just to make fifty, sixty bucks an hour - on average - instead of losing twenty bucks an hour. You would have put months in preparing for this, but if you do it right you'll make maybe two or three grand for a week of work. And that's work - don't kid yourself. It's not like going down to A.C. with six hundred bucks, getting wasted and shooting craps for a couple hours and hoping you don't lose too much so you can afford a decent hooker later on. What you're doing is as dull as dealing cards, and a lot more stressful."

"For three G's a week, Neil" said Willie, "I can handle the stress."

"You didn't let me finish. When you finally get to that point, your ass is going to be planted in that casino forty or more hours every week. Even if you hop around between casinos, they're gonna catch on to you soon. They've got cameras everywhere, facial recognition technology and the casinos share information on this. In a couple of weeks, they'll put you out of business."

"What if I wore a disguise?" asked Willie. Already seeing his card counting career being stolen away from him.

"Willie" said Pete, "I signed up for a card counting class - starts next Monday. The guy's got a whole new system for keeping the casinos from catching you and better counting systems with flexible strategies based upon the counts. You should think about coming too."

"How much is the class?" asked Nick.

"Twenty five hundred, but you can pay with a credit card."

"Pete, you're already down two grand - how much more you gonna put into this?" asked Neil.

"Forty-five hundred with the class" said Willie, doing Pete's math for him. "That's only a week and a half pay - you said so yourself. Not a bad investment."

"He's just negative," said Pete. "Neil's gonna spend the next thirty years of his life crawling in people's attics and smelly basements installing cable TV wire, while we're flying all over the world playing cards and getting paid to do it, Willie."

Pete didn't have to do any selling to get Willie involved. The only issue for Willie was getting the twenty-five hundred cash. This close to his bankruptcy, Willie didn't have any credit cards he could charge the twenty five hundred dollars to. He barely had that in his checking account and his mortgage was due in a week. Still, Willie knew you can always pay your mortgage up to two weeks late before there's any late penalty, and you can hold off almost a month before the mortgage company really starts to hassle you for payment. Willie decided he would use the mortgage cash to pay for the school. Before the month was up he'd have made the twenty-five hundred dollars and more back, playing blackjack.

Before he left Pete's apartment for his evening shift at Madison Ave, Willie had borrowed twenty bucks for gas and a copy of Edward O Thorp's *Beat the Dealer: A Winning Strategy for the Game of Twenty-One* from Pete. "This'll get you started, Willie. It's not as advanced as the system we're gonna learn from Doc Lipton, but it'll give you a good background into it and you can start practicing counting."

The next Monday, Willie and Pete were in a conference room in the West Atlantic City Ramada Hotel. "I'm Doc Lipton. Only, my name's not really Lipton and I am not a medical doctor" said the grubby, middle-aged, white-bearded fat man.

"He looks familiar," whispered Willie to Pete. "I think he was a Sam's Way sales manager; I can't remember his name, though."

"I do have a PHD in mathematics" said Lipton, who had a semester and a half of math and computer science at Rutgers, "and I drink a lot of ice tea. It's for everyone in the room's benefit that I keep my real identity secret. There's not a casino in North, Central or South America, Europe, Japan, Singapore or Dubai that doesn't have my picture on file and that I haven't been thrown out of. Between 1985 and 1998 I made over twelve million dollars by playing twenty-one – blackjack - in casinos. In 1989, I had my nose broken and three ribs cracked in the back room of a Las Vegas casino, whose name I can't mention due to the terms of a settled lawsuit. By 1993, after I couldn't find a casino that couldn't spot me within ninety seconds of playing, I got a nose job, grew a beard and intentionally put on forty pounds - that I haven't been able to since shed - to disguise myself. That worked for only about two months, but I cleared over one million dollars in October of 1993 alone.

"In 1999 I wrote my first book - *Hookers, Heroin and Hard-cash on the House - the Lazy Man's Guide to Blackjack Riches.* By the time the book hit the shelves I had burned through all my winnings. The week the book was published, I was featured on ABC's 20/20 with John Stossel. Someone from Internal Revenue must have been watching. I hadn't filed a tax return in almost twenty years. Long story short, two months ago, after doing five years with Irwin Schiff as a guest of the government at the Fort Worth Federal Corrections Institute, I got out. Now, I'm back and I'm ready to go to war with the real criminals - the so-called legal casinos."

Lipton actually spent most of the past five years working various multi-level marketing schemes, selling Gold by The Inch at flea markets and selling half-filled, recycled toner cartridges out of the trunk of his 1988 Oldsmobile.

"You and I, if we few took a few bets on a Sunday football game or ran a small, regular card game in the privacy of a home, the cops would come and throw us in jail. The casino operators, though, they not only get to legally do what we cannot - they are allowed to cheat. I can't run an honest poker game in my own house, but Trump can start shuffling the cards after every hand of blackjack - to keep me from using my skills in an honest way - because he knows I'm a good player and I can beat him.

"Millions and millions of people come down to A.C. and literally beg Trump to take their money and then thank him for a so-called 'comp' - some room so they can stick around longer and throw more of their money away. But, if one person in ten thousand is smart and works real hard to get a small edge, they can't have that. They either throw them out of the casino - like in Vegas - or they change the rules . . . start shuffling after every hand . . . whatever. It's called cheating where I'm from.

"Many of you think I'm here to teach you a new career, a career in blackjack. I am not. The only career in blackjack is dealing cards, and that's a lousy career. You're here to learn how to make money playing blackjack and you're gonna have to make it quick. Your so-called career in blackjack is going to more resemble being a bank-robber than a card shark. You'll make a few big scores and then you're gonna get caught. Only you won't go to jail, because it's not a crime. They'll just put you out of business.

"So, if you're here - and you've already proved your commitment by forking over twenty-five hundred bucks - you're gonna learn how to beat these bastards and how to avoid being detected - for a while, anyway - and you'll make your twenty-five hundred bucks back in a couple of days or sooner. But eventually they're gonna catch up to you. Hopefully you've made fifty, a hundred thousand - maybe a million - before then.

"After this course - and it's a crash course - it's gonna be tempting to run right out and start counting. A lot of you - most of you, probably - have read Thorp or Humble and have already been making trips to the casinos, and probably losing. Stop. Don't step foot in a casino again until you know what you're doing."

"Where do I get your book?" asked Pete, interrupting. "It's not on Amazon."

"As soon as IRS cracked my balls" said Lipton, "I stopped promoting it and the publisher never ran a second printing. Anyway . . . first, don't even step foot into Atlantic City or Vegas – not even for a hamburger - until you're ready to go in there and hit them hard and quick. Those of you with mustaches and beards: be prepared to shave them off a week, ten days after you start playing. Those of you who are clean shaven - stop shaving. To the woman: prepare to cut and color your hair once a week once you get started. Wear a lot of makeup and, frankly, dress a little slutty. The cheaper and ditsier you look the less likely the pit bosses are going to suspect you're counting and, even if they do, they'll let you slide a bit until they see you're winning a lot.

"Now, once the course is over - you're free to go on your way, of course - but some of you . . . maybe all of you . . . are going to be invited to do something bigger. We're going to put together a team and hit the casinos like they've never been hit before. It's gonna be bigger than the Lufthansa heist. We're not going to sit there like good little boys and girls, grinding it out, simply for the privilege of the odds being in our favor fifteen percent of the time. We're not going to simply have a spotter and a player either. We're going to have swarms of spotters circling the tables. They're gonna pass the counts back and forth to each other. No one will be at a table for more than four or five hands. And then we're going to have our big fish drop in - only when the count is high in our favor - and bet big and hard and then walk away when the count breaks even. We'll bounce between the casinos, go to Vegas for a couple weeks, take some time off . . . come back . . . hit them again. And, before they know what we are up to, we'll have pried millions of dollars from them."

Lipton had been a marginally effective card counter for about eighteen months but his fat face was easily recognized by the casino pit bosses. He also lacked the bankroll to bet big and was too good at math to risk playing beyond his means. Willie, as usual, was easily sold. He showed up for his first card-counting lesson expecting to spend the next thirty years of his life earning a six-figure income sitting on his ass forty hours a week playing cards. Twenty minutes later, he was convinced instead that he was going to strike it rich in about three to six months and then be known worldwide as a dangerous card player and be banned by all casinos. Winning a million dollars in a couple of months was even more appealing to Willie than earning a couple hundred thousand a year for thirty years. He eagerly threw himself into Lipton's classes and let Lipton know that both he and Pete were interested in joining his card-counting team - The Army, as Lipton called it - after their lessons were completed.

The card counting army consisted of revolving five member squads who each had to pony up two thousand dollars toward the ten thousand per unit bankroll. The two thousand dollars bought each member a fifteen percent ownership in the squad with the remaining twenty five percent going to Lipton for running the operation. The two thousand dollar buy-in meant Willie was now two months behind on his mortgage and Pete was now a month behind on his rent. In spite of countless hours of counting practice, the accountant Willie was incapable of keeping an accurate count of the cards, even in a classroom setting. In a casino, Willie would have been completely lost. However, always dressed like a Park Avenue lawyer rather than a Madison Ave liquor-pourer, Lipton was convinced Willie could play the role of the hot-shot Wall Street scum-bag broker looking to show off for the ladies by placing one hundred dollars bets and bouncing around between tables like a fruit fly and, thus, escape suspicion of the pit bosses for a while. Pete, who barely graduated from Bayonne High School, could keep perfect count of the blackjack deck even while half-drunk on cocktails and with one eye on every short skirt in the casino. Willie and Pete were teamed up with three women counters by Lipton. Part of Lipton's scheme for keeping the squad's counting disguised from the pit bosses was to have Pete constantly following two of the women on the ruse that he was hitting on them. Of course, Pete used the tactic as an excuse to actually hit on and harass the women, who quickly dropped out of their unit and had to be replaced. The third woman, who was to signal to Willie when the count was right, and at which table Willie should play, was meant to appear like she was approaching Willie and, indeed, she and Willie began hooking up early on during the card counting lessons.

The early couple of test runs for the unit produced disappointing results. The complicated system of roving counters more resembled a Marx Brothers' routine than Henry Hill and Jimmy the Gent at JFK. Fifteen or twenty minutes would often pass between opportunities in which the squad counters could confidently signal to Willie that they had a table with an open seat and a count that gave them a two percent or more advantage. Even if the system was working right and Willie was only making one hundred dollar bets when he had a two percent advantage, placing only twenty five or thirty bets an hour meant the squad would only average fifty-five dollars an hour profit. Fifteen percent of the pie worked out to $8.25 per hour, two dollars and ten cents more than the minimum wage in New Jersey in 2006, before expenses. A run of friendly cards did have the unit up nearly sixteen hundred dollars after about twenty-five hours of playing. Lipton took his four hundred dollar cut and the players each got two hundred forty dollars, about what Willie or Pete could pull in on an NFL Sunday at Madison Ave. After the cards turned cold for a couple of days, the unit's bankroll dropped to eight thousand. Lipton ordered Willie to drop his bets to eighty dollars until their bankroll recovered to ten thousand, meaning they'd be playing for free for forty hours if their luck was average and their counting was perfect. Their luck was below average, though, and the fatigue and monotony of counting and circling the tables without the thrill of betting on hunches wore down the counters. Out of frustration, and without conspiring, the counters all began signaling for Willie to begin placing bets when the count was only slightly positive so that more bets per hour could be placed. Willie was at no better than even odds against the house most of the time. Suffering the same frustration as the counters, Willie remained at the table even when the count went negative, chasing his losses. The unit's bankroll dropped to six thousand. Lipton ordered the maximum bet be dropped to sixty dollars.

"It's gonna take us a month to get back to ten grand" said Pete, to Lipton. "We have to up the bet back to a hundred dollars." To Willie, Pete privately confessed he was close to quitting, hoping to salvage his share of the remaining six thousand dollars.

"Hundred dollar bets with a six thousand dollar bankroll is gambling," insisted Lipton. "Grind it out, follow the math. Look, sometimes some drunken schmuck walks out of the casino two thousand dollars richer even when he plays all the wrong moves. In the short run the cards can go against you. But, if you follow the system, we can't lose."

"*You* can't lose," shouted Pete. "We're the ones working and we put up the bankroll. I don't see you putting your four hundred bucks back."

"I've got five other units operating and they're all in the black. Martin and Sam have their bankroll up to twenty grand and are making two hundred dollar bets now. You guys just hit a soft patch, or you're not working the system right. I've got a new class finishing this week and I have two dozen people who'd be happy to buy your position out, Pete."

"Forget it," said Pete. "I'm sorry Doc." Pete and Willie walked out of Doc Lipton's office and spoke in the parking lot. Unknown to Pete, Willie was even more inclined to bailout than Pete, but he couldn't afford to. Between the course fee, the bankroll deposit and missed shifts at Madison Ave, Willie figured he was in the hole almost six grand and needed almost all of that to make two mortgage payments. "What do you say we up the bet to one hundred bucks, Willie? I'll talk to the other counters; they're just as frustrated as us."

"I don't know" said Willie, "we should probably just follow the system. In the long run, the math is with us."

"Okay, Willie, but I can't keep this up much longer. Twelve hundred bucks of that bankroll is mine and that would come in handy right now."

"Let's play it straight, one more time. Tonight, if we don't get the bankroll up to at least seventy-five hundred by midnight, we'll tell Lipton tomorrow we're cashing in."

That evening at Trump Marina Hotel & Casino, Willie and Pete spoke with the other counters who were also close to quitting. They all resolved to play cautiously and faithfully follow the system that evening. Willie played especially cautiously, walking away from the table even before the count reached zero. After an hour and a half, the unit was up about twelve hundred dollars. Willie walked up to Pete. "Pete, why don't you guys take a break? I gotta run to the bathroom."

"Willie, walk the hell away from me. You don't know me."

"Twenty minutes Pete . . . I don't feel well."

"Jesus" muttered Pete, while avoiding eye contact with Willie. "Whatever."

Willie walked away from Pete towards the adjacent room. There were bathrooms less than a hundred feet from where they had been standing and Pete saw Willie going off in the wrong direction but couldn't call out to him for fear the pit bosses would realize they were together. After Willie turned left behind a corner wall, he marched straight towards a roulette table. Drenched in perspiration, suddenly Willie wasn't lying. He was sick. Willie placed the entire bankroll - $7,280 of chips - on red. Red hit. Willie separated the $14,560 of chips into two piles and walked to the cashier and cashed in half - his roulette winnings - and walked to the men's room and entered a stall. Willie took the cash from his pocket and spread it out under his briefs so no cash bulge would show from his pocket. With his heart still racing, Willie splashed water on his face to cool off, and then returned to the other card room and walked up to Pete. "Pete, I'm quits. Let's get out of here."

"You do look sick as hell, Willie. I've had enough too. Let's split the chips up five ways - it should be close to fifteen hundred a piece. What do say if we get a room and call up for a girl one last time?" Willie would certainly have agreed, but he had $7,280 of cash stuffed in his underwear.

"You know, I really feel like hell, Pete. Besides, why pay for it down here when we can have all we want for free in Middlesex County?"

18 - Fannie LaBrutto

Short on cash, and without credit cards after his bankruptcy, Willie reluctantly returned for a third tax season to work for Bullo. Bullo's tax shelters brought him a slew of new clients and he began relying more heavily on Willie to prepare returns. Willie's third season with Bullo was better financially than his first two, but he continued to be intimidated and bossed by Bullo. Willie only challenged Bullo's abuse once, during the last week of January.

"Don't talk to me like that, Bullo."

"You wanna' step outside?"

Willie just shook his head. Bullo *did* treat Willie a little bit better for a day or two, feeling he had reacted too strong, but that feeling didn't stick. Bullo quickly returned to calling Willie 'Fucko" or 'Pedro' and referred to the Puerto Rican Willie as "the Mexican" when speaking to others.

For more than two months, the abuse from Bullo continued, only becoming more regular and cruel as the pressures of tax season, and the worries over his K-1 scheme, exhausted the little patience that Bullo had. Willie again vowed he would never work for Bullo, even though he was making good money now as Bullo came to increasingly rely on him. Bullo was always a week or more behind in paying Willie and he knew Bullo would screw him out of a week of commissions if he walked out before April 15th. So, Willie tried to hold on, only wishing to survive tax season, and then quit Bullo for good.

Willie's resentment grew. He often thought of revenge, but reporting Bullo to the IRS or SEC never occurred to him. Willie had too little regard for the law to grasp the seriousness of Bullo's fraud, anyway. Instead, Willie conceived a complicated scheme that could both win some goodwill – and, hopefully, abuse relief - from Bullo, as well as surreptitiously inflict revenge upon him.

Fannie LaBrutto was a legal assistant at Weasel, Silverman & Spinner in Woodbridge and a regular at Madison Ave. Willie and LaBrutto had hooked up on a dozen or so occasions at her apartment in nearby Edison. Willie and LaBrutto's relationship nearly ended before it began. Drunk at her apartment after Willie's Madison Ave shift, LaBrutto reached into her purse and attempted to hand Willie a condom after they had been going at it awhile on her sofa.

"Aren't you on the pill?" asked Willie, grimacing. Willie never used a condom unless ordered to by the woman. In fact, Willie never gave contraception any consideration at all. A gentleman left that up to the lady. Anything that diminished Willie's pleasure was anathema to him and using a prophylactic diminished Willie's pleasure considerably.

"I am," said LaBrutto. "But, it's better to be safe than sorry."

"Don't worry, I trust you."

"Willie, my last boyfriend was an HSV carrier. Now . . ."

"HIV?" asked a startled Willie, pulling away.

"No, of course not, calm down. HSV, *herpes.* But we always used a condom and I've never had any symptoms. I just want to wait a few months to be sure. I already tested clean. I just want to be a thousand percent sure."

LaBrutto was sexually permissive, but had reasonably high hygienic integrity. Her integrity must be qualified as reasonable, rather than absolute, due to the fact that she did indeed have the herpes virus. LaBrutto worked for one of the most powerful Democratic Party law offices on the East Coast and started there at the height of the President Clinton/Monica Lewinsky scandal. Compartmentalizing, moral relativism, parsing words and situational ethics was everyday stuff in her world. LaBrutto always insisted her partner wear a condom and she never so much as left her apartment for a gallon of milk without a rubber in her purse, just in case. So long as she required the man to use a condom, she felt her sexual ethical duties were satisfied. Her sexual perjury was just a misdemeanor and further sexual discovery motions would not be entertained on a one night stand.

Having done her part in protecting her partner, she always made sure the condom issue wouldn't derail the proceedings. She would wait until she and her new partner had reached such a point of amour that even warnings of a guillotine-equipped chastity belt would have seldom adjourned the proceedings.

Resting her case, LaBrutto pinched the wrapped condom between thumb and forefinger and handed it arm-stretched to Willie like she was tipping a shoe-shine boy a quarter. Willie demanded no further deliberation. LaBrutto continued to insist Willie use condoms during their next several hookups until Willie finally suggested, "It's been months, maybe you don't have herpes."

"Willie, my blood work came back from my doctor. I am HSV-2 positive" said LaBrutto. Then, adding a specious mitigating qualifier, "but *just barely so*. I still haven't had an outbreak and he says it's 100 percent okay to have sex so long as we use a condom."

Willie went along with this for a couple more encounters, but then he stopped seeing her, claiming to have a new girlfriend. It was beginning to get old anyway, and Willie couldn't help believing every itch and twitch on his body was proof he had contracted herpes. When Willie called LaBrutto, she was a bit surprised to hear from him.

"Fannie, I've got a friend who has been hanging out at the club who I think you'd like."

"Really?" asked LaBrutto. "What made you think of me?"

"Don't be mad . . ."

"No, I won't." LaBrutto laughed, wondering what odd thing might have put her in Willie's mind.

"Well, he mentioned one time that he has herpes."

"Herpes?! Seriously, Willie? Is that what guys talk about? Jesus."

"No, it's just he mentioned going to the doctors one time . . ."

"Willie, this is really embarrassing, what did you tell him? 'Hey I've got a girl you've got a lot in common with!'"

"I never told him you had herpes, I figured I'd leave that up to you. Actually, I haven't told him about you at all yet. He's an accountant I'm working with now. You'd like him, he's almost as big of an asshole as those lawyers you work for."

"Alright, Willie, give him my number. I'm so sick of rubbers, anyway."

Willie had his bait and Bullo was an easy rat to trap. The next morning at the office when Bullo was taking a few moments off from his screaming fits, Willie placed the cheese before Bullo. "This girl I used to see stopped by the club last night. I think you might like her."

"What do you mean, 'used to see'?"

"We went out a dozen times. Then, it was enough already."

The answer satisfied him. "What does she look like?"

"Not bad. Good. She could lose a few inches off her ass, but she's always game."

Bullo was sold. Willie's plan was working perfectly. Bullo treated him politely the remainder of the week, even entreating 'Willie', instead of 'Fucko', to "get me some coffee."

Bullo made plans to see LaBrutto Saturday evening. Willie hadn't mentioned how old Bullo was or that he wore a wedding ring and she quickly learned Willie wasn't joking about him being a giant asshole. Nonetheless, Bullo had invested in three martinis which were now compounding interest in LaBrutto's liver and her apartment was only a short drive away.

LaBrutto wasted no time once they were inside her apartment. She almost just wanted to get it over with. Bullo followed her as she walked straight into her bedroom and began undressing. Less than five minutes later, Bullo reached down for his wallet which was in the back pocket of his slacks, which were now on the floor besides LaBrutto's bed. When Bullo pulled out his condom, LaBrutto said, "Don't worry, I'm on the pill."

Bullo, being faux-married - and paranoid - always wore a condom.

"I still think it's a good idea" said Bullo, not even trying to disguise that he doubted she really was on the pill, and more likely was trying to get pregnant and hook him into some child-support.

"It's okay - I'm an HSV carrier too. And, I really respect that you. . ."

"What!?" screamed Bullo, frightening LaBrutto.

"Not HIV - *herpes* - Willie told me you had it too."

"What? I'll kill that little spic. You fucking disgusting cunt" shouted Bullo, lunging away from her, grabbing his pants and heading straight for her bathroom shower. An hour later he would leave Willie beaten and bloodied in the Madison Ave parking lot.

19 – The Outerbridge Crossing

Bullo's heart raced as he sped onto Route 9 towards 440 and the Outerbridge Crossing. Constantly checking his rearview mirror for police, he was enveloped in fear. He felt brief relief as his truck reached the beginning of the bridge, only to be consumed with a singular episode of gephyrophobia as he approached its apex. Ferocious wind gusts along with his frayed nerves made it difficult for him to even stay in his lane. Once he had made it to the Staten Island side, he turned onto Arthur Kill Road and drove to Curves Topless Bar. Bullo didn't go in, he just parked at the far end of the lot and tried to compose himself.

"You goddamn idiot, what did you do?" shouted Bullo. Surely someone had spotted Willie's body by now. If Willie was conscious, there were probably cops already waiting for Bullo at his house. Should he even go home? "It's almost worse if they're not there," he thought. "Then, he's still unconscious, or even dead." Bullo stared down at his bloodied, swollen right hand. "That'll be bad for a week or more."

If he was going to make a run for it, he'd need cash, and his cash was hidden at home. "Best to go home," he reasoned. "If the cops are already there, then. that's good. If Willie already ratted me out, that means he's not that badly hurt. I'll just deal with it – get a good lawyer and fight it. If the cops aren't there, I'll grab my cash and lay low until I can find out what happened."

In Woodbridge, a groggy but conscious Willie struggled to sit up on the blacktop while two drunk, underage girls laughed at the old beaten man on the ground. Willie managed to pull himself up and get into his Lincoln. The alcohol in Willie's system was enough to dull much of the enormous pain he'd be feeling in a couple of hours. Willie reclined the seat and slept until 4:00 a.m. when the fierce aching of his head woke him. Willie started the engine and drove himself to JFK Hospital, in Edison. Without insurance, the nurses just bandaged Willie up and released him the next morning with a prescription for a week's worth of Vicodin. Before he was released, Willie was required to speak to the Edison police regarding the beating.

Willie told Officer Gatto that he'd been jumped by three black guys in the parking lot whom he didn't recognize and wouldn't be able to identify if they were caught.

"They didn't try to steal your car or grab your wallet, Mr. Rocinante?"

"They were just cutting through the parking lot. One of them yelled, 'go back to Mexico, you spic.' I said, 'What's your problem?' I should have ignored him. Just forget about it."

Willie stayed in his mother's house while recuperating. Willie didn't think it was safe to return home. He was certain Bullo had left him for dead and was sure he'd attack him again. Willie made up his mind. He was through with New Jersey. He would take off for Miami to hide from Bullo, and begin a new life.

Bullo drove to Hylan Boulevard, then slowed to a crawl as he pulled onto the crossroad to his street. He leaned over his steering wheel and peered down his block. No police were in front of his house. Bullo was relieved. He dismissed the idea of grabbing his cash and lamming it until things quieted down.

"I'm making too much of this" he thought, shaking his head in frustration.

Bullo parked and went downstairs to the guest bathroom. He swallowed five Tylenol PMs and showered, as he normally did after returning from a rendezvous. Too keyed up to sleep, Bullo grabbed a bag of frozen peas for his swollen right knuckles and googled for news stories in Woodbridge New Jersey.

The first few days after the beating were the hardest for Bullo. He lived in constant fear the police would arrive at his door. The worry of getting arrested prevented Bullo from even relishing the memory of pummeling Willie, something he normally would have delighted in. After a fourth day of searching the web for news stories of a Woodbridge battery - and even the obituaries for

Willie - Bullo had a new thought.

"That worm, he wouldn't go to the police. That's too easy. He's spiteful. He'll go to the IRS or FBI. I should have killed the little rat. I should have killed him and buried him in Keasbey, under the bridge."

Bullo was desperately tempted to drive over to Madison Ave and peak in to see if Willie was working, or to at least ask around about him. He finally called the club from a payphone. A busy and disinterested waitress only could tell 'Ralph' that she hadn't seen Willie for a few days.

The dread of knowing he was going to get exposed and ruined – maybe . . . probably, even -, but not knowing for sure, or when, tormented Bullo. Normally surly but steady, Bullo became downright combustible and dysfunctional. Bullo swung from euphoria, from memories of thrashing Willie, to acute depression on his impending asset forfeiture after the IRS raided him, to fear of being arrested by the police. He mirrored Sparky's mania, but in a far more dangerous body. His mind was like a pot overfilled with popcorn kernels and olive oil, and with the burner knob set on high. At any moment, the exploding thought kernels of fear and rage could overrun the pot, toss its lid aside, and spew hot oil and crazy corn at whomever was in his path.

20 – Bankruptcy

"Alright, I'm off to Tamarack Golf course. If anyone wants me, I'll be in court all day," said Sammy.

"Who should I bill these hours to, the Lesbians?" asked Sarah Shah, Tony's former tax season receptionist and runner up Miss Metuchen New Jersey, 2003. Tony had recommended Shah, a Seton Hall law student, to Sammy. Not as a favor but, rather, as a failed attempt at revenge. Tony resented Sammy for failing to get the disorderly conduct charges against him dismissed after his pot-brownie mania arrest. Tony was certain the volatile Shah wouldn't last a week with Sammy. Instead, they got along splendidly. The hedonistic Shaw saw charm in Sammy's amorality, while Sammy simply saw a twenty-three year old pageant runner up who could answer the telephone, and didn't object to him seeing other women. Shah even put off her second year of law school to work fulltime for Sammy and moved in with him, but only after he swore that he would not be faithful to her.

"No, I took the Lesbians on a contingency basis, remember?"

For a change, Sammy was working on a serious legal case, or at least he was posturing as if he hoped to win a serious legal precedent, while simply looking to negotiate a larger settlement for his client.

"Contingency, right, I keep forgetting. You never did that before. You always told me the legal profession was simply a retainer-racket."

Like most small-league lawyers, Sammy's general-practitioner's operation consisted of delivering an impressive sales pitch to a client in some legal predicament during a free consultation, and then landing a large retainer fee. After that,

Sammy did little else besides avoid client phone calls. In civil cases, except for contested divorces in which there were family assets for both attorneys to prey upon, Sammy played - and usually won - a waiting game with the opposing attorney to see who was the worst procrastinator and forced the other attorney to finally make the friendly, compromise call. In criminal cases, Sammy did literally nothing until the day of the court hearing after the usual half dozen or so court date reschedulings so that neither lawyers nor the judge would miss a tee time. On the way to the hearing - Sammy's cases never went to trial - Sammy made sure to pull over into the parking lot of a Burger King or McDonald's and take the case file out of his briefcase to do a cram-refresher on the details of the case, making particular effort to try to remember the client's name. After arriving at court, the judge, showing professional courtesy and gratitude for Sammy picking up the check or green fees the week before, would either let Sammy's client off on a reduced charge or impose just a nominal fine. Retainer earned, off to the next case.

"Retainers pay the bills, but my one third of the settlement on this Lesbian lawsuit is going to send us to Europe for four weeks in August. Bill the golf hours to the Jew, Shah."

Sarah Shah had taken to being called by her last name. Tony had begun exclusively referring to her as 'the Shah of Iran.' After some research, she learned the first Shah of Iran had outlawed wearing the hijab for which Sarah recognized him as her patron saint, quite an honor coming from a devout atheist.

"Which Jew, Sammy? You've got open files on two Jews. The divorce case? The one whose wife ran off with the golf pro?"

"Nah. That would be in bad taste, billing a Jew whose wife ran off with a golf pro while I'm golfing. The Old Testament Wall Street crook - bill him for my golf hours. The other Jew . . . I was thinking of him in the shower this morning and in the car coming in today. Bill him for four hours this morning."

"So, what's the story with the one-armed Lesbian? You keep promising to tell me."

"She lost a hand reaching for a trapped golf ball at a miniature golf hole with a windmill obstacle."

"No wonder she's a Lesbian. The one time she reaches for a ball she loses a hand."

"Anyway, the liability insurance policy for the golf course

had a half million dollar limit, which they've agreed to pay . . ."

"Oh shit, Sammy! A third of that's almost a hundred fifty thousand dollars!"

"Actually, a third of five hundred thousand dollars is *more* than one-fifty, but I'm not a part of that; the insurance company is not fighting that. The liability policy also allows for double damages in the event of loss of consortium: the inability to have relations with one's spouse."

"She's married, the one-armed Lesbian?"

"No, they're domestic partners."

"And, how does having only one arm prevent them from . . . consorting? Lesbians don't need any arms to consort."

"Consortium. I'm going to argue that their particular, personal sexual relations and rituals and preferences revolved especially around use of the hand that was lost."

"Sammy, that's ridiculous. I'm going to have to swim across the Atlantic if I want to see Europe this summer."

"You don't understand the courts in New Jersey, Shah. They're very progressive - especially on the social issues. They're frustrated that the New Jersey legislature is dragging its heels on gay-marriage, all because of the embarrassment Governor McGreevey caused when he came out of the closet and resigned. They're looking for any excuse to convey full marital rights to gays - such as consortium - on their own. Just the threat of taking this to court and giving the New Jersey Supreme Court the opportunity to make this a test case - I hope - will scare the insurance company into settling for an extra hundred thousand or so."

"Okay, not bad."

"Now can I go golf?"

"Oh, just one more thing: Willie Rocinante called, something about you 'redoing' his bankruptcy. He sounded almost suicidal."

"Of course, his *Chapter 13* is almost a year old; he must be in trouble again. Have him come in tomorrow before noon."

The most difficult part of Willie and Sammy meeting was that Sammy liked his workday to be done by one in the afternoon and Willie was usually just rolling out of bed around one. Sammy never compromised on his 'no appointment scheduled later than noon' policy, so Willie always looked a little ragged when he saw

Sammy, but he was always dressed like a million bucks. This time, he wore just a navy blue jogging suit. Only ten days had passed since Bullo had beaten Willie and his face was still bruised and swollen. Willie hadn't wanted Sammy to see him like this, but Willie was in a hurry to rid himself of his debts and leave New Jersey.

"Willie, what the hell happened to you? I warned you to stay away from married women. You got your ass kicked by some jealous husband, right?"

"Something like that" said Willie, somberly, but relieved Sammy had provided a story for him to falsely own up to. Sammy would have been furious had he learned Willie had returned to work for Bullo – much less gotten beaten by him – following the Amboy apartment fiasco, which Sammy blamed on Bullo.

"Willie, you look like hell - almost as bad as our mutual cousin in-law, Tony. You know about the shit he's been going through with that Bubba Tomatoes?"

"Of course, all he does is complain about it."

"Well, forget about Tony. What's going on with you, kid?"

"Well, Sammy, first this waitress at the club: she wants ten thousand dollars to have an abortion."

"Willie, when are you going to get a vasectomy?" asked Sammy, showing rare frustration with Willie.

Staring gravely at the floor and ignoring Sammy's question, Willie continued. "Pete knocked her up last winter and she only asked for two hundred fifty dollars to pay for the clinic."

"Willie, there's not really a legal solution to this problem. Where does she get the idea you've got the money to be shaken down, anyway? It's those five hundred dollar suits you wear to fill two dollar draft beers; half the people at the club think you own the place."

"I also made an investment. I bought into a horse," said Willie.

"A horse?"

"Raleigh Rider. I got a forty-nine percent stake in her for thirty grand."

"Cash? Where'd you get thirty grand? No one's lending you that kind of money while you're in *Chapter 13* bankruptcy."

"The seller held the note, a balloon payment. This nag came in last-place every time we ran her and in the last race, she came up lame. With the interest, I owe thirty-two thousand dollars the first of next month minus my half of whatever we get after she's sold for slaughter tomorrow; that's only a few hundred bucks, I think."

"Anything else?" asked Sammy, a bit impatiently.

Willie shook his head. "These monthly payments to the bankruptcy trustee . . . I thought bankruptcy was supposed to wipe out your bills, but all I do is pay every month. Plus, the lease is up on my Lincoln and they want almost eight hundred a month for a 2006."

"Eight hundred dollars for a car, Willie? You can almost walk to work - and you probably should with all the booze you drink while working. I don't pay a nickel for my car, never do. Don't you see that for sale sign in my window all the time? I've got a buddy with a used-car lot. He lets me drive one for free as long as the sign's in the window. Once in a while I've got to help him with a DWI or something."

"We're off to Cancún in a few weeks; maybe I should just stay there. A guy I used to work with at Madison Ave went to the Virgin Islands, blew all his money halfway through his trip and wound up talking a job at the Hilton while he was on vacation, and he never came back."

"Willie, you've got a wife, a couple kids, at least one bastard that we know of for sure, plus a house and half a horse" said Sammy, laughing now, but Willie just became more despondent. "You need to snap out of this, Willie. Maybe talk to your doctor about Lexapro or something."

"He's already got me on Buspar for anxiety, Levator for blood-pressure and Lomotil for IBS."

"Well, maybe you should ask for some uppers. Tell him you're having trouble sleeping. Maybe he'll get you on Modafinil. I told my doctor I had narcolepsy just to get on that stuff. It's legal meth, wonderful stuff. And, if you have a prescription, insurance pays for it."

"I let my insurance lapse after the bastard was born."

"Willie, I don't know what to tell you about this broad. Let her know you're in bankruptcy again and that she'll only get minimal child support. Tell her to talk to Marissa, if she doesn't believe you. As far as money goes, normally I'd advise you to play out the *Chapter 13* a little longer before we switched it to a

'7', but Bush passed this new *Bankruptcy Abuse Prevention Act* which is effective October 17. We've got to act soon while bankruptcy abuse is still legal."

"The sooner the better."

"It's not that simple, Willie, your house. This real estate boom is working against you. Even with your cash-out refinance you've got too much equity in it to keep it if you file *Chapter 7*."

"I don't want to keep it. I'm leaving, going to Florida. Leah and the kids will have to move in with her mom."

"You're splitting with Leah? I thought you were going to Cancún together?"

"I haven't told her yet. I'll let her know after the trip; it's already paid for."

For the first time, Sammy felt a twinge of contempt for Willie. Willie felt Sammy's disappointment in him but he couldn't tell Sammy he was fleeing to escape Bullo.

"Stop paying everything, except the child support – including your mortgage -, run your checking account down to nothing and keep your cash hidden. After you get back from Cancún we'll file for *Chapter 7*; we've got to do it by October, before the new law takes effect. Half the country is going to be filing bankruptcy in the next three months. And, Willie, get a goddamned vasectomy."

21 - Bubba Tomatoes

It was 3:00 a.m. on a Sunday morning and Tony was duct-taping the joint between an extension cord and his Shop-Vac, hoping to avoid electrocution. A nor'easter the day before had flooded Tony's basement and he finally had power restored. Tony's basement always flooded when Willie was on a cruise, or so it seemed to Tony. Willie was with most of the extended Magillicutty family on a Norwegian Cruise Line ship in the Eastern Caribbean. While the Magillicuttys stumbled drunk thought the halls of the Norwegian Gem looking for their cabins, Tony sloshed through his basement trying to minimize the flood damage.

The Magillicuttys began an annual vacation tradition the year Tony bought Tommy Potzandpan's tax practice. The vacation tradition brought nearly two dozen family members from three different states together each year and was always during tax season. Even Willie made the voyage, in spite of Bullo's complaints. The tradition caused Tony both resentment and relief. All of Tony and Gwen's babysitters were out of the state at the time of year he needed Gwen's help at the office and Tony and Gwen were stuck pet sitting for several of the family mutts. However, it did at least provide Tony an excuse to Gwen as to why they couldn't join the family vacation: it was tax season.

Tony was lukewarm at best when it came to animals. He was neither a lover nor a hater of them. Early in Tony and Gwen's marriage they had come to an agreement on which Gwen quickly, and regularly, reneged. They would have one pet - a small dog - and that was it. After a mouse appeared in their living room one evening, Tony consented to a single cat joining the family as well. An invited cat was slightly better to Tony than an uninvited rodent. That amendment to the animal accord was all Gwen needed. Like a well-skilled civil-liberties attorney, Gwen used Tony's cat-concession to blow a gaping hole into the Violette family pet-pact and soon began accumulating beasts. Parakeets, canaries, guinea pigs, gerbils, rabbits, more cats, a couple more dogs, aquatic frogs, fish, hermit crabs and probably a few others that escaped Tony's notice.

The animal population didn't grow in a straight, ascending line. Rather than an animal lover, it would be more accurate to describe Gwen as one who had a serial infatuation with pets. Gwen would come home with cages of guinea pigs, hamsters and gerbils, plus hay, feed and cage-toys, only to grow tired of taking care of them after a week or two when the novelty - temporarily - wore off. Tony half-seriously considered starting a business of pet renting - Pet Pimp. Tony figured that most pet owners, like husbands - and probably wives too, for that matter - almost all had buyer's remorse quickly after acquiring their new family member but that it was such a hassle to get rid of the new family member most people determined it was easier to adjust than divorce. Concerns about liability convinced him the Pet Pimp idea was impractical.

Getting rid of pets became an avocation almost as consuming to Gwen as her unpaid occupation of collecting them was. You can't really return a rodent to the store you purchased it from, even if you offer it back for free. Unless you know someone with a snake, you have to consider more sinister methods of disposing them. Tony would have been pleased to flush them down the toilet had he not been paranoid about it somehow resulting in an expensive plumbing bill, especially the guinea pigs and rabbits. The birds took care of themselves, or really, the cats took care of the birds. Not that the cats ever killed any of the birds directly, but no bird ever lived more than a month or two in the Violette house. The stress of being constantly looked at as a meal, and having their cages pawed-at, caused the birds to drop dead from heart attacks in their cages.

One time it was thought that Tabitha the cat had killed the parakeet, Noah. Tabitha managed to nose her way past an insufficiently closed bedroom door behind which Gwen was allowing Noah to fly freely, to the great amusement of her daughter Nicole. In seconds, Noah was bouncing off the walls and

Tabitha was tearing through Nicole's bedroom like a cheetah after a gazelle. Feathers filled the room like falling snow flakes. Noah disappeared. A tearful Gwen and Nicole chastised Tabitha and searched every corner of the room only to conclude that Tabitha had eaten Noah. Tony felt badly for Nicole, but put his foot down nonetheless.

"No more birds . . . that's it. They make a mess . . . it's a waste of money . . . and it's a miserable life for the birds, anyway. They all drop dead in a couple weeks, from heart-attacks, because the cats eye them like a snack all day. You want another bird? Look out the damn window - there's birds everywhere."

"I know," said Gwen. "I hear you. I don't even enjoy taking care of them anymore. I just need fifty dollars for cat food and some hay."

"What do you need cat food for? Didn't Tabitha just eat Noah? That should hold her off for a good week."

Tony went back to whatever he was doing that afternoon only to learn the disappointing news a couple hours later. "There's great news," said Gwen. "Tabitha didn't kill Noah after all. We just found her under Nicole's bed."

"Dammit . . . but what I said still stands - Noah is the last bird we are ever going to own."

"I know, I heard you before."

Later that evening Tony was in his garage with a flashlight trying to determine the source of an odd noise he was hearing. "Do you hear that?" asked Tony to Gwen, who just walked in to see what Tony was doing in the garage this late at night.

"What noise?"

"Shush!"

The noise resumed. Gwen looked up. "Noah!"

"What?!"

"Tony, Nicole was so upset when we thought Tabitha had killed Noah that I took the money you gave me for cat food and hay and bought another Noah."

"Gwen," said a dejected Tony, "even Noah's Ark - which had two of everything - didn't have two Noahs, but now . . . *we* do."

Even though his family was the only branch of the Magillicuttys not on a ship, Tony had more empathy for the *human* Noah than usual. His house was flooded, he had even more animals than usual because of the pet-sitting and, worst of all, the rodent cages and cat litter boxes had to be brought up from the basement to escape the deluge. The dogs were barking ceaselessly at the guinea pigs and rabbits. The stench from the cages now on the first floor of their center-hall colonial was making its way up to the second floor where the bedrooms were. The musty, fetid basement stench, magnified by three feet of water, was making its way up to the first floor. Tony was subsisting on just four hours a night sleep for the past two months. Now, in the final weeks of tax season, he was now up in the middle of the night before his last off-day until April 16th scooping buckets of water from his basement.

"Enough," shouted Tony. "You're getting rid of these goddamn animals."

"Which?" asked Gwen.

"The rodents . . . at a minimum: first thing in the morning. After that, we'll get rid of the rest by attrition. The cats and dogs can die off on their own, and you're never bringing another new animal into this house again. And, if you do, I am putting it in my car, driving right over the Outerbridge Crossing and leaving it at Fresh Kills. "

"What am I supposed to do with them?"

"Why don't you take them for a drive, now while it's still dark, and let them all out in your sister's neighborhood?"

"Tony!"

"Or go to the pet store - before it's open. Leave them in the cages in front of the store - let them worry about it. I want the cages gone too, anyway."

"They have cameras in front of the pet store. Not for robbers, but to catch people abandoning their pets. They catch people all the time - they call the cops on them. There's even a sign - 'no doggie dumping.' You get a fine and everything."

"Alright, then. Just bring them to the park. Let them be free. If I can't be free, at least let the rodents roam free!" roared Tony, less agitated now and feeling a bit punchy from his lack of sleep. "I'll take the cages to the office Monday and throw them in the dumpster."

10:00 a.m. that morning, with a foot and a half of water still in his basement, Tony was passed out on his bed in a sleep that could have been no deeper even if the half-drunk glass of Bardolino on his end table had been spiked with GHB.

"Tony, Tony . . . there's some type of cop at the door . . . Tony!"

"Wah?"

"He's got a gun. He's some type of sheriff or something."

"I have to sleep, Gwen. Tell him to come back in May."

"The gerbils. Somebody caught me this morning. They took a video."

"What? Gerbils? What the hell were you doing with gerbils?"

Loud banging on the front door could be heard all the way into the master bedroom. "You have to come down, Tony. He told me he would give me five minutes to get my husband out of bed. He's coming in, Tony."

"What the hell is going on, Gwen?" The pounding on the door got louder. "Is he really a cop? Let him in before he breaks the door in."

Gwen rushed downstairs and opened the front door. Tony grabbed his robe and stumbled down his hallway, dragging his right shoulder against the wall and knocking pictures askew. He reached the stairways, grabbed the railing with both hands and allowed his body weight to pull him down the steps. When he reached the bottom floor, Tony stood up and looked at the squared-shouldered, uniformed, revolver toting, crazy-eyed, mega-moustached, polished-bald-headed Bubba Pazza - better known as 'Bubba Tomatoes' - standing in his vestibule. Tony squinted to read the gargantuan patch on the left shoulder of the blue police-like uniform that read 'SPCA'.

"Are you with the CPA police?" asked a groggy Tony, not able to make sense of what was happening. "I've never heard of that . . . I'm allowed to prepare taxes with just an accounting degree."

"Monmouth County SPCA" said an unflinching Tomatoes, not even trying to make sense of what Tony was saying. "I'm Sheriff Pazza. I'd like to take a look around."

"This isn't Monmouth County . . ."

"Your wife was spotted at Lake Lefferts Park in Matawan this morning. A civilian spotted her releasing four animals - three gerbils and a hamster - into the park." The crazy-eyed Tomatoes reported this like he was announcing Gwen had been found holding the heads of four orphaned children underwater.

"Well, if you're here to thank her, just give us the reward and let me get back to sleep."

"You don't get it, pal."

"It's tax season, I've got six feet of water in my basement and we're watching pets for ten different relatives who are hopefully floating in punctured rubber tubes in shark-infested water outside of Cuba." Willie and a couple of Tony's uncles were actually on a bus at this time for an excursion in a Mexican port taking them to watch some Mexican Short-Knife cockfights.

Tomatoes' crazy-eyes were now bulging. His eye brows stood up as if being pulled by a static electric charge. "That's what I was worried about - you've got more animals in this house. I can get a warrant in thirty minutes, but I assure you this will be easier on both of us if you allow me to search the property."

"Get the hell out of here before I call the real cops."

"I hear your dogs barking, that's a distressed bark. Probable cause for more animal abuse. Step aside, sir. I'm coming in."

"Animal abuse? What the hell are you talking about? I am the only animal abused in this house."

"Step aside, sir, or the eight tickets I've already written up on your wife will be the least of your problems."

"Eight tickets?! For what?"

"Four tickets for abandoning three gerbils and a hamster and four tickets for failing to provide food and water to a domestic animal. The tickets are a thousand dollars apiece."

"Eight thousand dollars for four rats?"

"You don't get it, sir" said Tomatoes. Tomatoes always said 'you don't get it' whenever anyone failed to share Tomatoes' extreme animal rights perspective. It wasn't simply a matter of Tomatoes mistakenly believing that the other person was misunderstanding his view. It was pure fascism.

Lack of empathy for, or even cruelty to, animals is common among psychotics. However, there is a certain type of sociopath that, while devoid of concern and empathy for human beings, have a hypersensitivity for the feelings of animals. Abused and/or neglected in childhood, the animal-obsessed sociopath disassociates from fellow human beings but develops great empathy for helpless animals.

Tomatoes childhood was one of extreme cruelty and lack. He suffered daily beatings from his father and was bullied at school until his early teens, when he took up judo and boxing. Tomatoes trained obsessively at both arts and by age fifteen he had turned the tables and become the chief thug and bully at Perth Amboy High School. It wasn't just physical and emotional abuse that had traumatized Tomatoes. Although his family was working class, and not poor, Tomatoes suffered from severe deprivation. Tomatoes usually only had a pair or two of pants and a couple of shirts which he had to wear for weeks at a time between washings. Tomatoes looked more like a dust-bowl era Okee than a New Jersey working-class child in the 1950s. Tomatoes' parents simply endeavored to spend as little as was humanly possible in raising him. It was almost as if they knew what he was going to be like as an adult and they decided they disliked him as much as the people with whom he would interact with in the future did.

Every year Tomatoes' father grew a quarter-acre garden which consisted of nothing but tomatoes. Each week during the growing cycle he would plant a new row, so he would have fresh, free tomatoes for as long as possible throughout the year. When there were ripe tomatoes to be picked - and Tomatoes had to pick all the tomatoes - all Tomatoes was allowed to have for breakfast and lunch was tomatoes and fresh tomato juice.

This austere life, however, toughened Tomatoes up and provided him with a lifetime supply of resentment to fuel his bossy and unreasonable personality. Tomatoes' life was crap for his first twenty years and he spent the next thirty five years returning life the favor. Tomatoes had no feelings for human beings besides hostility, but he had a deep reservoir of love for animals. Not all animals, though. Tomatoes' animal-association and empathies were limited to domestic beasts and small animals of all kinds. Seeing a squirrel that had been run over by a car, a barking dog leashed to a chain or a chinchilla whose Timothy-hay bedding was overdue for changing, caused Tomatoes' crazy-eyes to leak buckets of tears. 'Here comes the tomato juice' was the phrase whispered behind Tomatoes' back every time he began weeping over a neglected ferret, or forgotten frog.

However, Tomatoes actually hunted large game. Shooting a deer or a black bear left Tomatoes as unmoved as had the suffering his extremism had caused in people's lives. Tomatoes' endeavors never had him cross paths with a chimp or gorilla, and it's not clear where his sympathies would have lied in that case, with apes being so close to human beings. Given a choice between and a man and a gorilla, Tomatoes likely would have sided with the gorilla, but should an orangutan have a conflict with a hermit crab, Tomatoes certainly would have sided with the crab.

The SPCA, of course, does do humane work by rescuing genuinely neglected and mistreated animals. However, in many jurisdictions, the SPCA has been given police-power allowing SPCA agents to impose radical animal-rights agendas. In Monmouth County New Jersey, it is better to be charged with killing a human being than an animal. A woman, whose ex-boyfriend had received a suspended sentence after being convicted of stalking and assaulting her, broke into her apartment, kidnapped her two cats, squeezed them into a bowling-bag with the ball still enclosed and threw the bag into Shark River. For this, he received a five year prison sentence plus a six-month suspended sentence for breaking and entering into her apartment. A grinning Tomatoes' image was all over the pages of the Asbury Park Press for weeks. Another time, a frustrated golfer, who accidentally brained a turkey vulture with a thrown pitching wedge on Hominy Hill Golf Course, had to settle for a three month sentence after Tomatoes tried to get him imprisoned for three years.

Tomatoes' main target were the animal trappers who people call when they had squirrels in their attic, skunks living under their deck or a raccoon sitting behind their fireplace screen. New Jersey statutes required that traps set for pests like moles, skunks and squirrels be checked daily by the exterminator but this, of course, is impractical. Normally, the traps were left out for the feral cats or raccoon and the home or business owner would simply call the animal-control business when an animal had been caught. Tomatoes had a pathological hatred for the trappers and obsessively monitored all the Havahart Traps he could, hoping to catch a trapper with an imprisoned squirrel or mole for more than twenty-four hours, so Tomatoes could fine him.

Tomatoes had a new mission now - raising the status of small pets, like hamsters and guinea pigs. Most people are horrified upon learning of abuse or the gross neglect of a dog or cat. A mouse or gerbil is another matter entirely. Although gratuitous cruelty to any living creature is repugnant, it is a sound impulse in a reasonable man that ranks a chimpanzee ahead of a ground mole, a dolphin above a guppy and an elephant higher than an earthworm. It was *this* hierarchy Tomatoes sought to tear down. To Tomatoes, a gerbil deserved as much status and legal protection as a German Sheppard, and Tomatoes was determined to make a public example of Gwen Violette's rodent-release.

While Tomatoes quickly canvassed the Violette's colonial, Gwen pulled Tony aside and earnestly explained that the rodent tickets were a much bigger deal than Tony realized. "Tony, a woman caught me with her video camera. I saw her taking pictures by the lake. She didn't say anything to me, but she posted it on YouTube. It's already a story on The Drudge Report. "

"Your mice are on The Drudge Report? What the hell is YouTube? This is all some big joke, right? Candid Camera? He does look a little like Alan Funt."

"The woman posted her video online and called the Monmouth County SPCA on me. They issued a press release this morning announcing eight thousand dollars in fines for a woman caught abandoning three gerbils and a hamster. That's when Drudge must have picked it up. I think it's all over the news."

"This is crazy, I have to get some sleep and get somebody here to help pump the water out . . ." began Tony as Tomatoes approached Tony and Gwen. Tomatoes intentionally didn't make eye contact with them and spoke loudly into his cell phone, wanting them to overhear.

"I need you to send backup - a couple of vans."

"Backup?" whispered Tony, to Gwen, "I think we have to get Nicole and make a run for it. This guy is deranged."

Tomatoes got off the phone and spoke to Tony. "You've got unacceptable conditions for the animals. You're not maintaining the house properly. There's a foot of water in the basement."

"We got flooded from the nor'easter! We just got power back seven hours ago."

"You also have traumatized rabbits - they should be kept separate from the dogs."

"We keep them separated - in the basement. We had to take the cages out of the basement to keep them from drowning."

"What the hell? You keep the rabbits down there? It's a hell hole."

"It's not normally a swimming pool - that's why we brought them up stairs. I only left the fish and aquatic frogs down there"

"You've got fish swimming in that mess?

"I was joking."

"Joking? You don't get it, pal. We're sending over a couple of trucks to rescue the animals."

"You're not taking any of my pets!" said Gwen. The same Gwen, whom thousands of internet viewers had already seen abandon four pets just hours earlier.

"Oh, now you want to keep your pets?" asked Tomatoes, sarcastically, while leaning his perspiring, bald head menacingly towards her. "You're unfit to keep animals."

"Can't we keep just one cat in case the gerbils find their way back?" asked Tony, intentionally trying to irritate Tomatoes, and succeeding.

"You're in a lot of trouble, pal. The animals are all going."

"They're not even all mine - we're pet sitting."

"Do you have a license for pet sitting?"

With that, Tony was done speaking to Tomatoes. "Gwen, call your jackass cousin, Sammy Riscatto. This is one case I think he'd be good for."

Bubba Tomatoes was out of his jurisdiction in Tony's Middlesex County home. Sammy got the Middlesex County D.A. to drop all charges against Tony resulting from the animals taken from his house and the dogs Tony and Gwen were pet-sitting were allowed to be returned to their owners, although Tony and Gwen's pets were still being held by the Monmouth County SPCA pending Gwen's trial. The removal of the pets from his house almost made Tony believe the eight thousand dollars in fines they still faced was a good bargain. Tomatoes, though was not done.

Angered that Middlesex County wouldn't press charges against Tony, Tomatoes stepped up his heat on Gwen, granting interviews to News 12 and WWOR 9 News and attempted to roll the pet abandoning charges into a disorderly person's offense that could have had Gwen facing six months in prison. It was the most commented-on story the entire week on the Asbury Park Press web site which ran nearly a dozen stories on the 'Middlesex County Woman Fined $8,000 For Abandoning Three Gerbils and a Hamster' in Lake Lefferts Park in Matawan'. Opinion among the posters were largely divided between people who thought Gwen was 'cruel and inhumane' and 'got what she deserved' and folks who were aware of Tomatoes reputation - many of them professional trappers - who used the controversy to expose Tomatoes' lunacy and extremism. Asbury Park Press beat reported Ned Johnstone covered Bubba Tomatoes and ran regular puff pieces of him rescuing abused dogs and neglected cats while down-playing Tomatoes' bullying and extremism. A final story of the week from Johnstone entitled 'the most talked about story in the Press this week $8,000 fine: just right or too light?' pushed Tony - already crushed under the weight of the final week of tax season, a looming eight thousand dollar fine and a growing mold problem in his basement - over the edge. Without consulting Sammy, Tony fired off an angry email to Johnstone, which the Asbury Park Press promptly, and eagerly, published:

> Mr. Ned Johnstone: I am Gwen Violette's husband. How do you have the most "talked about story" of the week and you don't even attempt to speak with the family who is the victim of this police abuse? How many people in Monmouth County understand that an extremist animal rights group has been deputized and if you <sic> neighbor thinks your dog barks too much, a firearms packing Bubba Pazza could be at your front door intimidating your wife and children while you're a <sic> work? Perhaps "Bubba" is (a) good contact for you, so asking him a few tough questions might interrupt your flow of human interest stories. The day this story broke on your web site, a 24 year old from Holmdel was killed in an automobile accident, but the rodent story was listed higher on the web page. Did you ask "Bubba" if he thought (that) $8,000 was (an) insanely inappropriate fine for gerbils? Did you even question the "sheriff" about engaging in the unethical practice of overcharging a defendant? Did you ask the "sheriff" if (he) was concerned about bringing down ridicule and embarrassment on his department for showing such extreme lack of

proportionality and judgement <sic>? Did you question Mr. Pazza about his extreme animal rights point of views? Did you ask Mr. Pazza if he felt (it) was ethical to use his police powers to attempt to impose his own subjective, and out of the mainstream, opinion? Also, why 8 tickets? If she had stolen eight dollars from someone would she be facing eight charges of stealing $1? How does he justify charging to <sic> tickets per rodent? One for abandonment and 1 for not providing food & shelter? By definition: once you abandoned a rodent you've stopped providing food and shelter. I phoned Bubba Pazza and attempted to reason with (him), but found it not unlike speaking to someone belonging to a religious cult. <u>Gwen understands that she used poor judgement <sic></u>. Sheriff Pazza does not understand that he used poor judgement<sic> to <sic>. Sheriff Pazza told my wife, "there's something wrong with you." Very professional! I (tried) explain (ing) to the "Sheriff" that his serving these citations to her, which requires a court appearance, caused such grief (and) anxiety for her that I had to send her to her doctor who put her on Xanax. THAT WAS BEFORE she became humiliated by the publicity of the case. When I told Pazza this, his response was to chuckle and say "make sure she doesn't watch channel nine news this evening because I'm giving them an interview this afternoon." I also appealed to Pazza explaining that these enormous fines he whas <sic> threatening Gwen with are going to fall on me, not her. Gwen doesn't work. So, there is no use in pretending that any justice or prevention of cruelty <sic> of animals is taking place. I explained to Pazza he is causing enormous stress to a family OF HUMAN BEINGS. I deeply regret sharing this personal information with Pazza because he seems to have an almost autistic-like inability to have empathy for human beings. His response to my sharing these personal details and the enormous pressure he was creating for my family (all before the publicity) was to lecture me about (how) I 'don't get it' for telling him that "This is not a chimpanzee, they're rodents". Gwen is an animal lover who has been a vegetarian for years and a vegan now for several months. I to <sic> have been a vegetarian for almost three year but plan on going straight to Outback for a steak and then on to the pet store to buy a mouse eating snake should she be convicted on these ludicrous charges. Pazza (is) an unbalanced lunatic! The "Sheriff", in my opinion, lacks the human empathy and intellectual judgement <sic> to wield such authority. Regards, Tony Violette

If Tony's objective in writing the email was to rein Tomatoes in, he failed completely. Of course, Tony really had no objective at all with his email, other than venting. The published email simply served to ramp up the hostility between Tony and Tomatoes and extended the controversy into another week. Unable to bring further charges against Gwen, Tomatoes took a new tactic in his counter-punch to Tony. Knowing Tony was going to need to make repairs in his basement due to the flooding, Tomatoes called a friend in the Woodbridge Home Inspections Department. The flood had ruined Tony's hot water heater which he promptly had replaced by a licensed plumber. When the Woodbridge inspector showed up the next week to approve the work, he rejected the newly installed hot water heater because the chimney vent-pipe wasn't insulated.

"I've never even heard of that," said Tony.

"It's new" said the inspector, not even lifting his eyes from his clipboard.

"Aren't I grandfathered in - they didn't say anything when we bought the house."

"Your old boiler was grandfathered in. New work: new rules."

"How much is that going to cost?"

The inspector just shook his head, "There are more problems."

"You're only here for the hot water heater."

"A couple things didn't escape my notice. You've got a deck

built around that pool of yours. I didn't see that on your original blueprints. Did you get a permit for that?"

"You study the blueprints of everyone's house before you inspect a boiler? It's not even attached to the house."

"I also see several locust trees from your backyard have been cut down without a variance or permit."

"I need permission to cut a tree down in my own back yard? They were blocking the sun. Plus, we had tons of leaves in the pool all the time."

"This neighborhood sits on a high water-table, sir. The roots from those trees would have sucked up most of the water that wound up in your basement." For a change, Tony didn't have a retort. "I'm afraid there's no way we can let you stay in this house, until certain repairs are made."

"What?!"

"Your home will be tagged 'unsafe to occupy' until you've been certified mold-free and have French drains and a sump-pump installed."

Even the normally paranoid Tony didn't see this coming. Worse, he didn't even smell a rat - or hamster or gerbil for that matter. Tomatoes' inspector friend played it beautifully. Tony, Gwen and Nicole had to move in with Tony's parents Eddie and Meryl while Woodbridge Township buried Tony financially in fines and repair costs.

22 – The Sunshine State

Willie's bankruptcy petition was filed. Leah and the children were out of their foreclosed Fords home and into her mother's Keyport apartment. Willie packed all his belongings and headed to Florida with no plan besides escaping Bullo and his creditors. On I-95 in Maryland, Willie phoned his Miami Cousin Lou and asked if he could crash with him for a while until he got settled. Lou was shacked-up with his girlfriend Nora in a one bedroom apartment in Fort Lauderdale and was ninety days behind on his rent. Lou eagerly welcomed Willie, expecting he would help him catch up on his back rent, and ordered Nora to remove her piles of laundry from the sofa to make room for Willie. Willie drove leisurely through Virginia, the Carolinas and Georgia, savoring the anticipation of his new life of rent-free freedom in the sunshine state.

By the time he reached the Florida state line, Willie's vision of Lou's apartment had evolved into a luxury condo with large bedrooms and a built-in swimming pool surrounded by bikinied blondes. Rather than look for a hotel room, an excited Willie increased his speed, eager to join his cousin that evening in his new bachelor pad. A speeding ticket in Jacksonville delayed Willie a half hour, but he still reached Lou's neighborhood by 3:00 a.m. the next morning. Willie's heart sunk as he drove up to Lou's street. Willie was almost afraid to get out of his car. He called Lou a half-dozen times until he finally woke and answered the phone. "Willie, what's up man? It's 3:00 a.m."

"I'm here, I'm parked a half block down the street."

"Damn, man – you drove all the way on your own in one night? Okay, it's cool, just keep it down when you get in, Nora's sleeping."

Willie grabbed his duffle bag of toiletries and a garment bag with a couple of suits and shirts and left the rest of his luggage for the morning. He took some solace in the fact that it was so late that even the hoodlums must have gone to sleep, and marched up to Lou's apartment. Lou was waiting with the door open and greeted him as warmly as is reasonably possible for a man awoken in the middle of the evening.

"Hey, Mister GQ" said Lou, while pointing to the sofa. "There's your crib. I gotta crash; we'll catch up in the morning."

Willie was too tired and stunned to even respond, but Lou was too tired and eager to return to bed to notice. Willie didn't even look for the bathroom. He placed his duffle bag down at the foot of the couch, laid his garment bag as neatly as he could on the adjacent chair and collapsed on the couch, fully dressed. At 7:45, Lou startled Willie from a deep sleep, shaking his shoulder.

"Willie, it's me? You forgot where you are, didn't you?" Lou laughed. "Willie, I don't want to wake you. Let me have your keys. My car's in the shop and Nora hates taking the bus to work." Lou was out of work but Nora supplemented her Social Security total disability income with an under the table job at a dry cleaners. Willie was too tired to object. He reached into his pocket and handed Lou his keys. "Which car is it, Willie?"

"The Lincoln."

"Okay. You need anything dry cleaned? She can get that done for you for free."

Willie only answered with a deep snore.

"Okay, I'll take that as a no. I'll be back in a half hour – I'll pick up some Dunkin Donuts." Lou and Nora walked out of the apartment only for Lou to return five minutes later. Lou shook Willie's shoulder again, "Willie, I thought you were parked out front. . ."

Fortunately for Willie, his bankruptcy hadn't been discharged yet and Sammy was able to add the auto loan on Willie's stolen Lincoln to Willie's bankruptcy petition. Willie's possessions were now down to two suits, a couple of dress shirts and only four hundred thirty dollars, most of which Willie would have to shell out for new shoes, socks and underwear, plus a bathing suit for a week's vacation in the Caymans he had already paid for.

23 – The Hotdog and the Hurt Dog

The weeks of worry had exhausted Bullo. Each day without the IRS, FBI or police at his door brought some relief, but Bullo had lost his edge. He had taken to going for long, aimless drives and parking by the water. This day he had driven down Victory Boulevard towards Fresh Kills Park. He stopped for a couple Sabretts and a can of Red Bull, but didn't have the appetite to finish them.

From his truck, Bullo watched the packs of stray Jersey-native hounds rummaging through Fresh Kills Landfill. One dog, a Spanish Water Dog mix, was limping along on just three legs. Moved by an odd emotion he didn't recognize, Bullo got out of his Mitsubishi, walked up to the mutt and offered him a half-eaten hotdog. The dog ignored the hotdog and, instead, dug its canines into Bullo's right forearm. As the mutt tore Bullo's skin he pounded its torso with three left hooks. The gasping dog could no longer hold Bullo in its jaw. Bullo followed with a swift kick to the animal's neck. The dog yelped and pathetically hopped back to the landfill.

24 – Tomato Soup

Tony and Gwen were more like stowaways than guests at Eddie and Meryl's house. Eddie and Meryl had become a bit cantankerous in the past couple of years and were ruthlessly set in there ways, while Gwen wasn't set in any ways. Like a driver on a long one-way stretch of road with a tailgater behind him and an eighty year old woman in front, Tony struggled to keep the conflicting, unhinged personalities apart while trying to maintain his own sanity. Tony spent as much time at his office as possible, trying to follow up with the typically unreliable contractors who were working on his house, and the Woodbridge Home Inspection Department, which was stonewalling him on every permit. The hours he did spend at Eddie and Meryl's left him feeling like a prisoner of war during an air raid. The hard-of-hearing Eddie and Meryl constantly attempted to speak to one another from opposite sides of the house.

"What did you say?" screamed Meryl.

"Huh? I didn't hear what you said," shouted Eddie.

"You're going to bed?' howled Meryl.

"You're going to see Ted?" cried Eddie. And, on and on it went then entire day. Neither Eddie nor Meryl would ever budge an inch during these failed conversation attempts, each believing the other one was not making a wholehearted effort to speak loud enough. Eventually, they would each give up with corresponding waves of their hands as if to say, 'the hell with him."

The worst was the television volume. Tony first tried earplugs and then picked up earmuffs from Ray's Sport Shop meant for shooting ranges, but it was not enough. "Canadian Geese migratory routes are even getting disrupted from this TV volume. I can tell what they're watching as soon as I turn off from Route 35, two miles from here."

As bad as the noise was, it was nothing compared to the stifling heat. Eddie and Meryl kept their thermostat on eighty-five degrees year-round, whereas Tony ran his air-conditioning at home straight into December.

"I'm gonna' die here," whispered Tony. "I can't breathe."

"Why are you whispering?" asked Gwen. "They can't hear anything."

"I don't have the energy to talk any louder. I've already taken four showers today."

"I know you have - your mother's mentioned it about five times already."

"She keeps track of them?"

"Are you kidding? She times them too. "

"Why don't you call Bubba Tomatoes? We're living like animals here - abused animals. Maybe he can get my parents locked up."

"Speaking of Tomatoes, Sammy called. He had my court date postponed again because it conflicted with his schedule. Willie's filing for bankruptcy again the same day."

"I thought Willie's filing date was next week?"

"It was, but Willie's going to the Cayman Islands next week instead. Willie won four thousand dollars betting on cockfights during their cruise and Sammy told him to spend the money right away otherwise it would go straight to their creditors. Willie spent it all on plane tickets and two non-refundable all inclusive packages for the Grand Cayman Marriott. And, he's not taking Leah . . ."

"You know" said Tony, sardonically, "when it comes to God, I'm agnostic. I'm too cynical to believe but too paranoid to be an atheist. But, as far as the devil is concerned, I know he exists just as sure as I know one plus one equals two."

Just when he was in his deepest despair, a phone call from Sammy, with indescribably wonderful news, rescued Tony from his anguish. "Tony" said Sammy, being a bit coy with his great news. "You can go home now. It's safe to go home now."

"What do you mean?" asked a suspicious Tony, with his left hand firmly over his ear trying to block the noise from Eddie's

TV.

"It's all taken care of."

Tony wiped the perspiration off his forehead. By the tone of Sammy's voice, Tony was convinced he had pulled some stunt that likely would bring him more trouble rather than less. "What have you done, Sammy? I'm in enough trouble as it is. I just want these repairs completed, the tickets reduced and to be back in my house."

"I wish I could take credit for this Tony, but sometimes it pays to be lucky rather than good."

"I know - but that only works for Willie."

"Tony, Gwen's going to have to plead guilty to one count of animal endangerment and pay a thousand dollar fine. A misdemeanor, no big deal. And, the 'unsafe to occupy' tag has been removed from your house."

"You kidding? How'd you do this, Sammy?"

"I didn't. It seems Mr. Tomatoes had a friend in the Woodbridge Inspector's department; not really a friend so much as someone who owed Tomatoes a favor."

"What are you telling me, Sammy? Tomatoes put Woodbridge up to all this inspection harassment?"

"Exactly, but that problem just went away."

"I have to pay off someone at Woodbridge, right? I'm not doing that. Tomatoes is just baiting me, probably to set me up on a bribery charge so I can get thrown into prison."

"You're so cynical, Tony. The problem went away on its own. I don't even want to tell you myself. Look it up, Tony. It's already on the Asbury Park Press website. NJ.com too. Drudge will probably have it linked any minute."

Bubba Tomatoes had been keeping particularly close tabs on a trapper who had been hired to catch a raccoon that had invaded the stables at a horse farm in Colts Neck. The evening before, Tomatoes had trespassed onto the property to spy on the traps, hoping to catch an imprisoned raccoon, so he could ticket the trapper. The farmer's security camera, however, captured Tomatoes engaging in an act of involuntary intimacy upon a colt. Word spread quickly. The next day, Tomatoes was mulching brush from a fallen tree in his yard from the nor'easter and got a call about the video, warning him that the police were on the way to his house to arrest him on bestiality charges. Tomatoes promptly threw himself into the woodchipper. Tomato Soup.

25- Pompano Beach Industrial Life Insurance

Willie returned from the Caymans to Lou's couch, and his two suits. Broke and without a vehicle, Willie began searching for work. Naturally, Willie went to every popular night club and bar in Miami, but new-in-town forty year old balding bartenders weren't in great demand in a town full of siliconed blondes and raven-headed Latina beauties also willing to pour drinks for a living. The Florida economy was already feeling the effects of a deflating real estate bubble. The only positions in the classifieds Willie could find were thinly disguised Sam's Way like multi-level marketing schemes or commission-only sales jobs. Willie finally answered the only one he could find which offered a minimum weekly draw, a sales position at Pompano Beach Industrial Life Insurance.

Industrial life insurance is the bottom rung of the insurance industry and Pompano Beach Industrial Life was the bottom rung of the industrial life insurance business, selling garbage policies in the poorest black and Cuban neighborhoods of Miami-Dade County. Industrial life insurance policies are extremely low face amount life insurance policies – often paying less than one thousand dollars upon the death of the insured – for poor people without checking accounts. The premiums are collected in person and paid for in cash. Even by life insurance industry standards, these policies are an incredibly poor deal for the insureds who pay more in premiums every couple years than the entire face value of the policy itself. It is also extremely dangerous work, collecting cash on a regular schedule in a neighborhood where checking accounts are out of reach to the inhabitants.

The well-dressed, bilingual Willie was hired on the spot to replace a soon retiring agent. In order to work for Pompano Beach

Industrial Life, Willie was required to get an insurance license and a carrying permit. Pompano Beach Industrial's sales manager arranged for stand-ins to pass the insurance exam and take the concealed carry license class, while giving Willie a crash course in insurance sales.

The selling of industrial life insurance more resembles a newspaper route in the days when twelve year olds delivered newspapers from their bicycles and knocked on their customers doors every Saturday to collect, than a regular financial sales position. Except that it is done in extremely poor and dangerous neighborhoods. Willie inherited a book of nearly 1,000 monthly policies to collect on. Willie's job was to go to each neighborhood once a month and collect cash premiums – often less than ten dollars - for the small burial life insurance policies. For this, Willie received a ten percent commission. There was seldom any salesmanship involved although new policies were constantly being written, not often to new customers, but to existing ones who often let their policies lapse because they were short of funds or just didn't happen to be home when the salesman came knocking the previous month. Willie *did* receive a higher first year commission on the new policies he sold but they were for such low amounts, and the paperwork was so time consuming to complete, he made no extra attempt to do so. After a couple of months on the job, rather than inform the customer that their insurance had lapsed, Willie simply assured them that he had gotten it reinstated and simply started to collect and pocket the cash premiums instead of writing new policies. Initially, Willie did this out of laziness, but after a couple of months he became accustom to the extra cash.

Willies main objective each day was to finish his collections before it got dark. This began to get increasingly difficult in the short days of late autumn. Willie carried a gun with him on his pickups but barely knew how to use it and never came close to pulling it. Not that he was never held up - he was several times - but handing over a couple hundred bucks always seemed wiser to him than trying to win a shootout. Besides, it was their neighborhood. Most of the stick-up men were almost polite as he handed his money to them. On more than one occasion they said, "thank you, man" as they ran away with the cash. No one had ever harmed him and he never went to the police nor did he report the crime to his company. He simply replaced the stolen premiums with his own funds. Many of the premiums weren't going to the insurance company anyway, so Willie was still ahead of the game.

It hadn't taken Willie long to realize that these policies were constantly lapsing for late payment, that even in these neighborhoods people don't die that often and that the policies weren't that large to begin with. So, when customers missed a payment, rather than attempt to collect back premiums to reinstate a policy, or sell a new policy, Willie simply pocketed the customer's future premium payments. Willie never issued a fake *new* insurance policy. A neighbor or friend who wanted insurance was written up legitimately by Willie. But, eventually, nearly ten percent of the premiums he collected on a weekly basis were for policies that had lapsed, effectively doubling his income from the ten percent commission on the active policies. In his first five months of collecting premiums for lapsed industrial life insurance policies, Willie only had to pay off on two death claims out of his own pocket, for a total of less than twenty two hundred dollars. That the insurance proceeds were paid in cash was not odd to folks who pay their bills in cash. In fact, the cash death claim payments Willie paid out of his own funds created such good will that it resulted in the sales of dozens of legitimate life policies after family members of the deceased learned of the quick cash payout. Willie simply required a copy of the death certificate, which he promptly destroyed, and would return within a couple of hours with a pile of twenty dollar bills. The Pompano Beach Industrial Life & Trust Company had another satisfied customer and it hadn't cost them a dime.

Between legitimate commissions and money collected from the lapse policies, Willie was earning a livable income but was missing home. An aborted holdup finally convinced Willie it was time to return to New Jersey. Willie was leaving an apartment complex on Washington Avenue after sundown. Normally, Willie started the day early enough to make his collections before dark, but it was December, the days were short and he was running behind this evening. A man jumped out from hiding in front of an old Datsun parked to Willie's left. Rather than the usual pistol or knife, this man was holding a sawed-off shotgun and appeared older than the typical hood that had usually robbed him. Worse yet, this was no polite business transaction – 'hand me your money and enjoy the rest of your evening, sir.' This guy was angry. "Give me your money" he said, holding the shotgun an inch from the scar on Willie's forehead. "Give me all your money you Cuban mother . . . whoa, whoa, hey . . . you're my insurance man,' he said, putting down the rifle, "you're my insurance man! I'm sorry, man. I didn't recognize you at first."

"Yeah," was all Willie could muster.

"I didn't scare you too much I hope? Ha, ha, I almost let you have it, too. Ha, ha, ha! You'd better get going, it's getting a little too late for you for to be in this neighborhood. I'll see you next month."

And with that, Willie's industrial life insurance career was over. It wasn't simply that he thought he was going to be killed. If he noticed Felix Williams hiding under the Datsun and pulled his gun and shot him, Willie himself would surely have went to jail. Williams' entire extended family had been paying Willie for lapsed life insurance policies for months, including Williams' cousin Will Williams. Will Williams had been knifed to death that October and was insured by a lapsed seven hundred fifty dollar life insurance policy which included an extra five hundred dollar benefit should the insured die of an accident. Willie had paid the twelve hundred fifty dollars cash out dutifully in front of more than a dozen of Will Williams' kin, many of whom immediately signed up for their own real policies on the spot. Many others in the room also thought they still had insurance like Will, but they were paying Willie for lapsed ones, too. Once news of a shooting of Felix had gotten out, including who the shooter was, not only would Willie's lapsed policy racket quickly come to light in the investigation, it is likely his self-defense case in the shooting may have failed as well even with the shotgun still in Felix Williams' dead hand. How do you plead self-defense for shooting a guy that you had been robbing yourself?

26 – The Truce

Already beset with anxiety from his tax-shelter scam growing out of control, Bullo's heart skipped a beat when he received a call from someone claiming to be Willie Rocinante's attorney. Bullo spent the weeks following his pummeling of Willie worried the police would show up at his door and arrest him for battery, only to have that fear eclipsed by the fear that Willie would rat him out to IRS for revenge. Each month, that fear had subsided a bit until he received the call from Sammy. Bullo realized he hadn't even thought of Willie for nearly a month.

"Mr. Cordardo, I represent an old acquaintance of yours – associate, really -, Willie Rocinante. Mr. Rocinante asked me to reach out to you on behalf of him regarding some of the differences the two of you had, and to see if we can't put them behind us."

"The son of a bitch is blackmailing me" thought Bullo. "I wish I had killed him."

"Why don't we meet for a cup of coffee; I'm sure we can settle this matter in twenty minutes."

"Alright."

"How's about two o'clock tomorrow afternoon at the Colonnade Diner?"

"Yeah, sure. Two's good."

Willie had been too embarrassed to tell Sammy that the main reason he had left for Florida was to hide from Bullo. But now Willie wanted to return to New Jersey but wouldn't do so unless he felt safe from Bullo. Willie confessed to Sammy that it was

Bullo who left him scarred and bruised when he met Sammy for
his bankruptcy filing prior to leaving for Florida. Willie detailed a
bit of the abuse Bullo had subjected him to and explained his ill-
conceived crack at retribution via the herped Fannie LaBrutto.

"Why didn't you go to the police and press charges?"

"He's a retired fireman. He knows a lot of cops. He does taxes
for dozens of them. They would have protected him."

"Then why didn't you come to me? You could have sued
him."

"You don't understand, Sammy. He almost killed me once. I
don't want to give him another reason to try again. It's not that
he's crazy . . . he's just a surly son of a bitch. He's got the worst
temper of any person you've ever seen."

"Okay, Willie. I'll give him a call to feel him out. I won't
threaten him, but I'll certainly imply that if there's any further
incidents, he's going to have legal problems at a minimum."

Sammy drove out to Staten Island to meet with Bullo and
ensure that Bullo understood he risked legal trouble should he
bother Willie again. Bullo drove over to the Hylan Boulevard
diner convinced he was about to be shaken down by some
scumbag lawyer and, worse, Bullo was prepared to meet almost
any terms. Bullo uncharacteristically arrived there first and waited
nervously for Sammy who arrived late due to traffic on the
Goethals Bridge.

"Are you Bullo Cordardo?" asked Sammy, who approached
the only middle-aged man sitting alone in the diner.

"Yeah" said Bullo, submissively offering his hand for Sammy
to shake.

"It's good you could meet with me over this."

"Anything I can do to put this stuff between me and Willie
behind us. . ."

The waitress arrived at the table and each man ordered coffee.
After Bullo requested milk and Sweet 'N Low for his drink,
Sammy, who always took cream and sugar with coffee, simply
said "black", further emasculating Bullo. "I want to speak frankly
to you. Can I call you Bullo?"

"Sure."

"Willie's usually not much of a hot-head, but it was all I
could do to try to calm him down and get him to see the best thing

is to try to put all this ugliness behind him."

"I agree."

"Why am I even telling you this - you know Willie, probably even better than me."

"I know, he's a good guy. I wouldn't mind even working with him again." Sammy just shot Bullo a cold stare. "Dammit, why'd I say that?" thought Bullo.

Sammy let Bullo dangle a few uncomfortable seconds before standing up and offering Bullo a firm hand. "I think we've got an understanding, Bullo." Bullo compliantly shook Sammy's hand as the waitress brought the coffees to the table. Sammy turned and walked out of the diner, like John Wayne.

"What the hell just happened here?" wondered Bullo.

27 – Poker Chips

Willie returned to Leah, Jersey and the kids like he had simply gone out for a carton of milk and was now back from the 7-Eleven. Willie got his bartending shifts back at Madison Ave and borrowed money from Leah's mom for the security deposit and first-month rent on a dreary duplex in Keasbey beneath the Driscoll Bridge.

After finishing his first football Sunday bartending shift in over a year, Willie headed out to Atlantic City with Pete. "What do you say we try some counting like the old days?" asked Pete, as they pulled into the Taj Mahal Parking Garage. "How much are you carrying, Willie?"

"I've only got two hundred bucks."

"Me too. Fuck it – do you still remember basic strategy?" Willie barely knew basic blackjack strategy even when he and Pete were in Doc Lipton's blackjack course.

"Sure."

"I'll walk the tables all night if I have to. I'll only signal to you if the count is sky high. Then, you go in with hundred dollar bets. Hit them hard, and then split."

"Let's do it."

Willie and Pete made an inconspicuous blackjack pair. No one seeing both of them would ever match them up. They arrived at Taj after both had worked an NFL Sunday shift at Madison Ave but Willie's blue-stripe Brooks Brother's suit, white shirt and silver paisley tie were without wrinkles, whereas Pete's rumpled

Chad Pennington jersey appeared to have spent the night rolled in a ball in spite of Pete's giant girth stretching away any creases. Pete stumbled around between blackjack games, looking for a table loaded with small numbered cards. Willie nervously jingled sixteen twenty-five dollar chips in his coat pocket while scouting the casino for unattached women. Finally, Pete made the signal. Willie sat, bet one hundred dollars of chips and was dealt a pair of sevens while the dealer held a five.

"I'll split those" said Willie, as he placed another hundred dollars of chips on the table. Willie was then dealt a three. "I'll double." Willie place four more chips down and received a nine to finish with nineteen. Willie's second seven received a two card and Willie doubled down again, emptying his pockets. Willie drew a Jack and held his breath until the dealer busted. "Yes!" said Willie, as he scooped up the thirty-two chips and stood up.

"Leaving so soon?" asked Rose Rosa, a liquored-up early-fifties year-old at third base at the table.

"I never hang around anywhere too long" said Willie, trying to sound suave.

"Well, I guess it's goodbye then" said Rosa, extending her hand to Willie, which held her room key. Willie smiled and shook her hand. The key caught him off guard but he deftly raised his left hand to join the handshake and help secure the key transfer.

Rosa was a bit over the hill and it wasn't that tall of a hill to begin with. Further, Willie preferred young ones to cougars. Still, Rosa possessed a kind of sexiness that women of means who manage to keep the extra weight off often possess. Rosa was always smartly dressed, impeccably groomed and perpetually flirtatious. She wasn't too attractive, but she was attractive enough, at least for a late evening romp. Rosa's husband Sheldon Gardner, a successful insurance executive from Florham Park, was playing poker, which meant he'd be occupied for six to eight hours.

Since his quasi-single stent in Florida, Willie had given up any pretense of quasi-fidelity. Rosa left the table and headed for her room. Willie walked to Pete and handed him his four hundred dollars in chips. "I'm taking a break, Pete. I've got a matinee. I'll be on my cell."

"What are you doing, Willie, you're hot? And, it's too late for a matinee."

"It's never too late for a matinee."

Pete took the four hundred dollars in chips back to the blackjack tables, and quickly gave it back to the house. Willie stopped to cash in his four hundred dollars of chips and headed to Rosa's room. "It's open" shouted Rosa, on hearing Willie's knock. Rosa poked her head out of the bathroom where she was freshening up. "The money's on the end table."

"The money?" asked Willie, confused. Willie looked at the end table. Twenty green chips were neatly stacked in five piles.

"That's what you get, right? Five?"

Willie paused for a moment. "Yeah, that's fine."

"What's your name, hon?"

"Willie."

"Do you live in Atlantic City, Willie?"

"Nah, Middlesex County."

"You come all this way to work?" asked Rosa, walking out of the bathroom wearing just an untied white terrycloth bathrobe. "I guess you gotta go where the money is."

"Yeah."

"Don't be shy, Willie. Pick up your chips."

Willie grabbed the chips off the end table and stuck them in the ticket pocket of his jacket, as his cell phone went off. It was Pete. "What?"

"Willie, I blew through the four-hundred. I'm completely busted. I need to borrow some of your chips."

"Fine. Room 504. Make it quick." Willie was annoyed, but didn't want to argue with Pete in front of Rosa. "A friend who I drove down with needs my keys to get his wallet from my car."

"It's okay, Willie. We'll have a couple of Jim means in the Beam time" said Rosa, laughing at her drunken malapropism.

Ten minutes later, Pete knocked. Willie walked to the door while trying to inconspicuously take the chips from his pocket. "Sorry Willie" whispered Pete, as Willie pinched the last couple of chips out of his pocket and dropped them into Pete's cupped hands. "How many chips are here?"

"Five hundred," whispered Willie.

"Five hundred? You held out on me, Willie."

"Forget it, we'll talk later."

"You robbed me fifty dollars" said Pete, as a pale-blue Sheldon Gardner stumbled down the hall towards the suite.

"Who is that doing at my door?" asked the drunk Gardner.

Pete squeezed the chips into the pockets of his tight jeans. "Are you talking to me?"

"Who the hell are you?" asked Gardner. Pete backed a few feet away from the door as Gardner approached and saw Willie. "What the hell are you doing in this room?" Gardner had left the poker tables early, sick from too much Jack Daniel's. "Are you robbing me?"

"No" said Willie, "I'm the bellhop - Willie."

Gardner squinted. He recognized Willie. Gardner was a regular at the Bourbon Street go-go bar in Sayreville and once watched Willie nurse a single beer and a stack of three singles for two hours while trying to interest the dancers in Sam's Way. "You're not bellhop Willie - you're Bourbon Street Billy!"

Willie tore for the elevator. The bulbous Pete struggled to follow, while laughing hysterically. Gardner vomited outside the door. Rosa was rolled up in a corner hoping Gardner would pass out before discovering her in the room.

The next evening at Madison Ave, Pete shared the story to anyone who would listen, and to some who *wouldn't* listen. Wilfredo Rocinante was no longer Willie, he was Bourbon Street Billy, although it quickly got shortened to 'Bourbon Billy.' Willie, being a Wilfredo and not a William, was never known as Bill or Billy, but he immediately took a liking to the 'Billy' part thinking that being a Billy would make people think he was only half Puerto Rican.

For years Willie passed himself off as half-Italian based on an evolving misunderstanding after learning his great grandmother - whom he had never met -'s last name was Ciocia. "We're Italian?!" shouted an excited Willie, to his slightly annoyed mother.

"No, grandma's husband was Italian. Your blood great-grandfather was Puerto Rican just like you."

Although his mother's explanation put a damper on this brief but exhilarating misunderstanding, a spark of the misunderstanding took root as a small distortion. Willie casually told a few friends that his great grandfather was Italian. It was sort of true. After all, it was his step-great grandfather. So, when one junior high school classmate, better at fractions than Willie, asked

"So, I guess that makes you one eighth Italian, right?" Willie agreed.

"I guess" said Willie, with a shrug and frown to feign disinterest. That was all the permission Willie needed. Immediately, Willie became one eighth Italian for the rest of junior high school. In high school, Willie became a quarter Italian. After all, his great grandmother did have an Italian name too, so he was sort of two eighths Italian. In college, Willie became half Italian. After all, he did sort of have Italian on his mother's side, so he was sort of half-Italian.

After asking around about Willie at Bourbon Street, Gardner got a tip and found Willie working at Madison Ave. Willie recognized Gardner as he approached the bar, but Gardner wasn't there to confront him. He was there to hire him. When the plastered Gardner confronted Rosa about the sleazy bartender whom he found in their hotel room, Rosa convinced the credulous Gardner that she was merely trying to hire him to bartend at their annual Halloween party they threw at their house for the executives and salesmen at Mutual of Hackensack Life. "I'm sorry I frightened you last week at the Taj, young man. I had a little too much to drink - a *lot* too much to drink." Willie was speechless. "Anyway, I hope your still willing to bartend our Halloween party this year."

"Sure" said Willie, "no hard feelings."

"Just one condition: you're not Willie. We already told everyone that 'the famous Bourbon Street Billy will be serving the drinks.' Rosa said you get five-hundred for the parties, right?"

"Yes."

"Don't worry, you'll double that with tips with my group. Just make the drinks strong."

Willie, rather Billy, worked the Halloween party for Gardner and Rosa. He even had a hundred business cards printed up – 'Bourbon Billy's Bartending' – and picked up a couple more private bartending gigs from the guests. He also made good on Rosa's five hundred dollar poker chip payment after Gardner had passed out and the rest of the guests had left.

While Willie poured drinks that night, Tony juggled bills.

"Gwen, did you see this Allstate bill?" Of course, Gwen hadn't. Gwen never looked at a bill in her life. "I don't understand this. We're supposed to have 'no-fault' insurance in New Jersey. Then, some guy with no insurance hits *your* car and my insurance goes up?"

On the other side of Woodbridge Township, a drunk returning from the Gardner Halloween party slammed into a ten year old Dodge Caravan. The driver was a twenty-four year old date of one of the Mutual of Hackensack Life sales reps, with no insurance, no money and facing twelve months in jail. The owner of the Caravan dropped collision coverage after the van was paid off. Now they had over five thousand dollars in medical bills and a ruined van. With the twenty-four year old penniless, the Caravan owner's attorney filed complaints against Bourbon Billy's Bartending and Sheldon Gardner.

"My client, Wilfredo Rocinante, is an unemployed accountant" said Sammy, to the Caravan owner's lawyer. "He doesn't have a pot. He was just tending some bar at a party to make a few dollars cash. Bourbon Billy's Bartending isn't even a real business. He's not registered. He's got no tax ID number. All he did was get a hundred business cards printed up; that's twenty bucks at Kinko's: nothing. He lost his house in bankruptcy a couple years ago and his wife is a nurse's assistant making only thirty K a year. Plus they've got two kids and Mr. Rocinante has child support for a third child, which he's six months behind on. I don't even know how he's going to pay me for this phone call. Go after the homeowners, my friend. If they're paying for private bartenders in tuxedos at a party at their house in Florham Park, they've got the deep pockets here."

With that call, the case against Willie was dropped, deemed unworthy of the expense. Willie hardly knew the details. Sammy let him know that the case was taken care of and that the fee was either five hundred dollars or a hook-up with one of the Filipino girls at the club. Willie sent a girl.

28 – Barry Goldwater Glasses

Looking morose as usual, Willie stared at the television rebroadcasting the previous night's Devil's game. Willie wasn't often forced to work the weekday afternoon shift at Madison Ave, but he resented it terribly. The money was bad and the quickly imbibed young women Willie preyed on were still making coffee and answering phones for men with regular jobs and wives and offices and all that depressing stuff. On most days that Willie worked the lunch shift, he would be allowed to leave around two and return after five. This gave Willie almost three free hours to matinee with one of his desperate housewife buddies or catch a nap. Even at Madison Ave, the hottest club in Central Jersey, empty bar stools filled most of the rooms at these hours. The few patrons were mostly old men and the occasional salesman between appointments. What a waste of his time and potential it all was, until this day. Willie was about to pour some scotch for a man who saw in Willie all the potential for success Willie felt entitled to.

Marv Dudley was a late-fifties, grinning, pink-faced sales manager with Barry Goldwater glasses and wearing, as always, a bad sports coat. Dudley had mastered the art of the lying, charming salesman you knew was lying to you but you trusted anyway because he was so transparent about his dishonesty. Besides him at the bar was a young, credulous looking Vince Dante. Dante wore a too bright red tie and a pin striped black suit, shiny from too many ironings.

"You must be the owner of this joint" said Dudley, as Willie approached the two men.

"Nah" said Willie, "just filling in for the afternoon girl. She had to take her kid to the doctor or something."

"Alright then, let me have a Johnnie Walker straight up and a Coca-Cola for boy wonder over here" said Dudley, pointing his head towards Dante, who was no boy wonder. Willie poured their drinks as Dudley began seducing Willie like Willie worked the twenty two year-old receptionists at the bar at 1:00 a.m., on their fourth gin and tonic. "Vince, tell our friend here . . . what is your name, buddy?"

"Willie."

"Tell Willie about the big sale you just made and . . . uh . . . what we just saw at our last appointment" said Dudley, with an even more devilish grin that normal.

Dante's Italian face turned nearly as pink as Dudley's Irish one as he shook his head with lips sealed, feigning that he didn't want to tell the story. Dante was a new recruit at Bates & Swisher Equities whom Dudley had taken a slight liking too, thinking he had a chance to be the one in five hundred or so of new hirees who had a chance to stick around awhile. Dante was smart enough to follow directions, but too naive to see through the racket that Bates & Swisher was. Dante had an honest face but an indifference to any business ethics. He was a bit too bashful though, so Dudley had decided to bring him along on a few appointments. Dudley hoped to cultivate some aggressiveness in Dante while maintaining his non-threatening demeanor. Dudley also wanted to get to know Dante a little better and make sure Dante didn't harbor any moral sentimentality below the surface. Otherwise, it wouldn't be worth the effort to try to make a salesman out of him. But most of all, Dudley wanted to whet Dante's appetite a bit regarding the lifestyle of a career salesman.

"A woman who's got a small whole life policy through one of our companies called the office. I think her nephew or cousin used to work for the firm."

"Something like that" said Dudley, trying to move Dante further along in the story.

"Anyway, it turns out the woman just had a scare . . . thought she felt a lump or something on her breast, got it checked out and she was fine. Just a pimple or a mole or something. Still, it got her thinking about things - you know, she's got a couple of young teenagers . . .a single mom, and she didn't have much life insurance. Forty three, but still not a bad looking woman." Dudley playfully rolled his eyes a bit towards Willie at the implication that a forty three year old woman was old and that it would be a surprise that she could still be good looking. Willie gave Dudley a nod of empathy as Dante continued. "So, we get to her house – this crappy two family place in Nutley. Anyway, we knock on her door, 'are you the salesmen?' she asks."

"No" said Dudley, unable to resist telling his standard storyline. "No, we're from the service department. I spent two weeks in sales thirty years ago and they told me I was either moving to the service department or I'd have to find another line of work." Then, with a wink, "I couldn't sell a thing."

"'Good' she said, as she was letting us in, 'I can't stand salesmen'," said Dante. "Then she asked if we knew Timmy. 'He worked in your sales department for a couple of months, but sales weren't for him, he's too nice. Everyone in the family bought a policy from him, we felt so bad.' Anyway, we're in her parlor. She's sitting in a chair. Marv is right next to her on the corner of the couch and I'm on the other end with Marv's open briefcase between us. Now, she's telling us, what I told you. She's got two kids and only a ten thousand dollar whole life policy and wants to know what it would cost to increase it to one hundred thousand. Plus, she's worried because of the scare she just had with the lump, if she could qualify. So, when she tells Marv how the doctors ran all sorts of tests and that her breast is fine and she's got no cancer, Marv puts on this skeptical, concerned look and makes a loud 'hummm' sound and then kinda looks down towards her blouse. The woman, without blinking, undoes three buttons of her shirt, reaches in and pulls out her left breast from her bra!"

"Ha, ha, ha," roared Dudley, his pink face now almost purple with blushing.

"He stares at it for, like, three or four seconds and then gives her a firm nod. He then starts grabbing blank forms out of his brief case. Before she's all buttoned back up, he's got the pen and forms on the coffee table."

"No way" said Willie, now out of his gloomy mood, although feeling a twinge of envy for the two guys. "She didn't say anything?"

"Just, 'how much is it going to cost?' Marv told her there was no charge in the first year because she was a longtime customer of the firm. We're gonna' use the money from her old policy to . . ."

"Forget about that" said Dudley, not wanting Dante to discuss industry secrets with an outsider. "Just be grateful, you finally saw your first pair of tits. No wait . . . your second pair. You told me in the car your mother breast fed you until you were nine."

"I thought he only saw one." Willie was paying close attention for once.

"You're right" said Dudley, then turning and pointing to Dante "you didn't see a pair; we'll just say you're up to your third tit, now."

Dante chuckled, staring into his coke, as Dudley went in for the next sale: Willie. Dante may have had potential, but Willie looked like the real deal. He was tending bar in a five hundred dollar suit. Heck, his tie had to cost more that Dante's entire suit, even before it had been worn fifty and ironed forty nine times. Willie looked the part of a financial advisor and tending bar in a club like this, Willie was certainly no ethical sentimentalist. "What's a young buck like you bartending when you could be out seeing tits like us and making real money?"

Willie grimaced, "Life insurance? I tried that once, it's not for me. Besides, I've got an accounting degree."

"It's not life insurance," said Dudley, "it's financial planning. Stocks, IRAs, mutual funds . . . Life insurance only plays a small part in it."

Willie's appearance made Dudley very interested in recruiting him, but when he heard Willie had an accounting degree, he had to have Willie. In Dudley's experience, few accountants matched the stereotype of the number crunching introvert, an anathema to a life in sales. True mathematical geeks went into engineering, not accounting. Accountants were unsentimental and ambitious. They wanted a shortcut into the business world. They wanted to make money. Also, an accounting degree gave them credibility and just enough knowledge about the investing and insurance side of finance to be useful, without spoiling them. Economics majors on the other hand, with the logical educational background for financial sales, made for the worst financial salesmen. Dudley would sooner hire an art history major – or a high school dropout, for that matter – than an economics major. Economics majors all took themselves too seriously. They all thought of themselves as financial planners talking asset allocation and modern portfolio theory to housewives and truck drivers. Dudley wanted life insurance and mutual fund salesmen, not wannabe Warren Buffets.

"And, it's not sales, we're servicing existing clients. We've got names and addresses of over forty thousand clients but less than one hundred agents to service them." Pointing backwards with his thumb, "Did you see that Cadillac I drove up in?"

Of course Willie hadn't seen his car and Dudley had dated himself a bit thinking a Cadillac would impress somebody born after the 1950s. Still, Dudley had hooked him a bit and he knew it. Now he was going to reel him in. "Look, if you're not making twelve thousand a month by January, I'm going to fire you anyway."

Simultaneously, a rush of excitement swept Willie and a pile of shame fell on Dante, as he stared back down at his coke, struggling to swallow. The big sale Dante just made to the woman with the breast was Dudley's sale, not Dante's. Dante was six months with Bates & Swisher and, at age twenty four, was still borrowing gas money from his parents - with whom he still lived - for his 1987 Le Baron. When he had an appointment with a prospect, he would park around the corner, lest they should see what type of vehicle he was driving. Yet, Dante was one of Bates & Swisher's young stars. Just lasting six months and having made a handful of sales beyond his family and friends put Dante into the top one percentile of Bates & Swisher hirees. Still living with his parents enabled Dante financially to last a while and pretend to himself and others that he was beginning a career with Bates & Swisher Equities and not simply being a stooge supplying future leads to their inner circle.

29 – Virginia Ham

It was Thanksgiving Day, 2006 in the Cordardo home. Bullo stared lifelessly at his television screen from his plastic covered armchair while his hands blindly replaced *Grand Theft Auto* with *Saint's Row* on his Xbox, the fourth time he had rotated the games in the past six hours. Only four bathroom trips necessitated by six Heinekens had budged Bullo from his perch all day.

"What time are you stepping out, Bullo?"

"About an hour, mom."

Since pummeling Willie in the parking lot, Bullo had stopped visiting Madison Ave, the closest thing to a social life he had. With the mounds of cash he was accumulating from his tax shelter and accounting clients, it was no longer a financial burden for Bullo to restrict himself to prostitutes. Whores were also less work. Bullo didn't need to expend energy trying to be civil to them or even have to pretend that he gave a damn about their feelings. Bullo also despised the phony conflict single girls professed when snagging a 'married' guy. Bullo knew envy motivated women more than power or money. His dad's wedding ring worked better than a BMW convertible attracting shallow women, but Bullo resented even the meager 'we're just staying together until the kids are grown' or 'we've got an understanding' role playing that was expected of him.

Sparky brought a square, weathered folding table into the living room, opened it up and slid it in front of Bullo. Bullo lifted his Heineken from the floor and placed it on the table. "What have we got tonight?"

"Virginia Ham," said Sparky. Bullo was pleased, but just nodded. Bullo changed the television over from his video game to some college football game. Sparky brought Bullo his salad and rye bread first, then his Virginia ham, mashed potatoes and carrots. The game served mostly as backroom noise. Bullo occasionally looked up at the screen to watch a play or two while eating, but he couldn't tell you the score or even who was playing.

When he was through, Bullo pushed the folding table far enough away for him to stand up. He went downstairs to the guest room. After washing up, he opened the refrigerator. It was jam-packed with cash held together in irregular bunches with rubber bands. "I need another fridge" thought Bullo. He pinched a quarter inch of bills out of one of the packs and briefly flipped through them, making sure there was at least a few hundreds and fifties to cover his cost for the night.

Bullo left through the garage exit and headed out over the Outerbridge to a South Amboy hotel on Route 35. An hour later he returned home and sat back down on his armchair. Sparky brought him a decaffeinated coffee and a plate of biscotti. After he finished, he pushed the table away, turned on his television set and began a new session of *Saints Row*. Sparky cleared the table, returned quickly to remove the table, finished the dishes in the kitchen, and retired to bed.

30 - There is no such thing as a Puerto Rican

"This is just like that prodigal son story" said Tony, with half-serious contempt. "He abandoned his family and now he gets a party for coming back? We should be throwing parties for men who don't abandon their families for a year."

"Are you arguing with me or Jesus, Tony?" asked Gwen. "Can't you just be happy for Leah and the kids?"

"He's been back a half-year already, anyway."

"I think your parents just wanted to make sure he was really returning for good before they threw the party."

"It's just backwards to me, rewarding bad behavior. Like when everyone makes a fuss over some drunk or junkie who comes back from re-hab. How about making a fuss over us who remained sober our entire lives?"

"Are you through?"

"I'll give you another one – bachelor parties. A night of decadence and debauchery for a guy who's been single his whole life? It's the guy who's been married ten or twenty years who's earned the right to have a night when everyone looks the other way."

"He's coming over," whispered Gwen. "Be nice."

"Wilfredo! You've still got that Florida tan, or is that your Spanish genes?"

"Don't mention Florida, Tony. It is the worst place in the world. I planned on settling down and then bringing Leah and the kids, but the goddamn Cubans are worse than Columbians."

"Cubans? They're frigging Spanish people, just like you, Willie."

"I'm Puerto Rican, Tony."

"Puerto Rican? There's no such thing as being a Puerto Rican, unless you're from Puerto Rico."

"Tony!" said Gwen.

"You were born in Union City, weren't you?"

"West New York, Tony."

"Okay, that's still America."

"Puerto Rico's part of America too, Tony. I'm a Puerto Rican American."

"Puerto Rican is not an ethnicity."

"Spend thirty minutes with a group of Puerto Ricans" said Uncle Freddy, "and then tell me they're not a distinct ethnicity."

"It's just a place your ancestors stopped off for a few generations before landing here. If your four grandparents had traveled to Sweden before settling in America, would you be claiming to be Swedish? The Spanish stopped off at Puerto Rico for a few hundred years before colonizing Hudson County – that's not long enough to evolve into a distinct ethnicity. All these tiny countries in Latin America – El Salvador, Guatemala, Belize – we're supposed to pretend like they're all separate people?"

"They're all part of the Latin race" said Willie, suddenly missing Florida and the Cubans. "Just different groups."

"Latin race? We used to have just three races –white Europeans, black Africans and yellow Chinese, plus your various brown mixes who filled in the cracks. But now, all of a sudden, we're supposed to believe that one nation, Spain, spawned its own race? Latinos?"

Willie wanted to leave, but he needed to speak with Tony about Bates & Swisher. It wasn't that Tony had offended him, he just found Tony's ramblings pointless and exhausting. "Different countries in Latin America are made up of different mixes."

"So, what if American never became the United States and the individual states became their own countries? Would Kansas or Pennsylvania be separate ethnicities now? My grandmother was from Maine, does that make me *Maine*?"

"Yes" said Gwen, "you're a damn maniac." Most in the room laughed but Willie walked out to the deck like a wounded puppy. "Tony, go talk to him."

Tony followed Willie through the slider onto his parent's deck and grabbed a Yuengling out of the cooler. "So what's going on, Willie? I hear your back at Madison Ave, are you doing any accounting work?"

"Actually, I wanted to talk to you about that. I'm starting up with a financial planning firm that hires accountants to service their orphan investment accounts. I know after Sam's Way you probably think it's just another scam . . ."

"Actually, Willie I was thinking of looking into something like that, myself. I need to expand my business past tax season. I was thinking about offering bookkeeping and payroll services, but that's tedious stuff."

"I already told them my wife's cousin is an accountant too. They said you're welcome to come to the Wednesday morning meeting and check it out, it you want."

31 – Am I under arrest?

Willie was woken from his late morning sleep by loud
pounding on his front door. Willie didn't know why they were
here, but he knew immediately who it was. There is as certain
knock that is distinct to police and Willie had his share of visits
from the police. So, it was with great relief that Willie heard: "Mr.
Rocinante, my name is Sean O'Kelly, Federal Bureau of
Investigation, and this is agent Michael Murphy." Willie had some
DUIs and other small beefs with the cops, but if it was the FBI on
his porch, certainly they were not there for him. Perhaps they were
seeking his help, possibly questions about one of the regulars at
Madison Ave. "We'd like to talk to you about Felix Williams. You
may have had some dealings with him when you worked for
Pompano Beach Industrial Life Insurance."

Willie's face turned white. "I worked there for less than a
year, there were thousands of customers."

"But, do you remember Felix Williams, an African-American
man in is early forties?"

"A lot of black people are named Williams."

"Well, he had a lot of family, a lot of them named Williams . .
. in his neighborhood . . . and they all recall a Willie Rocinante -
an insurance man they paid each month, who just stopped showing
up one day."

"What do you mean, '*had* a lot of family'?"

"Mr. Williams wound up on the losing end of a dispute
involving fire arms."

"Well, I don't know if I can help. Like I said, I'm not even
sure if I even met this person."

"Well, here's how you might be able to help us out, Willie . . . is it all right if I call you Willie?"

"Yeah."

"Willie, see, after he was killed his mom called Pompano Beach Industrial Life looking to put in a claim, only to be told Felix's policy had lapsed months earlier." Willie's heart began racing. "She told them, 'No, that can't be' our insurance man comes by every month' and that she pays 'for four policies', one for herself, one for Felix and two for grandchildren." Willie froze. "Well, Pompano Beach Industrial Life looked it up but it turns out all four policies had lapsed months earlier. And then it gets even stranger, Willie. When the service woman from Pompano Beach Industrial Life asked if she was sure her agent was submitting her premiums, Mrs. Williams went on to tell what a wonderful, honest man Mr. Rocinante was, and how he'd delivered, in cash, an insurance claim for her nephew Will Williams just a couple months before. Only, after checking, it turns out that Will Williams no longer had a policy at the time of his death."

"Am I under arrest?" asked Willie, close to fainting.

"Not at this particular time, Willie. We're just talking. Can you help us out here? We just want to understand what went on down there."

"I think I want to call my lawyer."

"Now" said agent Murphy, speaking for the first time, "you're under arrest."

The next morning, Sammy drove out to the Federal Detention Center in Philadelphia. "Willie, there's an Old Italian saying that goes something like: 'If you're going to steal, make sure it's something you wouldn't be ashamed, to get caught stealing.' Willie, they've got you dead to rights. You are going away for years, a lot of years."

"Years? Sammy, Felix Williams' policy was only one thousand bucks."

"Willie, if it was just Beulah Williams' word against you, maybe we could drag this out and eventually they'd lose interest and settle."

"There are no receipts for any of the cash she paid me."

"What about Will Williams, Willie? FBI says they have more than a dozen witnesses of you paying his family a death benefit, in cash, on a policy which Pompano Beach Industrial says had long lapsed. FBI knows you weren't paying a death claim unless you were collecting on a bunch of fake policies. How many, Willie?"

Willie stared down at the table, no longer able to look Sammy in the eyes. "Less than a hundred . . ."

"A hundred, Willie?! The Dade County prosecutor is going to jump on you like a rabid dog. These are poor people. He's going to look like Elliot Ness and Ralph Nader rolled into one and you're gonna look like Ivan Boesky and O.J. Simpson rolled into one, when this is all over. Plus, the Florida Insurance Department would love any excuse to put Pompano Beach Industrial out of business, so Pompano Beach Industrial is fully cooperating. Especially, since they were pissed at you anyway for quitting without any notice."

"So . . . what can we do?"

"Willie, just because there's a problem, doesn't mean there's a solution."

"Can't you make a deal with them, Sammy?"

"A deal? You don't have anything to offer, Willie."

Willie shot a calm, cold look at Sammy. "What about Bullo?"

"Bullo?" asked Sammy. "You're not getting the seriousness of this, Willie. So he smacked the shit out of you one time, at this point that's making him look sympathetic."

"He's running an accounting scheme, Sammy, I know, I saw the returns."

"Willie, I know what you're thinking, but you don't understand the seriousness of these charges. Sure, you steal a few thousand in premiums while he exaggerates tens of thousands of deductions. He's the bigger crook, right? But it doesn't work that way. The crimes are not comparable. Not remotely."

"I'm not talking about him lying on people's taxes. I mean, he's running a fraud – a Ponzi scheme or something."

"Come on, Willie. He's a retired fireman. You said it yourself, he does only a few hundred tax returns a year."

"No, not that. He's selling investments in phony rental properties."

"You mean like your South Amboy apartment fiasco? That's not a Ponzi scheme."

"Sammy, listen to me. He's got dozens, maybe hundreds by

now, of investors who pay him tens of thousands of dollars each year to invest in apartments that don't exist – only on paper – and they write off thousands of losses. They're bigger crooks than me and half of them are cops too."

"Cops?"

"Mostly fireman, but some cops too."

"He's ripping off cops? Maybe I can get them to give you a reduced sentence, if he's stealing from cops."

"Sammy, he's not *stealing* from cops, they're in on it. They pay him to create fake tax shelters and they write them off, nine or ten thousand a year in fake losses."

"Crooked cops, huh? Willie, it's a 'hail Mary' pass, but it maybe all you got. Let me dangle it in front of them."

32 – Bates & Swisher Equities

Tony couldn't decide what was more appalling, that he was sitting in a classroom being schooled on selling life insurance and mutual funds, or that it was Willie who convinced him to come. Worse, Willie had Leah call Tony last minute to tell him he couldn't make it. Tony's accounting practice was foundering. He knew he needed a second income source. Once Willie told Dudley that his wife's cousin was also an accountant, and with his own practice, Dudley insisted that he bring Tony in.

The Bates & Swisher Equity racket emerged out of the brutal 1973/1974 recession, the deepest since the great depression. Dominick Bates and Tom Swisher had met while attending Rutgers in 1965. Swisher had been a fledgling stockbroker during the nifty-fifty boom of the late sixties who didn't survive the layoffs after a fifty percent stock market correction. Bates had worked his way up to regional sales manager for Tupperware sales, only to lose his job around the same time due to the poor economy. While commiserating on their woes and cursing the vicissitudes of corporate life, Bates and Swisher hatched a scheme. They would take the Tupperware sales party idea to Wall Street. The idea is not as simple as it seems. You can't simply call your five best friends, sell them mutual funds and then sell them on the idea of selling their other friends some mutual funds, in exchange for a piece of the action. Investment sales are heavily regulated and reps need to pass a securities exam and get licensed. Bates and Swisher's genius was turning these obstacles into opportunity. They decided to open a school to get people trained and licensed to sell securities, regardless of their background. The economy was in the dumps and unemployment was high. They ran "be your

own boss" and "become an independent investment broker"
classified ads in the help wanted sections of local newspapers,
inviting interested parties to seminars where they'd sell them on
the "unlimited potential" of being their own boss in the business of
financial sales.

Bates and Swisher had reversed the hiring process of
traditional investment firms. In fact, they stood it on its head.
Instead of the expensive process of recruiting, licensing and
training investment professionals – all collecting paychecks during
the process -, only to have ninety percent fail out of the business in
five years and have half of those who survive move their skills to
other firms, Bates & Swisher were charging people for the school
and licensing.

The licensing school quickly became a success. Bates' canned
rah-rah speeches from his Tupperware sales force days easily
translated into the financial services school pitch, particularly
since nearly no one attending the seminars or enrolling in the
school had any financial background. The 'students' were laid-off
warehouse workers, failed furniture salesmen, truck drivers and
housewives. The second part of their business plan, however, was
not panning out. The new licensees were bringing in almost no
commissions. For one thing, the NASD licensing exam was
proving too difficult for most of their students and more than half
would drop out during the four week training course. The
burgeoning army of mutual fund peddlers was not fomenting as
they had envisioned. Even the students who did pass the series-six
security exam and became licensed were bringing in almost no
revenue to the firm. These were largely blue collar workers
without contacts. Bates & Swisher's prospects appeared grim,
until an unlikely attendee showed up at one of Bates' now sparsely
attended seminars.

Marv Dudley had been a stud salesman for Mutual of
Hackensack Life, but was beset with compliance issues and legal
complaints for his unscrupulous sales practices. Mutual of
Hackensack's policy of tolerating Dudley's malfeasance came to a
screeching halt when he been caught cuckolding Mutual of
Hackensack's vice president, Sheldon Gardner, with his first wife,
Constance. Dudley sat through Bates' sales pitch for his securities
licensing school, and on the prospects for ambitious self
employed to strike it rich selling mutual funds, and Dudley was

greatly impressed. Not at the prospect of selling mutual funds across the kitchen table to blue collar families. Dudley knew that was nonsense. Further, Dudley already had a series-six securities license to sell mutual funds, which he rarely used. What Dudley loved was the Bates & Swisher operation. Bates & Swisher Securities School generated an almost endless stream of new agents. Bates & Swisher's problem was that these new agents were generating almost no commissions from their working and middle-class contacts, if you could even call them contacts. Dudley, however, was an expert in earning top commissions from poor and working class people. Dudley turned Bates & Swisher's army of housewives, laid off factory workers and college drop outs, into a brigade of policy churners.

By the time Tony had joined Bates & Swisher Equities, it had lost a little steam. However, thirty years of recruiting and licensing thousands of failed life insurance and mutual fund salesmen had left Bates & Swisher Equities with thousands of insurance policies and mutual fund accounts for its managers to prey on and churn like vultures. The revolving recruiting door and insurance school continued as always. New licensees were directed to first sell products to their friends and family, and then rely on referrals - 'the true secret to success in sales.' Why waste money on marketing, or try the human spirit by making cold calls, when your existing clients can send you all the new prospects you need?

The myth of instant and numerous referrals is one of the cruelest perpetrated on new insurance and investment sales trainees. 'I get referrals after every sale' and even 'I require referrals - five to ten at a minimum' is a lie told by sales managers to every new insurance or investment salesman. Naturally, having to demand referrals from a new client fills the fledgling salesmen with even more dread and apprehension than calling on his friends and family to begin with. Having made a sale and grabbed a check, most new financial salesmen are out of the client's house faster than Jesse Owens. New salesmen, already under tremendous pressure to make sales, are left to feel like failures - even after having made a sale - if their appointment book isn't filled up with the names of all the friends and family members of the new client they had just victimized.

Bates & Swisher Equities had a couple of tricks and techniques to work around the awkwardness of soliciting for referrals. When a sale to a new client was made, Dudley required that the salesman have the client complete a 'reference referral sheet'. The reference referral sheet was meant to trick the client into believing it was part of the application process. As if to say, 'Thank you for your thousand dollar check for this overpriced insurance, Mr. Applicant, but in addition to medically underwriting your application to make sure you're healthy enough to qualify for this insurance, this four billion dollar life insurance company needs to call five of your closest friends to determine if you are of good enough character for them to take your money.' Having picked up a deposit check and an insurance application, the salesman now also had a list of five people to call on, needing their reference for their friend. "Bob, this is Marv Dudley from Bates & Swisher. Your friend Al Smith just applied for a new program with our company and listed you as a reference to help him get qualified. Would you have five minutes to spare some time this week so I can stop by and get this reference form completed for your pal Al?"

Vince Dante had used this technique with some success. It mostly had him driving around town filling out phony reference reports, but a few did lead to new clients beyond his friends and family, and that was enough for Vince to be considered one of Bates & Swisher's bright new stars. When the reference referrals ran dry, Dudley went to marketing plan number two for his new salesmen. Throughout the years, Bates & Swisher Equities had sold tens of thousands of life insurance policies and mutual funds. While only a fraction of these remained on the books, Marv Dudley still believed the names and addresses of these former policyholders had tremendous value. 'Lapsed leads' they were called. Each week, new recruits who showed some potential would be given crudely photocopied lists of a dozen or fewer names and addresses of former policyholders. Many of these names had been called on by dozens of previous Bates & Swisher trainees and were from policies that had lapsed sometimes ten and fifteen years earlier. Dudley still handed these lapsed leads to the new licensees like he was handing out buckets of Krugerrands. "These are the names and addresses of people who have already shown a willingness to purchase insurance from Bates & Swisher Equities and, better still, their insurance has lapsed! They need a new policy!"

"What do we say when we call them up?" asked Tony

"You don't call them - you just go," said Dudley. Dudley knew ninety-nine percent of those calls would go down in flames and neither Dudley, Bates or Swisher wanted to spring for the 4-1-1 charges required to get the updated phone numbers many of the names would need. Better the salesman waste his own gas. "You knock on the door. You're from the service department. Act a little confused. "The company asked me to follow up on your policy, but we didn't have a working number."

"What do we say when they tell us they don't have insurance with us anymore?"

"Always act a bit puzzled, look like you're struggling a bit, that takes people off the defensive. 'I'm sorry, who do you have your insurance with, ma'am?' Prudential, Metropolitan, Hancock . . . it doesn't matter what their answer is. 'Oh, yes, we service them too, ma'am.' If you're half-a salesman, nine out of ten times, you'll be at the kitchen table five minutes later reviewing their policies - whatever they are - shaking your head, 'Ma'am, I sure am sorry I didn't stop by a year ago before they put you in this garbage' and so on. You should come back with five sales and twenty-five reference referrals for every list of ten lapsed leads."

Dudley half believed what he was saying and he might have been the one salesman who could have pulled it off, had he not had a lists of thousands of active accounts to feed on for his own sales.

33 – The Offer

"Mr. Riscatto, let me save you some time" said agent Murphy, to Sammy. It was an easy case against Willie and it would play great in the press, in spite of its relatively small scope. "Your shit-stain of a client is small potatoes, but his crime is a prosecutor's dream - dozens of poor people swindled by a crooked financial guy? I don't care if most of them were robbed less than a thousand dollars. We have an almost unlimited number of charges to bring up on him and we're hitting him with them all. Probably even more than he deserves, and that's saying something."

"Willie's got some information on a far more significant ongoing operation, much bigger dollars involved."

"Let me guess. That night club he works for off the books, Madison Ave, isn't claiming all its receipts. That's some bait you're tempting us with."

"No, not that. Willie has firsthand knowledge of a growing accounting and Ponzi-like scheme."

"You are going to have a hard time convincing me that that inconsequential insect would have any knowledge of anything worthwhile to us." Feigning boredom, Murphy frowned and impatiently tapped his fingers on the desk, letting Sammy know he needed some red meat right away or the meeting would be soon over.

"Willie worked off the books for an accountant who not only prepares fraudulent returns – you know, mostly puffed up deductions and whatnot – but has created phony partnerships showing big losses which generate huge write offs for his clients, in exchange for pocketing the proceeds."

"Okay, well . . . we can probably figure out who that is without his help. But, if it's real and his information is useful, and his testimony makes our lives a bit easier, maybe we'd be willing to keep his sentence under ten years."

"Ten years? No, Willie walks for this."

"Mr. Riscatto, we're not interested in trading one smalltime crook for another, especially when we can find him ourselves and wouldn't need Willie's testimony anyway, if these partnerships are genuinely fake."

"Eighteen months, then. Minimum security prison."

"Not a chance, Mr. Riscatto. Willie is a dream bust. Easy case and great headlines. If we let him off easy – a human interest case like this – those headlines would boomerang back right at us: 'Another financial crook gets a light sentence for exploiting the poor'."

"What if he could give you some cops?" asked Sammy, showing his only ace.

"Cops?" asked Murphy, suddenly a little interested.

"A number of the investors are cops."

"So, cops are getting swindled?" asked Murphy, shrugging his shoulders.

"No, you don't understand – and I'm saying more than I should, in good faith that you'll take this into account when charging Willie – it's not a Ponzi scheme so much as a tax shelter scheme. The cops and other investors know the partnerships are fake. They're paying for fake write-offs on their returns – huge ones."

"Hmmm. Let me run this by my supervisor" said Murphy, now intrigued. "Let me see if there's anything I can do to help your client."

Sammy tried to temper Willie's expectations for a deal while he anxiously awaited FBI's offer. A week later, Agent Murphy called Sammy in for another meeting and requested that Willie attend this time. Willie and Sammy sat alone in the small, grey interrogation room and waited for Murphy and O'Kelly to arrive. "Remember, Willie, don't say a damn thing. Don't nod, or frown or smile. The only thing you're allowed to do in here is breathe, unless I tell you otherwise."

Murphy and O'Kelly entered the room along with a third man, a stern Internal Revenue veteran. "Mr. Riscatto, Mr. Rocinante, this is IRS criminal investigations special agent Todd Owens." As nervous as he already was, and in as deep of trouble as he already was, having an IRS agent in the room increased Willie's anxiety further. "Willie . . . is it all right if I call you Willie?"

"It's all right" said Sammy, answering for Willie.

"Willie, I'm sure Mr. Riscatto has made it clear to you the kind of trouble you're in. We have a slam dunk case against you that will send you away until you are sixty years old at least. Now, Mr. Riscatto has informed us you have some information about some accounting and tax-shelter scam. I've got to tell you, Willie, that doesn't interest us much. Not that you couldn't be of some use helping us to find some things sooner which IRS would have found eventually anyway. We might be willing to shave a few years off your sentence, but I'm guessing – from where you're sitting – fifteen years instead of twenty doesn't sound like much difference. Your life is ruined either way."

"Okay," said Sammy. "Well, I'm sure you didn't invite us and Mr. Owens here just to tell us what we already knew."

"It didn't take us long to figure out who we're talking about here, Brunello Cordardo." Sammy shrugged his shoulders and nodded. "Cordardo by himself is small potatoes – almost as small as you, Willie. But, his clientele and his neighborhood interest us a great deal. The word on the street, Willie, is that you and Mr. Cordardo had a falling out. Is there any way you might be able to convince him to hire you back?"

"A wire" said Sammy, understanding where this was heading. "He and Brunello Cordardo have come to a bit of a truce. Whether Willie could convince him to hire him back . . . I'd say it's fifty fifty."

"Well, here's what we're offering" said Owen, inserting himself into the conversation. "Or, rather, here's what IRS is interested in, and if you can get us what we want, well, I'll let Mr. Murphy tell you what he's offering. Setting up a sting operation is not only expensive, but it's not looked upon too kindly by the courts. However, if we can get a mole into an existing operation, then the sky's the limit for us. If your client can resume his relationship with Brunello Cordardo – not only get in his office and give us the files – but wear a recording device for two or three tax seasons . . ."

"Bullo will kill me – he almost already did once."

"Willie!" shouted Sammy.

Murphy took over for Owens. "Believe me Willie, the guys Cordardo is selling those phony tax shelters to are a lot more dangerous than he is. The people we plan on steering towards Cordardo even more so. Mr. Riscatto. . ."

"Sammy."

"Sammy, we're not only interested in crooked cops. Staten Island is loaded with wannabe wise guys and connected guys and the easiest way to take them off the streets – or flip them – is with the IRS. We have some assets on the street who may be able to refer them over to Cordardo. If Willie can do that – get back with Cordardo and wear a wire -, he not only walks, but we'll put him in witness protection – we'd have no choice - and set him up somewhere in a business. A little tavern maybe." Willie's eyes opened wide. For the first time in ten days he felt a gleam of hope.

"And if Cordardo won't take Willie back?"

"Then, like I said, we'll ask the judge to slice a few years off the recommended sentence in exchange for his information and testimony, but we're only talking different shades of grey here. Willie, if you want to walk, con your way back into Cordardo's office like you conned those poor folks in Miami out of their insurance premiums."

34 – The Deal

Willie was granted temporary release from custody so he could try to get himself rehired by Bullo. "There's no way Bullo's taking me back" said Willie, returning to New Jersey in Sammy's car. "I'm gonna split . . . I mean, I'll try talking to him, but it's a million to one. If it doesn't go right, I'm splitting."

"Willie, FBI will have you back in custody five minutes after you cut that ankle bracelet off."

"I know lots of people at the club who can get me a car. I'll take back roads. Once I'm in Mexico . . ."

"Willie, you're not lamming to Mexico and you're not talking to Bullo. I am."

"Won't that make him suspicious, Sammy, if you call on him again instead of me?"

"He'd eat you alive, Willie, it won't work. He's a bully, Willie, and a coward. That's the only spectrum he works on. You either tell him what to do, or he tells you. There's no negotiating or reasoning with him. He's too insecure. And I'll tell you something else, Willie. If this works, you're gonna have to eat a lot of shit and take a whole lot more abuse from him, and for a long time. Just remember, every time he yells at you or even hits you again – he's taking your place in prison . . . only he doesn't know it yet." For the first time in weeks, Willie laughed.

If he had a chance to do it again, Sammy would have popped in on Bullo rather than call him for another sit down. Their first meeting had left Bullo humiliated. Sammy hadn't blackmailed him like he expected, he had only intimidated him. Memories of the sit down festered in Bullo's gut while fears of Willie blackmailing him vanished. Catching Bullo off-guard would have let Sammy maintain the upper hand, but his second call only left Bullo wondering why he had let Sammy steamroll him during their first meeting.

"Bullo, this is Sammy Riscatto again."

"Why is this asshole calling me again?" wondered Bullo. "Yeah?" said Bullo.

"In light of the progress we made at our last meeting, Willie asked me to see you once more."

"Why?"

"Business; Willie thinks you and he might work together again."

"Nah, I don't think so."

"You mentioned at the Diner a few months back that you wouldn't mind working with him again."

Bullo grinned, he smelled weakness from Sammy over the phone lines. "You caught me in a rare good mood that day." Still, Bullo thought he actually could use Willie's help, if he didn't despise him so much.

Sammy felt Bullo slipping from his grasp and knew he had to raise the hint of a threat without alarming Bullo too much. "Willie told me he was uniquely qualified to work with you."

Sammy's hint was so oblique, Bullo missed it. "I'll be honest with you, Mr. Riscatto. Willie *is* useful to me. It's just that I can't stand the little spic's face." Then, after an awkward pause, Bullo simply added, "I'll get back to you" and hung up.

After not hearing from Sammy for a couple of days, Willie called to see if he had contacted Bullo yet. "I'll be honest with you Willie, I'm been procrastinating."

"You haven't called him yet?"

"I mean, procrastinating calling you. I spoke with Bullo."

"He said no?"

"Not exactly, he said he'll think about it."'

"Think about it? Sammy, FBI only gave me one week to make a deal – three days ago."

"I know, I'm going to make a second run at him, Willie, but this time I'm going to have to roll the dice and basically blackmail him, which is going to raise flags with him and probably not work anyway."

"How did you leave it with him, Sammy?"

"He conceded that you would be useful to him, he just . . ."

"Maybe I should try talking to him. What's the worst thing that happens? He beats me again? Kills me, maybe? That's still better than twenty years in prison."

"No, seeing you is the last thing he wants."

"Well, how can I work for him if he doesn't see me?"

"What are you doing right now, Willie?"

Sammy hopped in his car, picked up Willie in Keasbey and crossed the Outerbridge towards Bullo's office. "What are we going to do, Sammy? Ambush him?"

"Explain to me Willie, exactly your benefit to Bullo. What did you do for him? Why should he hire you instead of someone else? No disrespect."

"I was a combo free-receptionist/tax preparer. Last year when I was in Florida, I hear he paid a fulltime receptionist and just did all the taxes himself."

"Why didn't he hire another accountant? Isn't his business growing?"

"Too risky, whose he gonna trust?"

"Exactly" said Sammy, as he pulled into the parking lot of Bullo's office. "Stay in the car." Sammy slammed the door of his car and marched into Bullo's office.

"What the hell are you doing here?"

"I've got someone I want you to meet in my car?"

"Willie? I'll lay him out again."

"No, you're not going to lay a finger on him. Who else are you going to trust to prepare taxes for you?"

"Why do you care so much if I hire this little shit or not?"

"Willie can be useful – you said so yourself."

"I get it now, he gets you laid. Just be careful who he sends over."

"He's gonna keep pestering me to pester you until you say yes." Bullo felt a twinge of fondness suddenly for Willie, believing now Willie somehow genuinely missed working for him.

"Bring the asshole in."

Sammy walked out to the parking lot and knocked on the

passenger side window of his car. A daydreaming Willie hadn't seen him coming. "What did he say?"

"He said bring the asshole in."

"He's probably gonna kill both of us."

"Come on Willie."

Willie followed Sammy into Bullo's office. Only the pleasure of seeing the scar on Willie's forehead kept Bullo from exploding again in Willie's presence. "It's not gonna work, Riscatto. Get him the hell out."

"Do you have someone else who can help you with 1040s, Bullo?" asked Sammy.

"You know what, if he wants to open his own office somewhere, maybe I can direct some of my overflow to him. I've got too many damn nickel and dime returns to do now anyway. We can split the fees."

"Split the fee on some lousy short forms and he's got to provide the overhead? Come on."

"Nah, not just short forms. I've been doing a lot more business and partnership returns since Willie left and these partners all want me to do their personal stuff too; it's too much. These are three hundred dollar returns."

"The three hundred dollar returns, Bullo – and you only keep a third. That's the deal." Willie shot a puzzled look at Sammy.

"Please, a third . . . for my own clients? And, what's Willie going to do? Rent space at Madison Ave? Forget it."

"Willie's wife's cousin's got a small, struggling accounting practice over the bridge in Edison. He's already offered Willie the office space. He's straight as an arrow this guy. All your client's returns will be way under the radar screen with Tony Violette's tax ID on them. The fees from your clients get split between you, Willie - for preparing the returns - and Tony, for providing the overhead."

Bullo desperately wanted to reduce his workload and having his fake tax shelter clients get their returns prepared under the banner of a small, conservative accountant would also reduce the risk of an audit. Best of all, he wouldn't have to see Willie. "Alright, maybe we can give it a try."

The three men shook hands and Sammy drove Willie back to New Jersey.

"Sammy, what the hell did you just do? That wasn't the deal

the FBI agreed to. Besides, he was starting to soften up; I think he might have agreed to hire me if we stayed at it."

"He might have agreed, but he would eventually backed out of it before tax season. The deal is contingent on this sting operation actually operating, not on Bullo's promises. He's worried about all those partners and their returns – didn't you see how quickly he offered up the very returns IRS is interested in?"

"Either way, there's no way in hell Tony is going to let us set up a sting in his office – and he's never offered me use of his extra space."

"Tony can never know there's an IRS sting going on in his office – it'll be limited to the returns you do, anyway. It's your job on selling Tony. He's been struggling financially. Let him know he'll net a third of fifty or sixty thousand in fees for overhead he's paying for anyway. I'm the one with the tough sell, Willie, convincing the IRS and FBI to accept this amended deal.

35 - Road Rage

"Look at this woman in the old Tercel in front of us," said Tony. "She's got a 'proud to be a massage therapist' bumper sticker right on her car. Do you think she's a hooker?"

"Don't say 'hooker' in front of Nicole" said Gwen, as they drove home from a party for Tony's Aunt Lorraine in Ringwood. "Willie sure had a lot to drink tonight, huh?"

"How can you tell the difference with Willie?" asked Tony. "And, 'prostitute', whatever. She's also got a 'vegetarian chick on board' sticker too, which makes her sound more like a hippie-health-nut legitimate-massage-therapist type. But, she's smoking a cigarette, so she's no health nut. Also, that Clinton-Gore 96 sticker would suggest she's a bit of a sexual hedonist, or at least non-judgmental of debauchery. And, there's a little Playboy Bunny sticker too on the bottom of the back windshield. Sammy told me it was against the law to put anything on your back windshield. What do you think, Gwen? Is she a lady of the evening?"

"I have no idea, Tony" said Gwen, barely paying attention to Tony's ramblings.

"I'll try to pass her. I have to keep an eye on the road. Try and get a look."

"You're going to get a ticket."

"A hooker in a ten year-old Toyota? There are no middle-class prostitutes. They are either rich or poor. They're either making ten dollars a pop, and they can't afford a car at all, or they're making five hundred dollars an hour and they're driving a BMW, or something."

"How do you know so much about what hookers charge?" asked Gwen. "And, I think smoke is coming from the car, Tony."

"I don't see any smoke, besides her cigarette."

"No, our car -look!" shouted Gwen, as she pointed to the hood of their Plymouth Voyager.

"Oh, shit. There's a diner up there. I'm going to pull over." The radiator hose in Tony's van had sprung a leak. "Thank goodness there's a diner every two miles in Jersey. The Greeks are good for something, besides debt and sodomy. I've got duct-tape to patch it up. I'll get some water for the radiator to get us home tonight. I can replace the hose tomorrow, but we're gonna have to hang at the diner for about ninety minutes for the engine to cool down first."

"I'm stuffed, Tony, and Nicole's half asleep in the back seat."

"So? Do you want me to call a cab for a hundred dollars to Woodbridge and then call a tow-truck tomorrow for another two hundred bucks? It's an easy repair. I can do it in the parking lot at Pep Boys in ten minutes in the morning."

"Alright, I'll wake Nicole up."

"Just order drinks first. We'll get a couple of appetizers afterward. We'll stretch it out. They're slow this time of night anyway; they want fannies in the booths."

The Violettes entered the diner. The 'seat yourself' sign allowed Tony to pick a booth where he could keep an eye on his van. "I'm Staci, can I get you anything to drink?" asked the waitress, with a bit of a puss, while dropping three menus on the table.

"Could we get a high-chair for the baby?" asked Tony. Without responding, the waitress walked to the other side of the diner. "She's got a 'tude already, this waitress."

"You always say that" said Gwen, as Staci quickly returned.

"All of our high-chairs are taken."

"This time of day?" asked Tony. Then he said to Gwen "Just prop her up for now." To Staci he said "Just bring it over when one becomes free."

"Do you know what you're ordering?"

"We just sat down. We haven't looked at the menu yet. A couple of diet cokes and a small milk."

"Make one of the sodas a root-beer," said Gwen. Staci walked away and Gwen picked up a menu.

"Take your time," said Tony. "We've got to be here for ninety minutes. I don't want to get scalded by the radiator fluid."

"Speaking of scalded - did you hear about Uncle Mark and his Lexus?"

"No. Did he try to add radiator fluid while the car was still hot?" asked Tony, as Staci returned with the drinks.

"Are you ready to order yet?"

"I haven't even looked at the menu yet" said Tony, as Staci walked away in half of a huff.

"No, remember he bought that ten year old Lexus last year?" asked Gwen.

"No. He always drives a piece of crap car."

"That's why everyone was so surprised. It was ten years old, but still looked like new."

"Okay, so?"

"It turns out he bought in on Craigslist."

"What the hell is Craig's list?"

"It's an internet classifieds thing" said Gwen, sipping her drink. "This isn't root beer - it's Diet Coke."

"Internet classifieds? That's for hiring hookers."

"All of a sudden, you're this expert on hookers today. Was that what you were talking to Willie about all day at the party?" asked Gwen, as Staci returned to the table.

"Are you ready to order?"

"Actually, her soda's a diet - she asked for a root-beer."

"You both ordered Diet Cokes."

"Well, regardless, can she have a root-beer instead?" Staci picked up Gwen's soda and left.

"I said three words to Willie all day, which brings my lifetime total to seven."

"I saw you speaking with him for over an hour."

"He wants to come work for me at the office."

"You're serving liquor, now, at your accounting office?"

"He wants to prepare taxes."

"I thought you didn't even have enough business for yourself last tax season, that's why you're trying this investing thing."

"He has his own clients."

"Willie? Since when?"

"He has a guy who has too many and is referring them to Willie for a third of the fees. Willie will keep a third of the fees for preparing them and I'll get a third for providing the office."

"Why doesn't the guy just have Willie work out of his

office?"

"According to Willie, he had a falling out with the guy, so he doesn't want him in his office."

"It sounds suspicious. You're not going along with it, are you?"

"I agree it sounds suspicious. I'm only considering it because Willie says Sammy negotiated the terms. Your cousin's a sleaze-bag, but he's not stupid. He wouldn't propose something like this if it wasn't real."

"Sammy's not a sleaze-bag. You're so judgmental."

"Anyway, there's no way I'm letting Willie near any of my clients. But, I'm already paying for the extra room. Any income Willie brought in would be gravy. I'm gonna call Sammy when we get home. What were you saying about Uncle Mark?"

"Oh, yeah. Uncle Mark was at work a week ago and these New Jersey Motor Vehicle Police show up."

"Motor Vehicles has its own police force?"

"It turns out, the car he bought was stolen - they confiscated it right in the parking lot. Lorraine had to pick him up, and insurance won't cover it."

"Of course not, if the car was hot. No wonder he had a Lexus. He probably got it for two grand. What did he think? That it wasn't hot?"

"He paid ten grand, and New Jersey won't even refund the six hundred he paid in sales tax" said Gwen, as Staci returned with a new soda.

"Can I have your order?"

"Look, hon," said Tony. "We're gonna be here for at least another hour. So, we want to spread the order out a bit." Staci walked away again, this time in a *full* huff. "Ten grand? Ouch! You know, I was with Uncle Mark all day and he never mentioned anything about the car."

"Maybe he didn't think of it."

"Uncle Mark? Ten grand - are you kidding? He gets his sneakers at the thrift shop. Losing ten grand will haunt him the rest if his life."

"Aunt Lorraine did say something about Mark complaining all week about how he had just gotten the gas tank filled up too. This soda is Diet Coke too."

"This waitress . . . this is the waitress from hell."

"It's alright."

"But that's my point - Uncle Mark. He's got a story like that and he doesn't tell you. He's one of these holdouts. What's the point of knowing somebody, if they don't share their stories?"

"Not everyone likes to share everything."

"So? What is the point of knowing them? I mean, you need to know a dentist and a plumber, an electrician, maybe . . . but friends and family? Everyone's a burden to know, but at least for every new person in your life, you get a new set of stories. That's the whole point of knowing people, the stories."

"Some people just like to spend time with each other."

"Please. Uncle Freddy too. Remember that story on Sixty Minutes, or something, about cryogenics and Ted Williams?"

"I don't know who that is."

"He was a famous baseball player - they froze his head."

"Not a clue. They do that to all baseball players?"

"Only the ones who hit four hundred. Anyway, when some news story came on today about his kids fighting over the frozen Ted-head, Freddy launches into this story about how when he was like eight or ten years old, he was at Yankee or Met's stadium. It was Ted William's first day as a manager. Freddy goes up to him and gets his autograph. And, Ted was a surly son of a bitch, he never signed autographs. Then, he walks up to Bowie Kuhn, who had just been named baseball commissioner, hands him the Yankee program that Ted Williams just signed. Kuhn sees it and tells him, 'Wow, young man. Ted Williams never gives anyone his autograph. This will be worth a lot of money someday,' and then Kuhn signs it too. Well, Freddy left the signed program in his bedroom for years, until one day his mom cleaned out his closet and threw it out. He could have sold that on Greg's list for a fortune today."

"Craigslist."

"Whatever. The point is, he had that Ted Williams story all that time and he never mentioned it. Twenty years I've known him. Another holdout" said Tony, as Staci returned to the table.

"Look, guys, my ride's here. If you're going to order something, you have to do it now because I have to close the check."

"'My Ride's Here' - that's a Warren Zevon song. He just died a few years ago, but I don't think they froze his head."

"Who?" asked Staci.

"Warren Zevon - the musician."

"The magician?"

"Never mind. I'll take the check, but I'd like to order twenty large waters to go - for my radiator."

"Twenty large waters?" asked Staci. "I don't think we can do that."

"Look" said Tony, "just give us the check for the drinks and then send a different waitress over. We'll start from scratch with her." Staci rolled her eyes, placed the check on the table and walked away, in a huff and a half. "What the hell was that? I just let her off the hook. It was a good solution."

"You're not good with waitresses," said Gwen.

"You understand my point about 'stories'? I tell everybody I know about getting held-up at gunpoint and being taped up - with my own duct tape -at the restaurant, or when I got arrested for eating spiked brownies."

"No one believes you about eating the pot-brownies by accident, by the way."

"Look at this waitress Staci" said Tony, pointing out the window. "She's already left and she's walking towards our van. She's probably gonna slash our tires." Staci then walked up to a parked Jeep by Tony's Voyager, opened the driver's seat door and sat behind the wheel. "What! Her ride's here? It's her car. Her ride is her own car!" shouted Tony, as Staci drove off. "We should talk to the manager. This broad is a cancer for this place."

"Just let it go, Tony" said Gwen, as Tony waved the evening shift manager over to their booth.

"How can I help you, sir?"

"Look, I used to be in the restaurant business, so I wanted to give you a heads up. This last waitress, Staci, had a real attitude from the moment we arrived. Then she told us we had to close our check because her 'ride is here'. Then, I just saw her get into her own car. Her ride was her own car!"

"I don't normally work with her. I'll let the regular evening manager know when I see him."

"Alright" said Tony, "but could you send another waitress over? We'd like to order now."

"I'm afraid I'd like you to leave sir."

"You'd like *me* to leave?"

"The young woman said you were rude. We don't tolerate abuse to our staff. Do you know how hard it is to find good waitresses?"

"Obviously, it's a little *too* hard for *you* to find them."

"Sir, I'd like you to go."

"Okay. Can you just do me a favor? My radiator hose leaked. Can I get a couple of gallons of water - in a used bottle or something - so my van doesn't overheat?"

"You've got the plastic cup from your daughter's milk - you can fill that in the men's room" said the manager, as he abruptly turned around and walked away.

Fifteen minutes later, after two dozen trips to the diner's men's room, Tony had the van back on Route 23 headed home and had resumed his stream of conscious commentary concerning the other drivers. There was inexplicably heavy traffic for a Sunday evening. "Look at the guy in front of us, he keeps drifting to the right like he's going to change lanes and then he pulls back. He's stupid too. He should have changed lanes, because it's moving faster than ours. There must be an accident or something up there. His head is bent too. What is he doing? Talking on the phone? What could this guy have going on in his life that's so important? He's driving a twelve hundred dollar car. What is he doing, negotiating some big deal? Ha, ha. Can you imagine the poor bastard on the other end of the phone? They probably have the phone on speaker and are making mocking talking gestures with their hands."

"Like *I'm* gonna start doing," said Gwen. "I'm going to try to sleep. It's going to be three in the morning before we get home, at this pace."

"He's got big ears too, this guy," continued Tony. "I can see them from here."

"You've got big ears, daddy" said Nicole, from the back seat.

"I have appropriate sized ears," said Tony.

"Did you know daddy's ears wiggle when you touch them, Nicole?" asked Gwen, as Nicole giggled.

"I've got very sensitive ears," said Tony. "I probably have that thing like bats have, where they can see in the dark. What do you call that?"

"I don't know" said Gwen, sorry she mentioned Tony's

moving ears.

"I betcha if I ever went blind, in a couple of years I'd be able to drive again using my bat-ears. Look at this now" said Tony, glaring at his rear-view mirror. We're merging into one lane and this bastard behind me comes up to an inch of my bumper every time I stop. It's like sodomy. Vehicular sodomy."

"He's tailgating?" asked Gwen.

"He's not a tailgater. Every time we pick up speed he falls five car lengths behind. Tailgating and vehicular sodomy are two distinct car-crimes, although they sometimes overlap in some particularly psychotic drivers. This is where my fluorescent LED light sign in the back window would have been great." Tony had tried to patent an idea to have an LED sign that would attach to back windows so the driver could communicate with the driver behind him. One button would have the sign light up to read 'stop tailgating', another 'your blinker is still on', etc. After Sammy Riscatto explained to Tony that it was illegal to post any sign, or non-transparent material upon a car's windshield, Tony reluctantly gave up the idea.

"'Vehicular sodomite? I thought you called them 'pacers'."

"No, 'pacers' are the guys in two-lane highways who get next to someone and then go the exact same speed, so everyone gets trapped and can't pass them. This guy is an eighth of an inch from the rear bumper now. I'm gonna put the van in reverse and slam him."

"Tony, we don't need another incident, especially with Gwen in the car. You've already got a record."

"Alright, just hand me the flashlight from the glove department, I dropped my ring again" said Tony, as flashing police lights could now be seen a half mile up the road. A drunk Willie had been in a fender-bender, which had caused the traffic jam. A wallet full of PBA cards from Willie's customers at Madison Ave kept Willie from being put in handcuffs. Leah was sliding over from the passenger side to the driver's side of their Jeep and Willie was getting into the passenger seat as Tony's van approached the scene. "That's Willie! How is he not getting arrested? He was plastered tonight."

After stopping the flow of traffic to allow Leah to pull away, the police officer turned off his warning lights. Tony was only thirty yards away now, but forced to stop again after the police officer stopped traffic for Leah. The car behind Tony pulled to within a millimeter of Tony's van. Tony rolled down his window and pointed his flashlight directly on the front windshield of the car behind him. As traffic began to move, rather than take Tony's hint from the beaming flashlight, the driver behind Tony put on his high beams and began tailgating Tony's van. Tony kept his flashlight fixed on the trailing car's windshield. The police officer, who had let the intoxicated Willie slide after causing an accident, turned his lights and siren on and pulled Tony over.

Tony was arrested for careless driving and reckless endangerment. Allowed one phone call by the Wayne Township Police, Tony called his attorney, Sammy.

"Tony, is that you? The caller ID says Wayne Police Station. Are you okay?"

"You can tell Willie, the answer's no!" Tony slammed the phone down.

36 - Live within your means

"First off, Willie, the Bourbon Billy parties are over" said Sammy, to a glum Willie seated in his office. "And, you're gonna have to go on the books at that club."

"We're having a hard time making it as it is."

"Third: I hear about you getting pulled over for again for drunk driving, I'm telling the FBI myself to lock you up for twenty years." Willie was taken aback by Sammy's sternness. Sammy had always been Willie's enabler, but now he was drawing a line on Willie's lawlessness. "You are a cooperating witness for the IRS and FBI, for God's sake. I'm not saying you have to declare every tip, but make it plausible, Willie."

"What's wrong with the parties?"

"You're not licensed, registered or insured, Willie. Have you already forgotten about the drunk driver and the minivan?"

"Have *you* already forgotten about Maria de Castro?" asked Willie, sarcastically and with immediate regret. Sammy stared at Willie, stun and stung that Willie would cheap shot him by bringing up the girl Willie had sent him to cover a legal bill. Willie continued, "I'm starting something legitimate now anyway – Bates & Swisher – an investment firm. Tony's already begun there too."

Sammy had to close his eyes for several seconds to process what Willie had just said. "You're going to work for an investment firm?"

"Insurance and mutual funds . . ."

"Insurance, Willie? You're staring at twenty years in prison for insurance fraud!"

"None of that goes on my record, as long as I get them

Bullo."

Sammy's fondness for Willie was finally, completely extinguished. "Willie, the terms of your deal preclude you from returning to either the accounting or insurance industries once the operation is over and you testify against Bullo."

"But, in the meantime . . ."

"No, but none of this matters anyway unless I can flip Tony."

"He liked the idea when I spoke with him at my aunt's house."

"He blames you for getting arrested on that road rage incident."

"He always blames everyone else for his problems. You couldn't get him off on that? One call from the FBI . . ."

"I could easily, only he won't let me represent him anymore."

"Just tell the FBI to call the Wayne police"

"That won't do us any good if Tony doesn't know it was me who intervened, and I couldn't tell him I got the FBI to intervene on his behalf without telling him why. For the time being, IRS and FBI think Tony's on board for this, but I can only pull their chains for so long."

"He's just an asshole. Anyone else, if it meant keeping their cousin's husband out of prison, would gladly cooperate."

"Any other accountant would welcome the IRS and FBI bugging their office even though they haven't done anything wrong, Willie?" Willie shook his head in disgust at the thought of Tony. "We're done here, Willie. Tend bar, live within your means and take a cab home when you've been drinking."

Willie wasn't far from taking a cab home from work, whether he was drunk or not. The Rocinantes had strictly been a one car family – Willie's Jeep – since Willie returned from Florida, with Leah borrowing her mother's twenty year old Plymouth Horizon. His lease payment was a month passed due and Willie soon woke one afternoon to find the Chrysler Finance had repossessed it.

The five thousand dollar retainer which Willie had paid Sammy in cash had depleted all of his savings. The household bills were paid from a checking account, funded solely by Leah's paycheck, which Willie never balanced. Overdrawn by several hundred dollars, Willie continued to write checks against it until Leah's last paycheck was completely seized to cover overdraft charges. Willie began sending Leah to an Elizabeth check cashing store for payday loans against her modest income, further reducing their cash flow due to the usurious fees.

Leah scrupulously, and without complaining, stretched her earnings as far as she could, serving rice and beans or pasta for nearly every meal, cancelling her cable television and forgoing a cell phone. Willie made due eating most of his meals for free at the club, but his extra-marital social life was suffering, having to chauffer Leah back and forth to work every day in her mother's car. A seven hundred dollar transmission repair on the Horizon forced them to skip their rent and cost Leah three day's pay when she had no way to get to work. They were only a few weeks from having to move in with Leah's mom.

Willie half hoped that Sammy would call and tell him that Tony wouldn't budge and that Willie was going back to jail. Not that he'd go, but it would give him the excuse he needed to lam it. The uncertainty was debilitating and Willie could no longer afford his Buspar prescription. His life felt as bad as a prison sentence and, to Willie, it was mostly Tony's fault.

"He won't let me work out of his office? I'm making him money – not a dime would come out of his pocket" said Willie, to Leah. "And, I'm the one who set him up at Bates & Swisher. Again, he's making money at my expense."

"Let me try talking to him, Willie. If he knows it will keep you from prison, I *know* he will help you."

"And, don't forget Sam's Way – he's your only cousin who wouldn't sign up; we could have made a fortune together."

"Or let Sammy talk to Gwen. This is crazy, you're practically related to Tony twice."

"No, confronting Tony's only a last resort and Sammy doesn't think he'd go for it, especially since we weren't up front with him to begin with."

"He will help you, I know he will. He'll do it for my sake, if not for yours."

"No, he's an asshole."

37 – Lapsed Leads

"Tony, I haven't been seeing you at the meetings the past couple of weeks" said Dudley, from behind the desk in his remarkably modest ten by twelve foot office. Dudley's sales were all 'out in the field', so an impressive office was unnecessary. Also, keeping a modest office helped Dudley disguise just how much he profited from the sweat and toil of the starving brokers who worked for him.

"Those 'rah-rah' meetings are not for me." Tony paused, expecting Dudley to respond, but the normally loquacious Dudley was silent and slightly annoyed. Dudley knew Tony was in his office to ask for leads, but Dudley had soured quickly on Tony. "Someone said I should ask you for a list of lapsed policy holders. Remember? You went over the script, what I should say when I knock on their door."

"What about your own contacts? I haven't seen any production from you."

"I told you, I'm not cold calling or soliciting my family."

"What about your tax clients, that's your goldmine. Are you calling them up?"

"I sent out a mailing letting them know about my new services."

"That's not the way this business works. You have to call them."

"I'm not calling them out of the blue. They're clients, not prospects. When they have a need they'll know to call me."

Dudley stared at Tony like a dejected father looking at a son who had disappointed him his entire life. "You should talk to Dante before you go out on these." Dudley opened the top left drawer of his desk and pulled out a sheet with the names and addresses of a dozen former Newark New Jersey policyholders of Lyndhurst Life Insurance & Retirement Savings Company, whose policies had lapsed in 1994.

"The last time I saw Dante was three weeks ago. He borrowed ten bucks to put gas in his car and has been avoiding me ever since."

"Well, I think he's good for it. He just picked up a five thousand dollar commission check today - and that's without the life insurance commissions. He's got another ten grand coming after those are placed."

"No kidding? How'd he do that?"

"I was beginning to lose faith in Dante, but the last two weeks he's been a dynamo. Five or six life insurance policies - all with 1035 lump sum transfers -, four hundred thousand dollars in annuity sales and more than that in mutual funds."

"Wow. When I talked to him three weeks ago it was in the parking lot. He pulled up to me in this old Chrysler with only one real tire and three donuts."

Dudley laughed, returning to his normal boisterousness. "It's more of a museum on four wheels than a car. If he's doing business driving that piece of shit. You should come back with eight sales from this list, driving that minivan."

"He did that business off of these leads?"

"What do you think I've been telling you? This is why you have to make all the meetings. You just keep plugging away at it until one day you catch a break, or you grow some onions . . . whatever."

Tony picked up the sheet of lapsed 1994 Newark New Jersey insureds from Dudley's desk, left his office and went to find Dante. Dante was in a cubical next to Father Droll, who turned to avoid making eye contact with Tony. "Tony, I'm gonna get that ten to you, I've just got to get to the bank and cash my check."

"Dudley said I should talk to you, to get some pointers about how to deal with the leads he just gave me."

"Are those lapsed policy leads?"

"Sure."

Dante's face then contorted as if he had a bad secret that would be a real hassle to share, until he came up with a better idea. "Look, after the bank, I've got to buy new tires for my car and return a couple of those donuts . . ."

"Why don't you just lease a new car?"

"I'm first generation Italian; we don't buy anything on credit."

"Except for gas."

"I'll get your cash back and then some."

"Don't worry about it."

"Look, run these leads yourself this afternoon - the way Dudley taught you. Then, tomorrow I'll give you your ten dollars, buy you lunch and let you know how I've been turning some sales around here the past couple weeks."

"I don't want to burn them."

"You won't. I won't be able to explain what I've been doing until you've tried turning them yourself."

Tony agreed and, after grabbing a quick coffee, got into his Voyager and punched the first address on his list into his TomTom, which didn't recognize the address. Tony chose the option to simply navigate to Bergen Street Newark and got on the Eisenhower Parkway. Tony repeatedly hit the electronic door lock button as he entered Newark, and drove down Bergen Street. He cruised slowly as he reached the house numbers beginning with two hundred. He was looking for two sixty-four Bergen Street, but after he reached two sixty-two Bergen he saw only two vacant lots and then two sixty-eight Bergen. "What the hell?" Tony thought. "A vacant lot. Must have been a bad address . . . and just as well, in this neighborhood. I'll have to remember to tell Dudley he owes me an extra lead, tomorrow." Then, after looking around to make sure no one was too close - or watching him - Tony pulled over and punched the second address into his TomTom. "Good, it found this one and it's only a quarter-mile away. That first address was just some mistake." Tony drove to the next address on South 10th street only to find a burned out, vacated building. "What the hell?" The third address, like the first, wasn't recognized by the TomTom and when he got to Clinton Avenue, sure enough, it was another vacant lot.

Tony was ready to head back to the Bates & Swisher Equities Livingston office to confront Dudley, but the next lead was also on Clinton Avenue, so he figured he'd give that a try before returning to the office. Tony pulled up to the address, which was actually an apartment in a decrepit apartment project. Tony's heart raced as he contemplated getting out of his van. It was broad daylight. The street was empty, except for a couple of drunken homeless men and an elderly deranged woman who approached him for money. Tony ignored the old woman and walked apprehensively to the entrance of the apartment building. Tony might have gotten mugged or beaten, had he not looked like he might be a cop or DEA agent.

The woman named on the lapsed lead was on the third floor, apartment B. Tony felt safer taking the steps, rather than potentially being trapped in an elevator with some hoodlum. The stench of urine grew stronger, and the stairway grew dimmer, as Tony reached the third floor. Tony was out of breath simply from climbing two stories of steps. "This is what people in their fifties and sixties are talking about when they complain about steps," Tony thought. "It's just my nerves." Tony composed himself for a minute and then knocked on the door of apartment B, setting off loud and vicious barking from what was at least two dogs. Tony quickly stepped back and considered leaving, but he heard what sounded like an old man's voice.

"Hear - right there," the man shouted. A minute later, the door opened as wide as the shortest of the multiple chain locks would allow.

"I'm Tony Violette, with Bates & Swisher Equities" said Tony, as a Spanish Mastiff and Rottweiler tried to squeeze their heads through the door opening. "Is Carole Jones at this address?"

"Are you the insurance?" asked the man, who could hardly hear, even without the dogs barking.

"I'm with the service department."

"Are you the insurance?"

"I'm with the service department," screamed Tony. The old man nodded, closed the door and began unlocking the chains on the door. When the door reopened, the old man was pulling the dogs back that were leashed to two thirty inch chains with three-eighth inch links.

"Come in," said the thin, but reasonably fit old man, inviting Tony with an underhand wave with his free left hand. Immediately inside the man's door was a tiny living room where a vestibule might be in a single family home, and not much bigger than a vestibule. The man pointed at a two seat couch on the left with heavily duct taped cushions where the dogs had chewed. "Sit down." On the right was a square folding table with two chairs and a huge, old black and white TV set with rabbit ears. Above the table was a picture of Martin Luther King Jr. and a frame holding a World War Two metal. The dogs continued to bark and growl, baring their teeth and eyeing Tony. Saliva dripped from their mouths. The old man, unperturbed by the dogs barking - which he could barely hear - pulled the dogs back with all his strength. "Are you the insurance?"

Tony was now drenched in sweat. Worried the old man would lose control of the dogs, Tony tried to figure out a polite way to leave. "When does Carole come home?" The old man just smiled and nodded as he struggled with the dogs. "Is Carole at work now? I'll come back tonight" said Tony, still being drowned out by the dogs.

"You're the insurance" said the old man, beginning to get irritated with the dogs whose barking jaws were only four feet from Tony.

"Yes, I'm the insurance" said Tony, nodding. Tony would have bolted for the door at this point, but he had no confidence he could open it and leave without the dogs overpowering the old man's grip.

"You're the insurance."

Tony pulled out a business card from his shirt pocket. He gingerly placed it on the couch arm and slowly rose, trying not to further irritate the growling hounds. Tony smiled foolishly and nodded his head. "It was nice to meet you." Tony began walking sideways to the door. He continued nodding his head and smiling to the old man. The dogs continued to bark, growl and leak saliva. Tony grabbed the doorknob behind his back and gently cracked it open. "It was nice to meet you," Tony repeated.

"You're the insurance" the man said, for a final time. Tony slid out, closed the door and ran to the stairway. He reached the street level and doubled over, struggling to breathe. He was glad to be alive and relieved to see his van still parked out front, but someone had keyed the passenger side of the vehicle. Tony was no longer interested in returning to the Bates & Swisher Equities office to confront Dudley. He just wanted to get back to his Edison office and be an accountant again.

"What the hell am I doing in downtown Newark trying to sell

life insurance?" wondered Tony, as he sped down South Orange Avenue towards the Parkway. "Even Willie had the sense to quit this."

38 - The Delaware Water Gap

"Murphy's been asking me why you haven't moved into Tony's office yet, Willie. He smells a rat. Have you made any progress with Tony?"

"He didn't even come to Christmas Eve. He took Gwen and Nicole to Cape May for the week, I think just to avoid the family."

"I've tried calling him too, but he won't take my calls. I've asked Gwen to intervene, but he's a hard-headed son of a bitch. We're gonna have to go to plan C, Willie, or you're going back to jail."

Willie was barely paying attention. "We're living with Leah's mom in Keyport. Five people in a one bedroom apartment, Sammy, and for what?"

"Five people in a one bedroom apartment beats two people sharing a jail cell, Willie."

"The club is slow with the economy now. I'm making half the tips I used to even before taxes - which I never paid before - and now they cut me down to four shifts a week."

"Tax season's less than a month away, you'll make some cash then, so long as we solve this problem. Of course, if we don't solve this problem, you're going to jail. So, either way, your money problems are solved."

"I can't even lam it – I'm too poor. Pete loaned me his siphon pump to steal gas, but once I left the club, what would I do for food? I even went to donate blood. I always thought they paid you for that, but they only give you juice and cookies. I don't need any more sugar, we've been eating continental breakfasts every day for over a month."

"What do you mean, 'continental breakfasts'?"

"The Best Western in Hazlet is less than two miles from the apartment. We just walk in every morning and eat for free. They think we're guests."

"You have to confront Tony, that's your only hope. Be straight with him and throw yourself on his mercy. Make sure Leah & Gwen are there too. And, you've got to do it soon – this week."

"What about Bullo, Sammy?"

"I spoke with him last week about the arrangements. I asked him if he's still okay with the cut. I told him it wasn't too late for you to work out of his office and you two split the fees without Tony, but he shot that right down. I think the issue is less him working with you, and more that he's simply afraid his tax-shelter scam has grown out of control. He wants to move as much as he can as far away from himself, as possible."

"And after Tony says no, Sammy, then what do I do? Just turn myself back in to the FBI?"

"Then we try to sell Bullo & FBI on you just opening your own office. They'd both have to say yes but I don't think either would. Go get Leah, Willie – and Wilma and John too – and drive straight over to Tony's house, and pour your heart out Willie. Tell him – and Gwen – that your life is over if he doesn't let you in his office. Tell him about Pompano Industrial Life, the arrest and the FBI – tell him everything, Willie, and don't leave his house until he either agrees . . . he either agrees or calls the cops on you Willie, 'cause, if he doesn't change his mind, you're going to jail anyway.

Willie didn't believe there was any chance Tony would change his mind. Worse, once he told Tony he'd needed the IRS and FBI to bug his office, Tony would call FBI and they'd rearrest Willie immediately. Willie was going to lam it. He could be in Tijuana in three days, but he was broke. He needed cash. He decided he would rob Madison Ave.

Lefty Ladro was Willie's weed dealer, an occasional cat-burglar and a semi-regular at Madison Ave. "Big day Sunday, huh Lefty?"

"What do you mean, Willie, football?

"Of course – Jets and Giants both in the playoffs."

"New England will beat the Jets by a hundred points."

"Probably, but the Giants and Eagles should be a great game."

"I guess. I should have been a bookie. They'll clean up this weekend."

"You can't sell pot and be a bookie at the same time?"

"I'm not Walmart's, Willie. Territory: you carve out a niche for yourself and try not to step on anybody's toes."

"If you're already making enough . . . why bother, I guess."

Lefty smirked. "Nobody makes enough, Willie."

"I don't know, what about these guys? We probably bring in twenty grand on a regular football Sunday. The playoffs? Jet and Giant playoff games on the same day?"

"How much, Willie?"

"It'll be at least forty – maybe more." Lefty shook his head. "That's a lot of weed you'd have to sell for forty K in cash."

"I guess."

"Of course, one of the managers makes a bank run mid-afternoon with a security guard, but by Sunday evening there'd still be twenty five thousand or more in cash, I'd bet." Lefty shrugged. "All cash, Lefty."

"What are you saying, Willie?" Willie had to step away to take drink orders for a new couple at the bar. Lefty certainly would have no qualms about stealing the money, but this sounded like a cowboy heist, not Lefty's style. Further, Lefty figured Willie probably expected a fat finder's fee for nothing other than some fairly obvious information.

"What do you say, Lefty?"

"What do I say about what, Willie?"

"Helping me take this place down."

"How do you figure we do that?"

"I can get you into the locked office, where they keep the cash and safe."

"And you know the combination?"

"No. I mean you'll follow in behind me when the manager's there."

"You've given this a lot of thought, huh Willie? This place is loaded with cameras and security - mostly off-duty cops. Stick to bartending, Willie."

"What about the take, Lefty? One of the partners leaves every night around ten with a brief case, and not to the bank. I've seen them – Pete too -, they turn left out of the parking lot, not right towards the Wachovia Bank. *That's* the cash they take outta this place."

"Probably. They take security with them?"

"Only to the car. They leave alone."

"If you're thinking about their home, Willie, forget it. Partners in a place like this have alarms, security cameras, hidden safes . . . I'm not saying it's not a good target for real pros. There could be hundreds of thousands of dollars in cash in a house like that, but you and I'd be surrounded by ten drooling Rottweilers waiting for the cops to arrive before we got twenty feet from the front door."

"What if we intercepted him before he got home?"

Willie and Lefty conspired to have Willie flag partner Barry Dunham down about a mile away from the club, under the guise of car troubles. A more secluded road closer to Dunham's home would have been safer, but it would have been implausible for Willie to have been in Colts Neck. Leah's mother's 1987 Plymouth Horizon breaking down a mile from Madison Ave was totally plausible. They were going to tape Dunham up, abandon his car and leave him in the woods by the Delaware Water Gap. With his half of the score, Willie would be off for Tijuana.

Willie left Madison Ave after 9:30 p.m. and parked on a side street, waiting for Lefty's call. At 10:15, Lefty spotted Dunham, with briefcase and bodyguard, leaving Madison Ave. Lefty called Willie as Dunham got in his Pathfinder. "We're on, bro."

Willie drove to Amboy Avenue, pulled over to the shoulder under a street light and raised the hood of the Horizon. Lefty followed Dunham in a stolen Taurus. Willie spotted Dunham's Pathfinder and began doing hysterical jumping jacks in the middle of the lane, trying to get Dunham to stop. Dunham's tires squealed as he swerved to avoid Willie and return to the right lane. "Rocinante? Goddamn it!" Dunham slowed down as he approached the intersection of Route 35 and Amboy Ave. Lefty, accelerating, slammed into Dunham's rear. Already upset from Willie jumping in front of his car, Dunham jumped out of his Pathfinder to confront the driver of the Taurus who just hit him. "What are you, some kind of maniac?"

"Why did you stop short, asshole?" shouted Lefty, leaping from the car.

"You're paying for this" said Dunham, pointing to his back bumper.

"Alright, let's just call it even, man. My insurance is lapsed, don't call the cops."

"Wonderful."

"How bad did I get it?" Dunham turned to view the Taurus's dented hood. Lefty hammered him on the side of his head with a tire iron and jumped into the Pathfinder while Dunham landed on the ground. "Willie, I got the brief case, meet me at the White Castle on Route 1 by the mall. Park by the dumpster."

Willie drove past the abandoned Taurus and saw Dunham unconscious on the ground. Ten minutes later, Willie pulled into the White Castle parking lot. Lefty was standing outside, leaning on the Pathfinder with the tire iron behind his back. Willie got out of his car and Lefty smacked him in the neck, intentionally avoiding his head. Willie fell to his knees, gasping for air. Lefty opened the back door of the Pathfinder. "Get in . . .get in." Willie didn't move. Lefty kicked Willie in the stomach. Willie buckled over and then crawled into the back seat of the Pathfinder. "You better have the duct tape." Lefty opened the front door of the Horizon and spotted the two rolls of duct tape Willie faithfully brought which were meant to tape up Dunham. Lefty grabbed them and returned to the Pathfinder. First, he circled Willie's head a half dozen times, barely giving him space to breathe through his nose. "Okay, Willie this is what you are gonna tell the cops when they find you here in the morning. You were pulled over to the side with car trouble. The car flooded or something. You finally got it started only to pull up to an accident. Like a Good Samaritan, you got out of the car trying to help only to see that one man was laying on the ground and the other guy, some Puerto Rican -blue-bloods like Dunham, if he's even alive, can't tell Italians and Puerto Ricans apart. Some Puerto Rican – no, two Puerto Ricans – one cold cocks you with an iron bar, Willie. Then they threw you in their car – the Pathfinder – and one drove off with your Plymouth. Then they abandoned you here and stole your car. You got that Willie? That's how it went down if you want to live, Willie. And, find someone else to buy dope from, from now on."

Lefty proceeded to tape up Willies arms and legs, circling and circling until he used up both rolls of tape. He left Dunham's keys in the Pathfinder, grabbed the brief case and sped off in the Plymouth Horizon.

39 – Dumpster Diving

On his way to telling off Dudley and officially resigning from Bates & Swisher Equities, Tony met Dante for breakfast. "How did those lapsed leads work out for you, Tony?" asked Dante. "Anyone let you in the door?"

"Actually, someone did let me in. I was this close to being lunch for two giant dogs."

Dante grinned. "How many people did you have to speak to before someone let you in?"

"He was the only one I did speak to. The whole list was vacant lots, burned-out buildings and apartment projects."

"Oh, Dudley gave you the real shit list, not that the others are much better. He's testing you. Either that, or you've really pissed him off, and he wanted to stick your face in shit."

"What about the business you've been doing? Did he send you to the slums in Newark too?"

"I've gone through about thirty of those 'lapsed lead' lists, knocked on about three hundred doors and made three or four tiny sales that didn't even cover my gas" said Dante, as he pulled out a ten and put it on the table.

"Dudley said you picked up a five thousand dollar commission check yesterday and have more than that coming when the insurance policies get approved."

"My check yesterday was closer to two grand, but I do have about three times that coming when the insurance hits. Five thousand was the gross commission. That's the way he lies. There's always a kernel of truth, some bogus thing he can go back on, 'Oh, I meant Dante brought in five grand to the office.' He knows it's bullshit."

"The whole business is bullshit" said Tony, "but you still

earned, what, eight grand the past two weeks? How?"

"Tony, I figured that place out the day I met Willie at Park Ave with Dudley. I spent the day with Dudley and saw what he does."

"So, why'd it take you three months to start selling?"

"Tony, you've been there two and a half months. How many new people have they dragged through that insurance school?"

" Every other week, there are eight to ten people per class."

"At least. Let's call it twenty people a month."

"Okay."

"Half the people leave right away or can't even pass the insurance exam, but still there's a hundred or more that stick around awhile and make a dozen sales or more every year. Some a little more, some a little less. That's fifteen hundred new accounts each year and they've been at this thirty years. That's forty-five thousand accounts."

"I know, I can do the math. I'm an accountant."

"Didn't he tell you when he hired you that Bates & Swisher had forty thousand accounts to service - that's what he was talking about. Again, there's always a kernel of truth when he misleads people. That's how he justifies it to himself."

"I get it. So what does this have to do with your sales?"

"There are only six managers in the place. Fifteen hundred to two thousand new accounts are opened up and abandoned every year - that's what they feast on. Eighty to ninety percent of those forty-thousand accounts are dead, either closed or already churned. These six guys just go in a year or two after you leave and churn the accounts, or, at a minimum, take them over for the servicing commissions. In two years from now, Dudley, Arthur, Dominick, Dan or one of those jerks, will be calling on your uncles and cousins or whoever you sold in your family telling them what a great guy you were, but that you just weren't right for the business and how you put them in all the wrong products. But - not to worry - because *they're* from the service department, and so on and so on . . . That's the scam and we're the suckers at the table, Tony."

"You're right, Dante. It makes sense, but how did you make your sales?"

"I swiped a stack of active account leads out of Gelman's office."

"And they don't know?"

"I thought Gelman gave me a couple of looks, but I think I was just a little paranoid."

"Didn't they recognize the names on your sales, if they're existing clients?"

"They may at some point, probably, but they're swimming in accounts - real accounts - easy sales, Tony. These are already our clients - I really *am* from the service department. A couple pieces of paper, the money goes from one company to another and I get paid. The only problem is, I already went through the leads I swiped."

"Can't you get more? Where'd these come from?"

"I told you, Gelman's desk. He and Dan were on the phone with the 4-1-1 operators getting updated numbers on some of the accounts to call on. They don't drive and knock on strangers' doors. They call existing clients and qualify them to see if there's any more business to be done. Anyway, they get a little bored calling the 4-1-1 operators, who are like robots and will only give you two numbers per phone call, so you have to keep hanging up and calling back. Anyway, they've got this little betting game when they get bored and get annoyed with the 4-1-1 operators. They'll bet ten or twenty bucks they can get an operator to say a silly word - a curse word or something. So, I'm walking by their office a month ago. They've got the phone on speaker phone and Dan's telling the woman, 'I'm looking for an electrician in Red Bank . . . Hubby Electric or Stubby?' 'No, she says, there's no business listed with that name.' So, he says, 'I don't know . . . maybe it's Flubby or Nubby . . .' finally she says, 'should I try Chubby Electric?' They both burst out laughing and Arthur throws a twenty dollar bill across the room at Dan. They see me outside the room laughing at what's going on and Dan invites me in and says 'let's bet Arthur ten bucks, ten to one, that he can't get the next operator to say breast. We'll go fifty-fifty on it, Dante.' I said 'Okay,' and fortunately we won, because I didn't have the fifty bucks to cover the bet. Anyway, there was a stack of Oppenheimer accounts on the corner of his desk. Actually, there are piles of account statements all over his desk. So, I was carrying some folders with me, which I laid on top of the statements. After Arthur gave me my five bucks, I pinched about a half inch of statements and walked out of there eight grand richer. Really, eight thousand and five dollars richer. Those five bucks came in handy too; my tank was below empty that afternoon."

"Well, that's a hell of a story, Dante, but how do we steal more leads?" asked Tony suddenly intrigued by the idea of scamming Bates & Swisher Equities, for revenge and financial relief.

"He keeps his office locked. They all do. And, there's a reason why they don't let us in the back office. There are stacks of thousands of statements of active client accounts, everywhere. They're supposed to file them, I think, but they're too cheap to pay for the extra file space. Why do you think Tom Swisher has his daughter working back there? She opens all the mail. Ninety percent of it, they just throw out."

"Don't they have to shred all that?" asked Tony.

"Maybe they're supposed to, but that would be a huge job every week. Didn't you ever see the dumpster? It's loaded with black contractor bags, all the time?"

Tony and Dante just looked at each other with jaws dropped. Nothing needed to be said. So obvious and so easy. "I'll drive if you dive. I've got the Voyager, that'll hold about eight contractor bags if I take out the back seat, but we can't empty them out at my house."

"My folks have a two car garage they hardly use."

Fourteen hours later, Dante was up to his neck in trash in the dumpster behind the offices of Bates & Swisher Equities. Bates & Swisher shared the dumpster with a gynecologist, a real estate sales office and a pizzeria. Dante's main worry was running into a raccoon rummaging for scraps from the pizzeria. Bates & Swisher was the only business to use black contractor bags, so they were easy to find. Dante tossed three of the black bags from the dumpster and left the forth so it wouldn't look suspicious in the morning in case anyone from the office was particularly alert. Tony was parked about thirty feet away, the closest parking spot to the dumpster. As Dante hopped out of the dumpster, red police lights lit up the parking lot.

When Tony sped away from the Clinton Avenue projects in Newark the afternoon before, after surviving the Spanish Mastiff and Rottweiler, little could he have imagined he'd be back in

Newark the next day, this time in the Essex County Correctional Facility.

"What are you doing here, Sammy? You're not my lawyer anymore."

"Gwen called me."

"I told her to pick a random name out of the phone book."

"Identity theft is a big deal these days, Tony. What did you tell the cops? I need you to remember everything you said."

"What identity theft? I was parked in the lot of the office where I have a job. Dante just stepped out to take a leak."

"At 11:00 p.m.? Were you and this Vince Dante ever at the complex after dark before? I need you to be one hundred percent honest with me, Tony."

"No, yesterday was the first time. We only came up with the dumpster diving scheme yesterday morning."

"Dumpster diving? Well, your buddy Dante is singing like a canary." Dante's parents hired a top criminal lawyer for him and he hadn't spoken a word.

"Willie" said Tony, shaking his head in self-disgust. "Willie's the one who talked me into joining Bates & Swisher."

"You can't blame this one on Willie, Tony . . . but maybe Willie can get you out."

"How do you mean?"

"It just so happens that the assistant D.A. in Essex County owes me a favor. A big one. One that I've been holding on to a long time. I think I can get you a pass, but on one condition."

"What?"

"Make things right between you and Willie. Take him up on his offer. Take him into your tax practice - it's only going to put money in your pocket, anyway. It's family Tony."

Tony shrugged his shoulders and nodded. "What's going to happen to Dante?"

"Identity theft, nowadays - high priority, they don't settle those. Dante's gonna be someone's girlfriend at Rahway State Prison for the next five to seven years."

40 - Little D & A

"Hillary, it's Sammy."

"I know, I see the caller ID. You shouldn't be calling me."

"I'm in Newark, at Essex County Corrections, I was hoping you had fifteen minutes for coffee."

"Sammy, I can't believe we're having this conversation again . . ."

"No, it's not that."

"It's over, Sammy. I'm married, we were a mistake. You were a mistake."

"This is strictly business, Hillary. I need your help – a favor from an old friend."

"I can't Sammy"

"Hillary, ten minutes: the Starbucks on Martin Luther, by Rutgers."

"Sammy."

"It's strictly a legal case, Hillary."

Hillary paused, she knew Sammy's persistence. "Ten minutes, Sammy. I'll be there at one."

Hillary was a married assistant district attorney in Essex County whom Sammy had a fling with while her marriage was on the rocks due to fertility issues.

Sammy was pouring the third sugar into his coffee when Hillary arrived with her Soy Earl Green Tea Latte already waiting for her on the table. "You look good, Hill."

"How are you, Sammy?"

"Good. How are you and Keith doing?"

"It's all good, the scars are healing. We just put a pool in, now we're looking for a patio guy."

Sammy rubbed his forehead. "Hill, I've got a case and, it's a client . . . and it's family . . . and it's a molehill. But, because of all the hubbub about identity theft lately, they're gonna make a mountain of complications for a lot of people."

"What do you want me to do about it, Sammy?"

Sammy stared at her, firmly. "I want you to make it go away."

Hillary turned her head away. "Sammy, no, you're reaching here."

"Let me explain. A couple of guys working for some low-end investment firm . . . They were getting jerked around by their superiors – not getting the leads they felt they were entitled to – so, they grabbed a couple of bags of garbage filled with account statements out of the company's dumpster."

"Now you're gonna tell me they weren't stealing their social security numbers, they were only stealing leads from their own company which they planned on working."

"That is what they were doing."

"Come on, Sammy." Hillary shook her head and laughed.

"It's the God's honest truth."

"Even if I believed it, Sammy, they were stealing people's personal account statements, private information."

"Information they themselves potentially had access to anyway. These were orphan accounts which dozens of these jackals from their office call on every day."

"Sammy . . ."

"These guys aren't opening fake credit cards on anyone, Hill. One of the guys is my cousin's husband; he's a goddamn accountant."

"Privacy is a big issue these days. And what kind of accountant goes rummaging through dumpsters to steal people's account statements?"

"It was an error in judgment. And, he was the driver, not the diver."

"Diver?"

"Dumpster diver."

Hillary laughed. "Look, Sammy, it this case gets handed to me, and I'm convinced they weren't involved in some identity theft scam, maybe they can plea this down to some trespassing offence."

"If? Hill, I need you to take this case. No one is going to fight you for it. My cousin's husband, Tony Violette, was just sitting in his car in the parking lot of an office in which he worked. That's easily thrown out. It's the other guy you need to plead out. He can't get crushed while Tony walks and I can't have Tony called if it goes to trial."

"Why not, Sammy? He was up to no good. Does he have a record? Any recents?"

"That's part of the problem, Hill. Two, and they were recent, but both blown out of proportion."

"What were they, Sammy?"

"There was a disorderly person arrest after someone fed him some pot brownies."

"So, he's a drug taking accountant that rummages through garbage to steal people's personal account statements?"

"He didn't know the brownies had marijuana."

"Please. What else?"

"He's facing an aggravated assault charge from some road rage incident that got blown out of proportion, as well."

"Facing? What's the status on that one?"

"I'm not his attorney on that case . . ."

"He sounds like a real asshole, Sammy. I know he's family . . ."

"He was just shining a flashlight in some other driver's face that was tailgating him, or something. He argued with the cop, that's why they didn't just give him a ticket. He's got a problem with authority, I think. He's his own worst enemy. In fact, I told you about him once. Remember the guy whose wife abandoned the pet mice?"

"Oh, yes. He went to war with the SPCA in the newspapers down there."

"Look, I know you're a vegan and everything . . ."

"Sammy, I understand he's your cousin's whatever, but he's an asshole this guy. Let him do nine months in Rahway."

"I need your help here, Hill. Just tell them a guy sitting in his car in the parking lot where he works is no case."

"I don't know what to tell you, Sammy. You can make that argument in court, but I'll bet the dumpster diver is gonna try to cut his losses and make a deal and he's gonna have to testify that your driver was in on it."

"How is Keith?" asked Sammy, coldly.

"He keeps juicing, Sammy, and pumping iron, trying to get his count up."

"I need you to do this for me, Hill, and I need to hear it from you. I need to hear you tell me you're going to get them to drop this case."

"Or what, Sammy? You're snitching on me? You want to call Keith? You want Keith's number, Sammy?"

"It doesn't have to be like this. I'm just asking you for a favor."

Hillary stood up and tried hard not to shed any tears. "Alright, Sammy. Alright. Just so long as you promise that I never hear from you again - the rest of your life-, Sammy. What's his name, Violet?"

"Violette."

"I always thought of you as a bit of a rapscallion, but harmless, Sammy. But I was wrong, Sammy. There's no 'there' there, with you. You're not harmless, you're heartless."

41 -Two Iron

The IRS-FBI joint sting operation against Bullo's tax shelter scheme was given low priority by each agency. No funds for renting space by Tony's office to conduct surveillance had been allotted, so Murphy and O'Kelly raided the Chinese prostitution enterprise down the hall, which operated under the guise of the Acupuncture Wellness Center. The Wellness Center consisted of a seedy waiting area manned by the stern, homely madam, Chunfu Ji, and three small offices with twin sized beds, linens, lotions and towels. Murphy made a deal with Chunfu. He would not bust her or her stable. In exchange, the FBI and IRS would be given full use of one of the three offices as a safe house to record Willie's appointments. Wires were easily run through the suspended ceiling tiles between the Wellness Center and Willie's office, although they had to be replaced twice in the first month after being chewed through by the building's rats. The FBI also photographed everyone entering and leaving the building via a car cam located in Chunfu's Mercedes, which now was endowed with a handicap license plate, allowing her to permanently park in the space in front of the entrance door.

It was early February and only a handful of Bullo's tax shelter investors had made their way to Tony's office to have Willie complete their tax returns. Murphy was hearing more from Chunfu complaining of the agents not paying for favors from her herd than he was from the agents with useful information. Still, the tax appointments were trickling in and they were providing actionable information.

"What do you think about Willie's clients?" asked Tony. "They're all assholes," said Rickie Rose. "And why do we have to keep their folders in his office behind a locked door?"

"It's better that way. I don't want his clientele infecting my practice."

"Clientele? He's got even less business than you." Tony frowned. "And, why is he so paranoid about his files getting mixed with yours? He's reminded me like twenty times to put his folders in his office, only he's never here. I have to slide the files under his locked door after I collate them. What if someone comes to pick them up when he's not here?"

"How many more scheduled appointments does he have this week?"

"Three. All of them jerks needing directions from Staten Island. Why are all his appointments from New York?"

"Where is he, by the way? His Jeep is parked out front."

"The Wellness Center. He said the acupuncture helps with his allergies."

"Do me a favor, when you collate his returns, make an extra copy of them for me. Don't tell Willie. I want to take a look at them."

From down the hall, they heard shouting. "That's not Willie, is it?"

"No, it's the Pakistani and the Indian again."

"They don't get along?"

"Of course not."

"Why 'of course not'?"

"Pakistanis and Indians don't get along. You didn't know that?"

"I can't even tell them apart."

"I know, to us it's like, 'what's the frigging difference'?"

"I just know one of them won't eat pigs because they're so bad and the other won't eat cows because they're so good."

"Maybe that's what they're arguing about."

"Yeah, it's like Melanie and Willie yesterday complaining about the Mexicans."

"Exactly! They're Puerto Ricans; it's the same damn thing, basically."

"I guess."

"I know the Mexicans are supposed to have some Mayan blood too, but they all look more like Don Quixote than Pocahontas to me."

"Oh God . . ."

"No, I've had enough of these Spanish people pretending to be Indians. It's identity theft, basically. *We* may have pulled a lot of crap on the Indians, but at least we never pretended to be Indians. We took Canada and America, they took every frigging thing else. We don't claim not to be white people anymore, but they're pretending to be Latinos. Latinos? They're frigging Spanish people. Stop pretending to be Latinos! Now they're demanding we give them Arizona and New Mexico back. Back? They belong in freaking Barcelona. It's like you and I rob a house together and then I see you with half the loot and say, 'give me my stuff back, Rickie.'"

"Okay, I'll make you copies of Willie's files if you promise to stop."

One by one over the next three days, Rickie delivered copies of Willie's returns to Tony. They were all nearly identical. Two retired cops, the other a retired fireman. All were implausibly generous to their church and all had five figure losses from S-corporations. "I knew it," thought Tony. "What was I thinking, letting Willie in here? Anything he's involved with has to be crooked." Tony nearly picked up the phone to castigate Sammy, but business was slow and Tony's curiosity was stronger than his fury. After Willie and Rickie had left for the evening, Tony pulled a webcam he had in his widow for monitoring the parking lot, with the idea of planting it in Willie's office to eavesdrop. Tony didn't have direct access to Willie's office – Willie had installed a new door lock – but Tony could see into Willies office by poking his head through the suspended ceiling tiles that separated their offices. Tony grabbed a flashlight to see precisely where the gauche picture of Marilynn Monroe Willie had hung in his office was. Tony figured he could run a webcam wire through the wall and poke a hole in the mushy old sheetrock wall behind Marilynn. He didn't need to see Willie in action; he only wanted to listen in on an appointment or two. Tony stood on his desk which he had dragged to the wall of his office, lifted a ceiling tile and spotted a thick wire running down a cleanly cut hole in the two by four ceiling joist between he and Willie's office. Everything above the ceiling tiles in the building was covered with dust, but the wire was shiny and clean and ran as far as Tony's flashlight could aluminate. Tony gently pulled on the wire and it came up without obstruction. Six feet of wire later, Tony saw the FBI microphone.

"What the hell is Willie up to?" screamed Tony over the phone to Sammy. "I just found a wire in his office."

"Tony, just give me a minute – I just got out of the shower." Sammy put his phone down and ran for his cell and called Murphy. "Tony found the wire. Get someone over there, now." Sammy rushed back to his landline. He could hear Tony screaming across the room even with the handle face down on his couch cushion. "Tony relax, don't do anything hasty."

Murphy called the Wellness Center and was relieved to find the agent had stayed past his shift to chat with the hookers. "Get over to Violette's office now– he spotted the wire."

Tony didn't get in more than a couple of sentences of screams and threats at Sammy when he heard pounding on his locked waiting room door. "Who's banging on my door, Sammy?"

"FBI, Tony . . . maybe IRS. Let them in Tony, I've got to take this other call."

Murphy called Sammy back. "You may have gotten lucky, Sammy, we still had an agent in the building. Violette had better co-operate and keep his mouth shut or Willie's deal is off."

"Willie's done everything asked of him."

"What can you tell me about this cousin of yours, Tony Violette? Anything we can use in case he's not cooperative?"

"He's stubborn as hell, I don't know. Have your IRS guys threaten him. Tell him they'll audit all his clients and put him out of business."

"How'd he find this wire, Sammy? It was buried in a wall."

"I don't know."

"Maybe someone tipped him off, Sammy; maybe somebody's been playing us."

"His restaurant . . . he had a restaurant a couple years ago. No privately own restaurant on Earth has clean books. Tell him IRS will audit his returns from the restaurant if he doesn't play ball."

Tony opened the front door of his office. "I'm agent Sean Reilly, FBI."

"Do you have a warrant to be in my office?"

"I have a warrant to have a listening device in the office of Mr. Wilfredo Juan Rocinante."

"I have a contact at the Asbury Park Press – Ned Johnstone. He helped me expose that Bubba Tomatoes."

Tony scrolled through his cell phone contact list looking for Johnstone's phone number. "Mr. Violette, I would advise against you interfering with an ongoing FBI investigation."

The office phone rang. Tony never picked up the phone at the office, but thought it might be Sammy calling back. "Violette Tax & Financial, how may I help you?"

"Violette Tax & Financial? I thought this was Tony Pepperoni Pizzeria. Did I misdial?"

"Tony Pepperoni? Who is this?"

"Oh, I'm sorry – Mr. Violette, right? This is Mr. Murphy, I just got confused a moment I had been going through the files from your restaurant, before I dialed you."

"My restaurant? That was five years ago."

"Still within the statute of limitations for fraud, Mr. Pepperoni. I mean, Violette. It came to my attention while reviewing your arrest involving some dumpster diving incident. Don't know how they let you walk on that one. Of course, that case is still open. Is my agent, Mr. Reilly with you?"

"Yes"

"Listen to what he has to say, Mr. Violette, and don't do anything rash."

"Fine."

"You're not under investigation, Mr. Violette, and Mr. Rocinante *knows* the wire is there, he's cooperating with us."

"That bastard . . ."

"You have nothing to be concerned about so long as you don't interfere with our investigation."

"Investigation of what?"

Reilly reinstalled the microphone and wire while Tony stewed. Reilly guaranteed Tony a meeting with his superiors to bring him fully up to speed. Tony promised he would remain silent for the time being, not even letting Willie know he had discovered the wire, but did so simply to get Reilly to leave. "Is it alright if I close up now?"

"It's your office, Mr. Violette."

Tony's instinct was to drive straight to Willie or Sammy's house and confront them but getting home late would alert Gwen to the crisis. Instead, Tony went home only to toss and turn all night and wake up for good at four instead of the usual five in the morning. "Why are you going in so early, Tony?"

"I left a lot of work on my desk last night. Go back to sleep, Gwen."

Tony got to his office at 5:30 a.m., climbed back on his desk and yanked the FBI wire from Willie's wall. Then, Tony pulled the Wellness Center end of the wire, which quickly snapped, sending Tony flying to the floor. After binding the thirty feet of wire with duct tape, Tony returned to his car and drove straight to Sammy's office, stopping only at a McDonald's drive through for coffee. Tony sat for two hours in front of Sammy's office until Sarah Shah arrived. Tony walked in right behind her, before she had even switched the lights on. "What the hell are you doing here, Tony?"

"I need to speak with my lawyer."

"What's the goddamn wire for?" Tony walked straight into Sammy's private office. "You can't go in there."

"Why don't you go to city hall and burn your bra, or something?"

"It's not the sixties, Tony, although I so wish it was. Sammy's not expected in this morning. He has court." Tony saw six neatly stacked boxes of Titleist golf balls on Sammy's desk with 'Pompano Beach Industrial Life' stamped on them. They were given to Sammy during a round of golf with Sammy, Murphy, IRS agent Owens and an executive from Pompano Beach Industrial Life when they hashed out the details of Willie's cooperation and witness protection deal. Tony placed the wire on Sammy's desk, lifted the boxes of golf balls and grabbed a two iron out of Sammy's golf bag which stood in the corner of the room. "What are you doing with those?" asked Shah, as Tony stormed back to his car.

"Reparations!"

Tony headed towards Edison on Route 1, turned onto Aspen Place and parked. The street was crowded with morning commuters. Tony grabbed Sammy's two iron and golf balls and walked west until he was across from the Internal Revenue Service Center. Tony emptied the seventy two golf balls on the grass, waited for traffic to pass, and began hitting shots towards the IRS building. The first two missed wildly. Then, Tony hit a line drive that bounced off the building's concrete exterior and bounded back to him. Tony kept swinging with mixed results until blasting through a window on his twelfth swing. Two cars stopped to watch Tony. The homeowner, whose lawn Tony was tearing up, shouted out a window, but Tony couldn't hear. Tony's twenty second shot also cracked a window. A suited man emerged screaming from the side of the building.

"What the hell are you doing?"

Cars were now backed up in both directions of the street. One driver shouted encouragement and laughed, while most of the other honked and cursed Tony. On his fortieth shot, Tony heard a police siren. With his four recovered bounce-backs, he still had 36 balls remaining and maintained his steady pace. Tony didn't hit his third window shot until his fiftieth. On his sixty first shot, he felt a blister start burning on his left index finger. "I should have taken his glove too," he thought. Tony was starting to take time between shots now and cars began accelerating through his shot line between swings. Two drivers had pulled to the side to film Tony on their cell phones. Before his sixty eighth shot, Officer Gatto's Edison police car pulled up inches in front of Tony, nearly running over his left foot. "I've got nine more shots," said Tony, before dropping the club to the ground and raising his hands.

42 - China Girl

Gatto grinned at seeing Tony behind bars again. "Well, you've got one call, Mr. Violette. Do you want me to get Sammy Sleaze on the phone for you?"

"He's not my lawyer anymore" said Tony, pensively, while Gatto laughed. "I do have a call I'd like to make, though.

Gatto opened Tony's cell and walked him to the interrogation room. Gatto slid the telephone across the table to Tony. "You've got five minutes . . . I'll be right outside the door."

"You don't have to leave" said Tony, as he began dialing Ned Johnstone at the Asbury Park Press. "Ned, this is Tony Violette – I've got an even bigger story for you than Bubba Tomatoes and the gerbils. The FBI and IRS have been using my office to run a sting operation . . ."

Gatto bolted from the interrogation room and phoned FBI in Newark to see if what Tony was saying was true, but Tony himself wasn't being investigated by FBI, so his name did not come up in their data base. After ten minutes on the phone, Gatto was convinced Tony was either pulling a stunt or maybe he was genuinely delusional. Another cannabis fueled fit of mania, perhaps. Gatto's absence gave Tony nearly fifteen minutes on the phone to rant to Johnstone. In less than an hour, the Asbury Park Press web site's top headline read: Former Bubba Tomatoes' Nemesis' Office the Site of FBI/IRS Sting. Twenty minutes later, while Gatto ordered a series of drug tests on Tony, the FBI put out arrest warrants for Willie and Bullo. It was before noon, so Willie was simply picked up at home. Bullo's cell phone coordinates sent Murphy and O'Kelly to a location in South Amboy.

"It four hundred dollars, up front" said Hóng, standing outside

Bullo's motel room.

"Four? The other China Girl was only three hundred dollars."

"Húong say you too rough, no come no more."

"What's your name?"

"Hóng."

"Well, Hó Chí Minh, why don't we call it three hundred fifty dollars?"

"Ewww, just one time three hundred fifty dollars" said Hóng, as she entered Bullo's South Amboy motel room. "Where is bathroom?"

"Take a guess, there's two doors and only one's a closet." Before Hóng had reached the bathroom, there was loud pounding on the door. Bullo was still standing just a couple feet away. "What?!" he screamed and opened the door to see O'Kelly and Murphy holding revolvers. "She's my girlfriend, assholes; I'm not paying for this."

"Ha" roared Murphy, "Cordardo thinks we're with the vice squad. FBI, asshole."

"I no know him," said Hóng. "Here by mistake."

"Run along, honey," said O'Kelly. "And you, Bullo, turn around and put your hands behind your back. You're under arrest for tax and securities fraud."

Sammy reached Murphy on his cell while they were taking Bullo into custody. "Why is Willie under arrest, Murphy?"

"Don't feel bad, Sammy – we just picked up Bullo too."

"This wasn't the deal, Murphy. You've got Bullo, Willie walks. He did everything you asked."

"Bait and switch. Someone screwed us, Sammy, and the odds all say it was you. Willie's your client, Tony's your cousin's husband. This was your idea, using Violette's office. I should have smelled a rat."

"I don't know how Tony found the wire, but I sure as hell didn't tell him, and Willie swears he didn't either."

"Well you're in a bit of an ethical dilemma, Mr. Riscatto, because either *you're* going to jail or your client is."

"I'm headed out to Philadelphia. Will I be able to see you there?"

"We can all have a great big get together, Sammy, I've got an agent picking up Tony from the Edison Police Station."

"Tony?" asked Sammy. "Stealing my golf balls isn't a federal offence, Murphy."

43 - Get me a Heineken

"The refrigerator is gone, Bullo. The IRS took every last dollar. They ransacked the whole house too, the sons of bitches."

"I know, mom" said Bullo, home on bail a week after his arrest.

"That's all the money we had. If you go to jail and lose your pension . . . how am I going to survive on only your father's twelve hundred dollar a month Social Security?"

"I'll take care of it. Who came by, besides the IRS and FBI? Tommy?"

"Frankie came first, asking a lot of questions. Were you 'cooperating with FBI?' and such"

"What did you tell him?"

"I told him the truth. I ain't talked to you and I don't know nothing. And, it's true, I don't know nothing. I don't know what you do."

"Who else came by?"

"Just Tommy . . . just Tommy and some punk I don't know."

"And?"

"He just told me to have you contact him as soon as you're out. He said it like five times. Like a parrot. 'Make sure he calls me, first thing when he gets out. Make sure it's the first thing he does.' Five times, over and over he says the same thing. The other guy just stands there like a dummy and stares. I told him I don't know nothing. I'll give you the message. That's all I told him."

"Get me a Heineken, mom."

"There's no beer left in the house. I haven't gone shopping since they arrested you. I haven't left the house."

With his thumb, Bullo pointed back towards the kitchen. "I

keep an extra one hidden in the back of the fridge, behind the pickles." Sparky left for the kitchen. Bullo stood, removed his belt and slowly followed her.

With her head buried in the refrigerator, Sparky shouted. "There's no beer in here."

"No, it's in the back of the cold cuts drawer, I forgot." Sparky bent down further and pulled the drawer open. Bullo came up behind her, lassoed her with the belt and pulled her, facedown, onto the linoleum. Bullo kneeled on her back with all his weight and pulled on the belt ends. Even after Sparky stopped flopping, Bullo held on until his strength gave out. Bullo left the belt ends fall to the floor, rose and walked to the bathroom.

Bullo opened the hot faucet in the bathtub and lowered the drain stopper. While the tub filled, Bullo undressed, lathered and grabbed his safety razor. Bullo shaved, deliberately, while regretting there wasn't a last Heineken in the house. As the tub reached three quarters full, he finished his shave, removed his father's wedding ring and placed it on the sink counter. Bullo removed the blade from the razor, sat into the tub, and opened his veins.

Epilogue

Three months later.

Tony sat across a metal table from Sammy Riscatto at the Federal Detention Center in Philadelphia as a guard watched on. "You're not my lawyer, Sammy. What are you doing here?"

"I'm still family, Tony and I'm not *anyone's* lawyer anymore."

"I know what it is: I never thanked you for not pressing charges against me for stealing your golf balls."

Sammy stared down at the table. "Tony . . ."

"Who was this Brunello Cordardo, Sammy?"

"A coward, Tony. He was the crooked accountant Willie worked for that Willie ratted out to the FBI, in exchange for a deal on some insurance fraud they had Willie dead to rights on."

"And, Willie? Where is Willie now? This public defender they've assigned to me doesn't tell me anything; he's worthless."

"Willie is in witness protection."

"Witness protection? Who's he in protection from?"

Sammy shrugged. "No one, really, especially with Cordardo dead. It's just the deal he made. I think he just wants to make a fresh start, where no one knows who he is, or where he's from."

"Ha! I already know where he is. He's going by that Bourbon Billy moniker. Gwen already found him on the internet. He's got a tavern in Arizona, or something. How'd he pay for that?"

"New Mexico. That's the deal he made. FBI set him up. He doesn't really have to hide from anyone, Brunello Cordardo is dead and the others they caught – a bunch of retired cops and firemen – they're getting their wrists slapped. Willie has nothing to fear from them."

"So, basically Sammy, you sold me out for two crooked accountants?"

"That's not the way they look at it. You impeded an investigation. They're furious about the newspaper article. They wasted hundreds of man-hours setting up a sting that lasted two weeks instead of two years, and they blame you. That golf ball stunt just gave them license to keep you here without bail." Sammy frowned and shook his head. "They're just being vindictive."

"What did you mean, before, when you said you're nobody's lawyer anymore?"

"This deal Willie made – any deal like that - you swear confidentiality. That includes the lawyers as much as anyone else. A month ago, I went back to this Murphy at FBI - the one Willie and I made this deal with - and I told him I was going to the press to corroborate your story and embarrass the FBI and IRS if they didn't drop these charges against you. They threatened me with disbarment, but I told them I was quitting anyway, which they didn't really believe."

"You're not the bluffer you used to be."

"I'm not bluffing, Tony. I'm quits."

"You're closing your office? Giving up law?"

"We're not closing the office. Sarah passed the bar exam, she's taking over. She's a true believer. I can't do this anymore."

"What are you gonna do, Sammy? Make coffee and answer her phone calls?"

"We're getting married."

"You're marrying the Shah of Iran?"

"And, we're adopting Willie's bastard."

"Willie's got a bastard kid? Since when?"

"He's almost five." Tony shook his head. "Yesterday, FBI called with a new offer. They know I'm serious now. You can walk Tony - today -, in exchange for a permanent gag order - from both of us. This whole thing has been a big embarrassment for them; that's your only leverage. The IRS still wants about fifty K in back taxes, interest and penalties they say you owe them from your Tony Pepperoni days. It's up to you."

"Sammy, my business is gone and my house is in foreclosure. I'm an accountant who's got a prison record and I owe fifty thousand dollars in back taxes without a job to pay them. I think

I'll take my chances with a jury. At least I can still write a book. What do you think, Sammy? 'The Accountant the IRS Arrested for *NOT* Filing Fraudulent Returns.'

The End

www.ingramcontent.com/pod-product-compliance
Lightning Source LLC
Chambersburg PA
CBHW020757250626
47155CB00003B/1111